CONGO CREW

A Novel

by

William Goodlett

Path Press, Inc.

Library of Congress Cataloging in Publication Data

Goodlett, William, 1932-
  Congo crew.

  I. Title.
PS3557.05827C6   1988   813'.54   88-25346
ISBN 0-910671-05-2

Published by Path Press, Inc., 53 West Jackson Blvd.,

Chicago, Illinois 60605

Manufactured in the United States of America

Congo Crew moves relentlessly toward a shattering climax as Chitown, while at a port in South Africa, becomes separated from the ship and is forced to live as an African in an angry, agitated shantytown. Black and alien in the most racist country in the world, Chitown must find the personal courage and skill to survive.

But there is more than boldness here. Subtle touches abound. As in most great novels, the visions of the spirit are in constant conflict with the demands of the flesh.

Congo Crew is one of the most complete novels ever written about Africa.

ABOUT THE AUTHOR

WILLIAM GOODLETT was born in Chicago, Illinois, and studied speech and drama at Kennedy-King College in that city. After discharge from the Navy in 1956, he became a train switchman and railway postal clerk, travelling throughout mid-America in the performance of his duties. In 1961, he entered the Military Sea Transportation Service and signed aboard the **U.S.N.S. General Blatchford.** Service c this ship took him to the ports so vividly described in **Congo Crew,** his first novel. Goodlett currently resides in Chicago with his wife and teenage daughter.

*To my wife, Peggy, whose love and faith
helped to make this book possible*

We have no heroes and no wars,
Only victims of a sickly state
Succumbing to the variegated sores
That flower under lashing rains of hate.

We have no battles and no fights
For history to record with trite remark,
Only captives killed on eyeless nights
And accidental dyings in the dark.

Yet when the roll of those who died to free our land is
called,
Without surprise; these nameless, unarmed ones will stand
beside
The warriors who secured the final prize.

—Dennis Brutus

BOOK ONE

Sail north to Congo, you bloody black,
Jolly good show if you never come back!

Chapter One

IT WAS a haunting night in Capetown, South Africa, Mid-December, 1961. The shadow of Table Mountain, with its long flat crown stretching between two high rising peaks, loomed like a giant sphinx on the far side of the bay. The wicked Atlantic wind howled from the mountain's crest and echoed down its home-lit slopes. The wind lashed out across the dark green harbor, causing the moon-lit tips of the water's countless white caps to dance a mad, inharmonious ballet. Huge rolling waves smashed relentlessly against the three lonely vessels docked at the pier, making them whimper as they tugged and strained at their bonds.

The USNS General Mitchell was tied up between a British freighter forward and a Japanese Maru aft. She overwhelmed them in size, and because of her pale Navy color, was nicknamed "The Gray Ghost". Unlike the other ships, the quarterdeck of the Mitchell was lined with heavily clothed sailors excited enough to brave the chill.

Just over an hour ago news had arrived that replacements were landing, and this information had buoyed the crew with anticipation. Many of the sailors, feeling they

1

now would be home for Christmas, had rushed to the quarterdeck, as though awaiting immediate departure.

It was in this spirit of expectancy, that they let out a joyous roar when four headlights turned off a narrow road and stopped in front of the old teahouse at the end of the pier. But the shivering, thinly-clad newcomers who were riding the vehicles to which the headlights belonged did not reciprocate. They only cursed upon debarking the two big brown busses. They had changed their winter clothes in Libya. It also had been hot in Nigeria and the Congo, two of the other points they had touched on their way to their destination. Now, here they were in Capetown and were finding the South African weather to be as mysterious as the rumors.

Soon the confusion settled and the men who debarked the busses moved into long thin lines and strode for the lights of the Mitchell. Conversation was harsh and mumbled through clattered teeth, as they took brief, snarling glances into that frigid wind from that awesome mountain, across that eerie looking bay.

When the first contingents started up the gangway, they were greeted by another roar, and shouts of "Welcome! Welcome aboard!" Other sailors, who would not be going home, had joined their shipmates on the quarterdeck. But they welcomed the new arrivals in the sense that misery loves company. And as the shivering sailors filed past them, they were told of long slow voyages, torturous days, sweltering nights, and lousy no-good chow.

Wilber Kane set his luggage on the warm steel deck and glanced around the compartment. It was small but neat, and smelled of fresh paint. Clean linen, towels, and blankets lay folded at the heads of the two double-deck bunks on opposite walls while bright orange Mae West-type lifejackets decorated the feet. Four tall gray lockers stood between the bunks on his left and a small sink leading to the entrance.

He sat down in one of the three folding chairs near a big wide metal desk and blew hot breath into his cold stiff hands. His thoughts drifted back to his old Navy days. The yearly voyages across the Pacific; and steaming up and down the Formosan straits with the Seventh Fleet. The nightly air raids by piss-call Charlie over the murky waters of Inchon harbor had taught him to sleep in everything but his shoes. Scars were still on his shoulders and legs from running to battle stations across pitch black, machinery clogged, cable-strung weatherdecks. It had been over five years since he was last on a ship, and experienced that grim ... captive feeling. The very idea of sailing into another war made him even more uncomfortable.

"Too late now!" he whispered. "Too goddamned late to turn back now!"

There was a noise in the passageway. The hatch flew open and Sonny Collins strutted in.

"Hey Chitown!" he shouted to Kane, "this the cat I was talkin' bout on the way over. Told you he would be here ... didn't I?" he nodded toward the tall copper-colored man sporting a neatly trimmed Van Dyke and dark blue beret, who followed him in and closed the hatch. Kane stood up, introduced himself and extended his hand.

"Rinco Styles," the tan man smiled as they shook hands, "Welcome to the USA ... Union of South Africa. If you're from Dixie, feel right at home."

"He from Chicago," Collins said, dropping his suitcase and stretching his long garment bag across the deck, "that's why we call him Chitown; have to keep reminding him there ain't but one real city ... and that's the Apple."

"Well" ... Kane hunched his shoulders, "Chitown sounds better than Wilber."

"They still call you Big Shot?" Rinco asked Collins.

"Yeah!" Collins grinned, "especially the bitches!"

"He's right about that," Rinco winked at Chitown, "he'll out bid anybody in any port we drop anchor."

"You better believe it if the bitch fine enough." Collins gave his wide smile, displaying bright even teeth that bit the tip of an ivory cigarette holder sticking out of his dark smooth face. All of his clothes were expensive, and he wore double soles with thick heels to heighten his short narrow body. "Just what the hell this ship doing over here anyway?" He took off his hat and wiped the sweatband with a silk handkerchief.

"Didn't they tell you?" Rinco lit a small cigar. "We are under the command of the United Nations ... who I don't think know what the fuck to do over here, except try to save white refugees. Our job is to haul troops back and forth to the Congo."

"What kind of troops?" Chitown asked.

"Indian and Malayan, but right now we don't even know who the enemy is. One month it's Tshombe, then there's Adoula or Kasavubu. President Lumumba invited us to help put down rebellions in Kantanga and Kasai, and we ended up fighting him. We're just pawns in a power play between East and West for control of the resources."

"No Europe?" Big Shot frowned "No Far East?"

"Nope." Rinco blew a ring of smoke. "Just India, Malaya, and Africa."

"Huh!" Big Shot grunted. "I see you still like your women like you do your coffee, black and bitter."

"You got that right," Rinco agreed. "I've been right here on the Ghost for nearly two years, swinging around the Cape of Good Hope like a horizontal pendulum. And I'm going to stay here for the duration ... not because of women, but because I believe what we are doing is much more important than chasing skirts."

"Well I ain't here to hunt elephants," Big Shot grinned. "I heard about these Capetown Coloreds ... fine friendly and frantic!"

"Just like stateside," Rinco nodded, "brown and round, yellow and mellow ... light, bright, damn near white. You name it."

"What's with this colored shit?" Chitown asked.

"The word colored means mulatto or half-cast," Rinco explained. "Their ancestors were Hottentots and Malay slaves from the East Indies, absorbed by early Dutch settlers, and visiting white sailors. They speak better English

4

than we do, drink like fish, live to party, and love fast-spending cats like Big Shot."

"Hear that Chi?" Big Shot beamed, but Chitown was more interested in picking a bunk.

"Are these bottoms empty?" he asked.

"Take your choice!" Rinco answered "I'm the only one left in this compartment, and I haven't slept here in a month."

"That's hip!" Big Shot said "It's just gonna be us three. A all-American crew ... we can call each other all the 'niggers' we want to!"

"There's so many of us on this ship that 'nigger's' out of date," Rinco said. "Here, you're either a baby or a mother-fucker!"

Chitown dragged his heavy bag across the deck to the bunks on their left. "You haven't slept here in a month," he said. "How long has this tub been in port?"

"Nearly two, we just got out of drydock last week." He looked at Big Shot. And we get underway tomorrow!"

"What!" Big Shot bucked his eyes and sneered. "You mean to tell me this pig-iron bitch been sittin here all this time, just waiting for us to bring our dumb asses aboard?"

Rinco rubbed his beard and laughed. "Why do you think you got such a grand reception? Those cat's bags been packed for weeks, but they couldn't go nowhere until you got here, nor could the ship."

Chitown just stood motionless with a forlorn look on his dark, cheeky face. Then he dropped his stocky six-foot body on the bottom bunk and shook his head.

"Man what the hell we waitin' on?" Big Shot snapped. "Let's hit that beach!"

"I think I'll stay aboard," Chitown sighed. "Drop my old lady a line and hit the sack."

"You got to be kiddin' dude, Big Shot said "With all that boss action out there, you mean to tell me you ain't gonna hit the beach?"

Chitown shook his head no.

"Well me an' Rinco gonna blind you with ass. Come on, Rinco." Big Shot unzipped his garment bag to get his coat.

5

"Look Chi," Rinco put out the cigar in a large brass ashtray on the desk, "tomorrow we head for the Congo, where there will be no liberty because of the war. Then it's straight around the Cape and across the deep-six to Malaya and India. So it will be a long time before you get another chance to go ashore."

"In that case," Chitown opened his grip for his leather jacket, "I could sure use a few drinks."

"Mellow!" Big Shot slipped into his trenchcoat. "Let's split, times wastin'."

"We should still be able to get a cab if we hurry." Rinco checked his watch, then went to his locker and got a denim jacket.

"What about our gear?" Chitown asked.

"It'll be alright. I've got the only key to the compartment."

"Let's split!" Big Shot said again and headed for the hatch.

"Wait-a-minute!" Rinco stopped him. "Before we go I want to tell you guys something. Now listen and listen good. There's more 'black only' and 'white only' signs in this one town than the whole state of Mississippi. We're not just hated by the hunkies, the colored cats don't dig us either. And these coloreds have a lot of street gangs just like the Apple. They all carry knives and will use them. A half-dozen crewmen have been cut up already. If a stranger stop you on the street for a cigarette ... or anything ... start running or fighting. And above all ... don't walk the streets alone at night. If you can't get a cab to pick you up, stay where you are ... believe me, it's the safest thing to do."

While he spoke Big Shot and Chitown stood silently, staring from him to each other.

"Why the colored gangs so hard on us?" Big Shot asked.

"It's a long story. I'll break it down later. Meanwhile I know you guys can take care of yourselves," he reassured them. "I just wanted you to know what's happening. Now let's get the hell out of here. Capetown's one of the best liberty ports in this part of the world."

They hurried up the ladder to the starboard passageway, forward to the quarterdeck, then down the long shaking gangplank to a small taxi waiting under the single bobbing light of a closed warehouse.

Rinco knew the tall slender driver with shining black hair, who turned to face the strangers in the rear seat and smiled as he was introduced.

"Jake's one of the few colored cats you can trust ... if he knows you," Rinco said.

"Where to? The party?" Jake asked.

"Yeah!" Rinco answered.

When they reached the Teahouse at the end of the pier, Jake made a sharp right turn onto a narrow dusty road. As the car approached a customs shanty near a railroad crossing, they were halted by two stout Europeans in drab brown uniforms.

"Any firearms?" the closest one barked, peeping through the windows.

"No firearms!" the passengers answered.

"Anything to declare?"

"I declare a end to this bullshit, so we can get the hell to town!" Big Shot snapped.

The officers looked at each other, shined their flashlights into the car, then waved them on.

"Why these hunkies so hung-up on firearms?" Chitown glanced back through the rear window. "That's all we heard from the time we landed ... got any firearms? ... got any firearms? ... hell, they told us before we left New York there would be serious consequences for anybody caught smuggling weapons into South Africa." He lit a cigarette and held the lighter while Big Shot stuffed one into his holder. "And when we came through customs, they checked every bag for firearms, and nothing else."

"This is a police state," Rinco said, half turning in his seat to face them. "Its main concern is to keep weapons out of the hands of non-whites."

"I knew something was wrong with these motherfuckers," Big Shot said, taking a long draw on the smoke and leaning back in his seat "by the way they frowned on us at the airport."

"What did you expect," Chitown laughed, "when they saw all those niggers strutting through the lobby like they owned the joint ... talking loud, flashing gold watches, diamond rings and big bankrolls? They probably never saw any shit like that before."

"Well they sho' didn't turn down one of that good ole American green at them magazine counters and souvenir stands." Big Shot flicked an ash on the floor. "But you could see them fuckers turn red when we whistled at them gray broads ... and they got even more pissed when we used the washrooms marked 'white only'."

"I'm hip!" Rinco unwrapped a cigar. "Apartheid is a bitch. Three million whites practically enslave over eleven million African, Asiatic and coloreds." He lit the cigar and his voice took on an angry tone. "In the parks they have separate benches, and string rope down the middle of bridges to keep the races divided. And that's only a fraction of their outrageous laws. Non-whites have to ride the top of double-deck buses. And the government has the audacity to run combs through people's hair to determine where they should live."

"Damn!" Big Shot grunted, "If the governor of Georgia came over here, he'd even say these motherfuckers crazy."

"Yeah," Rinco agreed, "right now we're riding in a second-class taxi. Only the whites ride first class. That's why you don't look for a cab after one o'clock. Blacks and coloreds can't be on the streets of Capetown. I would need a whole day to tell you how this country degrades black people."

"And you would take all night too, if we let you," Big Shot cut in, "but running off at the yap ain't gonna change shit. So let's talk about something interesting, like the time I broke up that crap game in Yokohama."

"Here we go again." Rinco faced the front and sighed.

"When I finished with them cats I had nearly two grand, and the weekend off. So I got with a couple square-ass dudes an we rented a whole bar for eighteen hours. I mean everything man, upstairs, downstairs, the booze, the broads, all of our food cooked and served . . . everthing a motherfucker needed."

"Damn!" Chitown said, "They don't call you Big Shot for nothing. That must have been one hell of a party."

"Sho was!" Big Shot smiled, "But them lame-ass dudes fucked up everything. I hope the niggers on this ship ain't like the one's I sailed with in the Orient."

"Niggers are the same everywhere," Rinco pointed at Big Shot, "and you're typical."

"Not like those silly-willies," Big Shot said, ignoring the implication. "Now there we was with a well-stocked bar, and ten boss broads . . . ten man! . . . that's three broads apiece, plus Mama-San to spare. Can you believe those dumb-ass dudes ended up fighting over one bitch. And them niggers was really humbugging, jack. I mean they was breaking up an' tearing up shit. Mama-San had to call the cops. She gave me half the money back an' reopened the joint. I shacked up with her while them cats spent the weekend in a Jap jail. Ole Mama-San was fine, too, man." He kissed his fingertips. "She called me Daddy Yen-Yen."

When they finished laughing, Rinco changed the subject again.

"Who's the new evaporator man?" he asked.

"Me!" Chitown rolled down a window and discarded his cigarette butt. "What kind of plant you got on that tub?"

"Two triple shells."

"Good! Those the kind I worked with in the Navy. But how are we going to operate with only two watchstanders?"

"We've got another . . . a white guy named Smitty. He sleeps in the next compartment."

"Ya'll talk about that shit later." Big Shot put out his smoke and stuck the holder back into his shirt pocket. "I got more sea time than both of you dudes put together, but I wouldn't sail as anything but a wiper. Fuck that watchstanding responsibility. I make enough extra bread shooting craps. As soon as that gangplank hit the dock, I

9

wanna be decked out in my silk wools, with my tough lids cooked ace-duce, peeping through my bad shades, with two pockets full of green. Now how much farther we got to go?"

"Not much." Rinco shook his head. "I'm dropping you guys off at Margo's. She's throwing a party for some of the cats who are cutting out tomorrow."

"What do you mean you dropping us off?" Big Shot asked.

"I'm just going to get you guys acquainted, have a drink or two, then head for Seapoint."

"What's at Seapoint?" Chitown asked.

"Seapoint" . . . Rinco said, "is where rich hunkies stay in exclusive buildings on the slopes of Table Mountain. I go with one of their African maids that live in the basement apartments. But don't worry Shot . . . there will be lots of chicks at Margo's."

"Mellow!" Big Shot hunched Chitown with his elbow. "Bet you glad you came along?"

"Not all that glad," Chitown said, "I'm just gonna have a few drinks and look around. I'll leave with Rinco. When he gets to Seapoint, I'll keep the cab and go back to the ship. I still want to get that letter written tonight." He turned and stared out of the car window.

It was only 10:00 P.M. and the streets were already deserted. In the quiet darkness, Capetown had the outward appearance of some of the American cities Chitown had passed through enroute from Chicago to New York. And it was from the window of that Greyhound bus taking him away from her that Jean's face had begun to haunt him. Staring out at the endless sky over the Atlantic, he had remembered their last night together. Her trembling voice tried hard to assure him that she would be all right. But the tears streaming down her lovely face pleaded for him to reconsider leaving her. The further he traveled, the more he missed her. It had been six days, almost a week since he had taken off from New Jersey on that big, slow-moving, four-engine Air Force transport.

10

The first stop was Iceland, where he brought more flight insurance and mailed her a card. Then during the two day layover at Wheeler Air Force base in Tripoli, with its scorching days and cold sleepless nights, he often whispered her name as he shivered under thin blankets, while low-flying jets screamed overhead. He bitterly recalled that refueling stop at Kano, Nigeria, where he sweated in the hot waiting room for over a half-hour trying in vain to make a long distance call. He tried again at Leopoldville in the Congo, but could not get his money changed before it was time to take off for Capetown.

"This is it!" Rinco said, as Jake pulled up and stopped in the middle of a block filled with dull, three-storied tenements that sat atop wide, dingy-looking storefronts.

Chapter Two

AS THEY started their climb up the narrow stairway
to the second floor of thirty-four Burke Lane, the gay
sound of female laughter accompanied the loud wail of a
slow American blues song. The door on their left was
cracked open, and they followed Rinco out of the dark,
musty hallway into a spacious, gaudy lit dining room
where red, blue, green and yellow bulbs glowed from a
huge chandelier, hanging over a long table covered by
dingy white sheets.

It looked and smelled like a Harlem rent party, with the
strong, spicy odor of frying chicken seeping through the
closed kitchen door on the far side of the room. All of the
furniture had been pushed back against the walls to create
a dancing area, where tightly snuggled couples moved
other parts of their bodies more than they did their feet.

"I'll be damn!" Big Shot whispered through a felicitous
grin. "Who the fuck need to go to Europe . . . will you look!
. . . wall to wall bitches, an' as boss as they want to be!"
He glanced around at the quantity and variety of women
out on the dance floor, huddled into little giggling groups
along the walls, or parading back and forth to the table for
drinks.

"I want to hip you to these cats," Rinco said, leading them toward the table. "They run the crap games, sell the booze, and handle the best smoke."

"Mellow!" Big Shot smiled. "Those the dudes I want to get to know."

They passed a wide doorway covered by thick orange drapes, where a big bow-legged man sat hooking up a mike to the phonograph.

"Meet Johnson and Brother Poe!" Rinco introduced two men the same medium size and height, the same dark color, who looked somewhat like twins in their starched khaki messjackets, and beaded African skullcaps pulled tight over their bald heads. Each was wrapped around a tall, light-brown lady.

"This is Big Shot and Chitown, new members of the crew."

"What's happening baby!" Johnson and Brother Poe said at the same time, and slapped them in the palms of the hands. Then they introduced the women, who smiled and nodded behind dark sunglasses.

"Welcome to Capetown!" Johnson said. "Nearest thing to stateside on the continent."

"And the bossest bitches too!" Brother Poe winked and squeezed one of his lady's breasts.

Rinco picked up a glass and motioned for Big Shot and Chitown to fix themselves a drink.

"Is this all they got," Chitown frowned, "gin and coke? What about ice?"

"This is the land of lush baby," Johnson said. "They don't dilute this shit with no ice. You lucky to get coke."

"Hell, you lucky to get gin," Brother Poe added. "At one time coloreds couldn't buy nothing but wine. That's what whitey used to pay 'em in."

Johnson's lady objected. "Only the people who worked in the vineyards received part of their wages in wine," she said, "and that was long . . . long ago!"

Chitown shook his head. "The more I hear about this country, the harder it is to believe."

13

"Believe it baby," Brother Poe seemed to amuse himself by embarrassing the women, "'cause these motherfuckers serious as cancer."

The most distinguishable characteristic between him and Johnson, beside the fact the he talked faster and flatter, were the gold caps on his upper front teeth.

"My man tell me you cats got some boss smoke!" Big Shot grinned and stuck out his palm.

"That's right baby!" Brother Poe slapped it. "Ya'll don't hafta drink that shit, 'cause we going back an' puff a little hash right now."

Rinco and Chitown declined, but Big Shot could hardly wait.

"Catch you squares later," he said, then followed Johnson, Brother Poe and the ladies through the doorway with the thick orange drapes.

"Man, I've got to admit, these colored chicks are gorgeous," Chitown said as he and Rinco fixed themselves a drink and moved to the edge of the dance floor. "I can see why the dudes are so pissed off at us."

"Yeah," Rinco agreed when they stopped to watch the horny dancers. "But it's mostly envy. Before Apartheid they had it made, but now they are damn near in the same boat as their black brothers. And a few of them still believed they live better than any non-whites. Then here we come, flashing more dough than they've ever seen and chasing after their women. But you've got to realize we sailors deal mostly with the fast life people . . . the hustlers, dope heads and boozers of the population. The coloreds are really more like American blacks than anybody in Africa, even those Toms in Liberia."

"You've been to Liberia?"

"I was born in Liberia."

"No shit, I would have never guessed you were African."

"I'm not, but my father was. My mother is from the Apple. She took me out of Liberia when I was four, divorced my father and never went back. When he was alive, she used to let me stay with him a few weeks every couple years. You know . . . like city kids visit the country on summer vacations." Admitting to himself that he was biased because of his mother's dislike of the country, Rinco changed the subject.

"Look around at the many contrasting skin tones," he waved his drink.

"Same as ours," Chitown said. "If we didn't know we were in Capetown, we could be back in any black neighborhood stateside."

"Right ... they copy our slang, mannerism and music more than any other urban Africans. It's a damn shame that a little educational and economic advantage make some of the coloreds think they are better than the blacks."

"And some black Americans think they're better than the coloreds," Chitown added.

"Right again," Rinco said. He wanted to tell him about the many other similarities between the two USAs. Beside the abbreviations, their history also showed similar parallels. At the same time the pioneers in the United States were heading west, killing off Indians, the Dutchmen in South African were trekking north, slaughtering Africans. He wanted to explain to this young brother seeing South Africa for the first time that the only reason he was not as oppressed as these people over here, was because in the U.S. he was a minority and posed no serious threat. And even considering the population percentages, things weren't that much better stateside. But he had to know Chitown better before really opening up. Had to be sure he wasn't CIA.

The music suddenly stopped. Everyone looked toward the phonograph where the big bow-legged man stood with a mike in his hand. He was almost a giant, nearly seven feet tall and weighed close to three hundred pounds. He combed his fingers through his long black processed hair as he cleared his throat.

"Testing ... testing ... one-two ... one two!" His loud heavy voice came over the four speakers placed in each corner of the room. As the crowd drifted closer, he turned down the volume and spoke a little softer.

15

"Now I want you people . . . I can't say ladies and gentle-men because I would be out of order."

The laughter interrupted him. But with a wave of his big arms, it was silent again.

"I want you people," he repeated, "to be quiet so we can hear a few words from our lovely hostess Margo!" He clapped his hands and the crowd did the same.

A pretty, green-eyed, well-stacked, copper-tone woman in a tight blue evening dress strutted from behind the orange drapes to a large round of applause, and a lot of help from a short, fat, flat-faced man, whose hands moved about her body with familiarity. She took the mike, smiled into it, and then spoke.

"This party is being given in honor of Mr. Edmond Pickins." She nodded in the direction of flat-face, who smiled and waved his cigar.

"He with other members of the Gray Ghost so very dear to us will be leaving tomorrow for America. I speak for all at Thirty-Four Burke Lane when I say we will miss you drastically . . . and do hope you return soon . . . good luck and happy landing."

There was another ovation while she cleared her throat.

"And to the new members of the *Ghost* who are in South Africa for the first time, it's with warm pleasure that we welcome you. I sincerely hope you enjoy yourselves and become fond of Capetown. May your stay be a happy one. Thank you very much." She handed the mike back to the big man as the eager hands of her friend led her back through the drapes.

A short golden girl, about twenty years old with narrow features and long brown hair, burst from the crowd and ran to the middle of the floor.

"Puti-Puti time!" she yelled, massaging her plump butt through skin-tight white slacks.

The room echoed with repeated shouts of "Puti-Puti!" followed by clapping, stomping and whistling, until it was all drowned out by a strange sounding jazz-like record that thundered through the speakers.

16

Everyone rushed back to the dance floor. Since the new Americans had not been exposed to the dance, many of them just watched. The Puti-Puti was created by the Zulus, with music similar to calypso but definitely African. And the way the coloreds did it was too sexy for the French stage. It made the average sultry dance look like an Eighteenth Century waltz, while arousing passion in both dancers and spectators. When in close, the participants simulated touching and feeling all parts of each others' bodies. Then they stepped back to make suggestive motions before moving in again. The footwork was a mixture of bebop and calypso, accentuated by occasional shuffles and stomps while the head and shoulder movement resembled the Watusi, and grew more vigorous as the dance progressed.

That particular record played over and over, with each dance becoming more torrid. Chitown's eyes kept drifting back to the girl in the white slacks, and how the thin cloth strained to contain her slithering body.

On the fourth dance, their eyes met and her knowledgeable smile embarrassed him. He told Rinco he was going for another drink and headed for the table. The record ended while he was filling his glass, and a fast beat lyric started.

"My name is Janet!" She walked up beside him and fixed herself another drink. "Yer new in Capetown, aren't you?"

"Yes!" he said after clearing his throat, "just got here tonight." He turned and extended his hand. My name's Chitown."

She took it, pulled herself into him and whispered. "I want to dance."

"Sorry baby! I only slow roll." He started back to where Rinco was standing, and she followed.

Johnson, Brother Poe, Big Shot and the ladies returned from their session dry-mouthed and glassy-eyed. They all went to the table for cokes, then Big Shot told them he was going to "look around and check out the broads!"

17

"Sho' plenty of 'em to check out!" Brother Poe waved as Big Shot started down the floor in the direction of the cracked door leading to the musty hallway.

Big Shot moved slowly, his eyes hypnotized by the many luscious bodies slicing through the thick smoke and deafening music. When he neared the door, a short man wearing black horn-rimmed glasses entered and bumped into him without an apology. The man just mumbled something to himself and hurried away, scanning the dancers through scornful eyes. Big Shot wanted to challenge him, but was much more interested in deciding which one of those choice bitches he was going to hit on.

When Chitown returned, Rinco was standing between two women. One was brown, but dark by colored standards, with short curly hair, wearing a tight low-cut pink blouse that revealed the top halves of her plump breasts.

"Polly, this is Chitown!" Rinco had to shout above the noise. "Chitown meet Polly!"

Polly gave Chitown a casual nod, but her face was filled with anger directed at Rinco. The other woman's name was Freda, and she was beautiful indeed, with long flowing jet-black hair, that hung loosely over her smooth pale shoulders. When Rinco introduced her, Janet, who had been following Chitown, grabbed Chitown's arm and spun him around.

"You my man!" she shouted. "I teach you to Puti-Puti. Then you dance with no one but me. If I catch you with another girl, I break yer jaw!" She put her tiny fist up in front of his wide face. When Rinco, Freda and Polly all started laughing, he didn't know whether to get mad or join them, so he just shook his head and said, "This woman is crazy!"

The man in the horn-rimmed glasses spotted Janet, then eased into the crowd at a distance so he could watch her unobserved.

"I see you got another one, eh," Johnson said to Janet, as the high-flying quartet joined the other group.

"That's right!" She hugged Chitown, slinging her perfumed hair in his face. "He dance with no one but me!"

18

They all laughed as Chitown tried to pull away without getting rough. "This broad's giving me the blues," he sighed.

The Puti-Puti music started again. Janet stepped back, snapped her fingers, and shook her hips.

"Come on!" She beckoned to Chitown. "I teach you to dance."

"No way." Chitown shook his head and took a stiff drink.

"Let's go baby," one of the crewmen came over and grabbed her by the hand. She swallowed her drink in two gulps, gave Chitown the empty glass and wiggled onto the floor.

Chitown was relieved. "What's wrong with that chick?" he asked.

"Beside being drunk," Johnson laughed again, "she's got the Puti-Putis."

"An' she got a puti-head ole man too," Brother Poe said.

"Them two crazy motherfuckers made for each other. You leave that bitch alone, Chi. She ain't got it all."

"Don't worry," Chitown finished his drink.

"Phillips must have the duty," Johnson said, "or he'd be hawking that whore like deputy dog."

Polly whispered something in Rinco's ear, and they eased back out of the crowd to talk alone.

"Is Creed coming ashore?" Freda asked.

"Naw!" Johnson answered. "You know how Creed is. He might fuck around and miss the plane, so he didn't want to take the chance. He said if I saw you, to tell you goodbye, and that he would write."

For a second she looked a little sad.

"But it's a cat somewhere 'round here," Brother Poe said, "I think you'll dig. I told him 'bout you."

"Oh . . . so you've been talking about me," she purred.

"Only 'bout how fine an' foxy you was baby, an' how you like to stay sharp an' get high!"

She blushed while the other girls looked at her and grunted.

"Speak of the devil!" Johnson spotted Big Shot strutting along the outside of the crowd and called him over.

19

"This the chick I told you 'bout." Brother Poe pointed to Freda. How do you like her?"

Big Shot was flabbergasted. "Well . . . " He grinned and stuck out his hand. "My man told me how boss you was, but I couldn't believe it 'til now. Sonny Collins," he said when she took his hand. "Big Shot Sonny Collins they call me."

"Freda," she smiled. "Pleased to meet you."

"Baby . . . " he sighed, "I've checked out every woman in this joint. And you are, without a doubt, the most fabulous of them all." He moved closer and the other women grunted again.

"Hear you use' ta go with some dude name Creed," he said.

She nodded, "Yes."

"Well I'm glad he's going back, 'cause I just got here baby," he slipped his arm around her narrow waist, "an' I'll be coming back for a long time. So we might as well get to know each other, 'cause I ain't gonna hit on nobody else. I done found what I want."

She gave him a look that assured she had developed an interest, then turned to Johnson.

"Now don't forget to bring me that ball of hash when you return from Bombay," she told Johnson. Before he could answer Big Shot spoke up.

"If he don't, I sure will! You wanna get high now?"

"No thank you," she smiled, "I smoked a joint on the way. Later perhaps."

"Anytime you ready baby." He kissed her on the cheek.

The crowd let out a roar that grew louder with whistling, clapping and shouts of "Take it off . . . Take it all off!"

The thick circle of people around the floor thinned out as everyone but Polly and Rinco, who were engaged in a heated argument, edged forward to see what was happening.

Janet's partner was just another spectator because she had taken over the floor, twisting and grinding her lovely body burlesque style to the slow beat of an American blues record. The encircling throng egged her on with cat-calls, clapping, and more shouts of "Take it off . . . Take it off!"

Janet pulled the tail of her blouse out and started to unbutton it from the top, until her eyes met the angry lustful eyes of the man in the horn-rimmed glasses. He gritted his teeth as she did a double spin, spotted Chitown and moved slowly in his direction. When she got to Chitown, she did a slow grind while her dark eyes bit into him.

The crowd grew louder and the circle tightened when she went into her climatic ending. With outstretched arms and in one fluid motion, she did a spin, dropped cross-legged on the floor and snapped her head forward, slinging her long brown hair down into her face.

The crowd yelled for more, but she fought off the eager hands helping her to her feet and dashed for Chitown. He saw her coming and had to admire the way she moved her body.

"Look baby," he said, shoving the empty glasses at her, "since you've taken it upon yourself to be my girl, why don't you fix us another drink? Make mine straight, with no coke." He tried to sound nonchalant, but realized her dancing had gotten to him.

"Very well," she said, taking the glasses and kissing him on the lips. "Don't mess around with any other girl. If I catch you . . . I break yer jaw."

"I've got to get away from this broad," he thought as he watched her wiggle off toward the table. He feared that instead of staying annoyed by her constant hugging, he might become aroused.

"What the hell's going on, bitch?" The man in the horn-rimmed glasses snatched her around just as she finished pouring the two drinks. "I can't be a little late without you chasing your funky ass at some son-of-a-bitch!"

"Go to hell!" she pulled away, put down the bottle and picked up the glasses.

"Goddamnit!" He pointed his finger in her face. You my woman! If not for me you wouldn't have decent shoes to put on your stinking feet!"

21

"Yer a damn liar!" She shook a glass at him, spilling gin down the front of his shirt. When he stepped back to wipe if off, she hurried through the sweating dancers back to Chitown.

"Where yo' ole man, Janet?" Brother Poe joked.

"He's my old man." She stepped back and looked Chitown in the eye.

"Not me, baby!" Chitown shook his head. "You better find the real thing."

A fat, white-looking woman with no upper front teeth, pushed the kitchen door open from the inside and shouted. "Chow's ready! Come and get it!" The loud cheers and stampeding feet almost drowned out the music, as a long line formed.

"Go fuck the black African!" Polly yelled at Rinco as they rejoined their little group. "Take yer ass to Seapoint ... see if I care!" She turned to the other girls and talked about him in Afrikaans.

"What you been doing to that broad?" Johnson grinned.

"It's what I haven't been doing," Rinco tried to joke.

"Polly ain't black enough," Brother Poe laughed.

"Yeah," Big Shot added, "that coffee got a little too much cream."

"Goddammit!" Brother Poe shouted at the women who were all jabbering at the same time, "knock off that Afrikaans ... I done told ya'll 'bout talkin' that shit 'round me ... speak English goddammit! ... so I know what the hell you saying."

"Maybe they just want to get back at you for calling them all those bitches," Rinco laughed.

"What!" ... Brother Poe frowned. "You the motherfucker they talkin' 'bout!"

Rinco threw back his head and laughed as the girls kept on talking in Afrikaans.

"What the hell's going on?" Big Shot asked Johnson.

"You know some of these coloreds think they're better than the blacks," Johnson answered, "and he put Polly down for a Zulu chick."

22

"Oh ... " Big Shot said, "so as far as these bitches concerned, he done stepped on his prick."

"That's right baby!" Johnson said, as his girl turned and spoke to him in English. "We're going ta 'ave a bite, coming along?"

"Naw baby," he shook his head, "you go on and grease."

The other men also declined, but Big Shot was reluctant to remove his arm from Freda's waist. He finally let her go.

"Man you cats sho' some mellow dudes." He slapped skin with Johnson and Brother Poe. "Turned me on some boss smoke, an' helped me tighten up with that sleek yellow fox." He watched her rush to join the other girls at the end of the line.

"Let them bitches grub," Brother Poe said, "I don't want no hot-ass chicken an' curry. We gonna pick up some steak dinners at the Zambesi on our way to shack-up."

"Put-up!" they call it," Johnson laughed.

"Shit!" ... Big Shot called after Freda. "My bitch ain't gonna eat no curry either", he commented to his companions when he got her attention. I'm gonna buy that fine motherfucker a steak too!"

Rinco and Chitown laughed as Johnson and Brother just looked at each other.

Suddenly, the man in the horn-rimmed glasses ran up to Chitown.

"You just got here, mon!" he waved his finger in the air. "You don't know what's between that girl and me ... Janet is mine!" He punched his finger in his chest. "She do as I say. You have nothing to do with it, mon."

For an instant Chitown was stunned, then quickly regained his composure.

"Now just who in the fuck are you ... and what in the hell are you talking about?" He shifted his weight to his right foot as the stranger inched forward.

"I'm Boatswain Phillips ... from the deck department, everybody know me!"

"Yeah!" Brother Poe cracked, "As a damn fool!"

23

"The steward department don't show me nothing, mon!" Phillips retorted.

Big Shot recognized him and snapped, "Everybody here ain't from the steward's department ... an' anyway, ain't you the motherfucker who bumped into me without saying shit?"

"I'm talking to this mon!" Phillips pointed to Chitown.

"Fuck that!" Big Shot moved in.

"That's okay Shot, I can handle it." Chitown waved him away without taking his eyes off Phillips. "If this silly son-of-a-bitch come within range," he thought, "I'm going up side his head like a air hammer!"

Phillips sensed the danger, shifted directions but talked all the louder.

"She know where her bread's buttered." He punched his finger in his chest again. "I warn you mon." He turned the finger to Chitown. "You see this woman coming, go the other way. If you know what's good for you mon, you'll keep away from her." He backed up and headed for the front door.

"See how dumb that motherfucker is," Brother Poe said. "He backed off a little cat like Shot, an' tried to sell wolf tickets to a big beefy dude like Chi."

"He did the right thing," Big Shot patted his pocket, "'cause I got something for his ass."

Johnson eased up to Chitown and whispered, "You got a blade?"

"Naw! I don't carry one."

"Well you better start." He slipped a knife into Chitown's pocket. "That cane chopper might be waiting outside."

"We hip ta these West Indians," Brother Poe interjected. "They bad as these Capetonians. They just soon cut you as look at you. An' don't ever let him get too close, or he'll butt yo' brains out."

"Here comes Jake," Rinco told Chitown. "I want to get out of here before Polly finish eating. You going back to the ship or staying?"

"Back to the ship," Chitown answered. "I don't want to be bothered with Janet, or her stupid-ass old man. Thanks for the shank." He offered the knife back to Johnson.

"Naw!" ... Johnson shook his head ... "you keep it baby. Me and Poe carry one in each pocket. Wherever we hit, we can't go wrong."

"Say man, you don't have ta fuck with Janet," Big Shot said to Chitown, "not with all these fine broads here. Why don't you grab another one an' party with us. Damn going back to the ship!"

"Maybe Rinco got one' a them Zulus waitin' for him at Seapoint," Brother Poe grinned.

"No," Rinco tried to remain calm, "he just happened to be married, man. Now remember what I told you about walking the streets at night," he gave Big Shot a final word of caution.

"Don't worry 'bout me," Big Shot pulled out a white handled straight razor. "This for hair or niggers, which ever come first."

As Chitown followed Jake and Rinco down the musty stairway, anger with himself had replaced bewilderment with Phillips. That sickening feeling which had plagued him from the time he left home, crept back into his stomach to enhance all those nagging doubts and strong misgivings about this whole venture. The woman he loved was thousands of miles away. And he had just been threatened because of a bitch he knew nothing, and cared less about. He put his hand in his pocket and felt the smooth hot handle of the knife. It gave him no comfort.

Chapter Three

IN CONTRAST to the night before, it was a beautiful morning, bright and clear, with only a mischievous crispness in the air. The Gray Ghost sat low in the water like a fat lazy duck squatting in the sunshine. Thin streams of pale smoke rose leisurely from her single upright stack, while glistening blue waves licked her wide curving waterline.

There were scores of women who had stayed up all night, or gotten up early, to see their boy friends off and lend more radiance to the day. Most were gold and carmel-skin coloreds in flat shoes and tight-waisted skirts, with skimpy breast-clutching blouses. The fashion-conscious Africans sported lightweight suits, full dresses and lots of wigs crowning smooth black and brown faces. The white women wore shorts, skin-tight slacks, high heels and sunglasses.

As in every aspect of South African life, there was the constant presage of apartheid. White police in drab brown uniforms ignored their women gathered under the fantail, but strutted up and down the pier watching the coloreds clustered amidship and strung along a warehouse wall, and

26

the Africans congregated around the benches of the old Teahouse.

Two brown buses, with an entourage of cabs, were pulling off for the airport when Big Shot's taxi reached the gangway. He paid the driver, jumped out and slammed the door. With only a casual glance at the women, he scampered up the gangplank, registered at the quarterdeck, then ran aft through the passageway. He was down the ladder in four steps.

"Where the hell you been?" Rinco looked at his watch and scolded. "It's almost ten o'clock!"

"I ain't saying shit till I get a drink!" He opened his suitcase and pulled out a half full bottle of Scotch.

"You know you missed muster," Rinco said, "but I covered for you, just like the old days. Better report to the Second Engineer as soon as you can."

"Mellow! . . . an' thanks," Big Shot breathed a sigh before he poured two inches in a glass, drank it down straight, then rushed to the face bowl for water.

"Man!" . . . he frowned and shook his head as the whiskey burned it's way down. "You told me not to walk the streets at night . . . you didn't say a damn thing about daytime."

"What happened?" Rinco and Chitown asked at the same time.

"I almost got wasted! . . . Me and Freda shacked up at a house called number nine."

"That's a rough neighborhood," Rinco said, sitting on the desk and leaning back against the bulkhead.

"You damn right!" Big Shot continued, "'cause 'bout seven this morning I went looking for a cab. I see these dudes coming my way, but since it's daylight I didn't pay much attention. Then I suddenly realize them cats was trying to surround me. I act like I wasn't hip, but dug 'em closing in with heir hands in their bosoms."

"How many?" Chitown asked as he affixed a stamp to his letter.

"I don't know! . . . three, maybe four . . . everything happened so fast. Anyway, I eased out my razor then dashed

27

for the middle of the street. That caught 'em by surprise, but one of the bastards tripped me an' I almost went down. He was right on my ass when I straightened up."

"You're lucky," Rinco said, "that would have been it. Those Skullys don't play!"

"I'm hip ... but he wasn't lucky, 'cause I spinned around"—he demonstrated making a complete turn on one foot, swinging his right hand back and down—"an' kept on running. Man, I can still see the shock in his eyes when my blade split his mug."

He poured another drink. This time Chitown and Rinco joined him.

"By the time he thought to scream, I was in third gear, widening the gap." He finally took off his hat and wiped his face with a towel from an empty bunk. "When I looked back over my shoulder, they was still coming an' cursing with the biggest shanks I ever saw. The one I had cut, with blood streaming down his face and shirt, stopped and drew back his blade to throw. I prayed an' put on more speed." He shook his head. "The handle caught me right here." He reached back and felt the sore spot between his spine and left shoulder blade. "When it hit me, man I thought this is it, until I heard the knife fall. Then I set a new track record gettin' back to number nine. I started hollering a block away. Freda had the door open an' was with the cops on the phone when I got there. The Skullys split, but them hunkey cops acted so nasty I didn't leave with them, so me an' Freda got high all over again and hit the sack."

Rinco and Chitown looked at each other, shook their heads and laughed.

"Let's go topside," Rinco suggested. "It's almost time for early chow."

When they stepped out into the sunlight, a bunch of crewmen were leaning over the lifeline, yelling down to the dock. The big bow-legged man who handled the mike at Margo's party was being chased by a half dozen police with their long clubs drawn.

"What the hell's going on?" Rinco asked.

"I don't know," one of the sailors answered, "but that's Nelson they after, I'm getting down there!"

"We'd all better get down there!" Rinco motioned, and the crewmen dashed forward toward the quarterdeck.

"Let me go! You red neck motherfucker!" they heard Nelson shout as they approached the hatch.

"Now wait-a-minute there boy!" came the southern, high-pitched voice of First Mate Ludlam followed by the sound of a short scuffle and a loud crash.

They scattered as Nelson jumped into the passageway. "Get out of my way!" he snapped, and streaked for the messhall.

In the short time it took him to run all the way from the Teahouse, and flop down at a table in the messhall, over two dozen seamen had been attracted to the scene, and more were on the way. They surrounded him, all talking at the same time, trying to find out what had happened. Large beads of water rolled down Nelson's face as he sat gasping. The collar, back and armpits of his dungaree shirt were soaked with perspiration.

"All right fellows! ... cool it!" Rinco yelled as he, Johnson and a few more crewmen waved back the crowd. "Give him room to breathe!"

"An' cut out some-a-that goddamn noise so we can find out what's going on!" Brother Poe added.

The voices slowly subsided, except a lingering giggle from the rear when someone said, "I ain't seen a big nigger run that fast since Jim Brown."

Nelson caught his breath and gulped down two glasses of water a cook gave him.

"What's this all about?" Rinco asked when silence finally prevailed. "What the hell those cops after you for?"

Nelson pulled out a handkerchief, wiped his face, and downed another glass of water.

"I went down to the ... ," he coughed and started again. "I went down to the Teahouse to get a paper, an' I dug this old hunkey pushing this little African kid around. He was really fucking with the dude, I mean slapping, shaking, an' all kind a shit ... pissed me off." He wiped his face

29

again. "So I pulled my shank an' put it round that cracker's neck, an' made the kid kick him in the nuts."

Everybody started laughing. Nelson joined them and went on. "He was kicking that peckerwood on the shins, knees, ankles . . . everywhere before he hit the balls." The more he told, the louder the laughter grew. "But when he did hit the bulls-eye, man that hunkey screamed so loud cops came from every which-a-way. So I hatted up."

"Clear the way!" Came the voice of First Mate Ludlam. "Come on, get out of the path!" The loud squeal of a Boatswain whistle momentarily froze everyone.

Ludlam was tall, pale and wiry, wearing a spotless white short-sleeve uniform that the crewman leaned and rubbed their hands on as he moved slowly through the crowd. He was followed by Boatswain Phillips and five white men in the drab brown uniforms of the South African police force.

"Where's Nelson?" Ludlam demanded, pretending to ignore what was happening to his clothes. "We want to talk to him!"

The farther they advanced into the horde of angry black faces, the quieter it got.

"There he is!" Ludlam pointed, then looked down at the short chubby, cross-eyed cop with the sergeant stripes. "This is your guy right here!" He turned back to Nelson. "I want you to go with these men!"

"That's right yank," the sergeant sneered, "you can't get away with that sort of thing you know! . . . come along now!"

"Fuck you, hunkey!" Nelson growled, "I ain't going no-where!"

Silence again engulfed the messhall.

"Damn!" came that mysterious voice from the rear, "you can hear a rat piss on cotton."

There was no giggling, only a tense stillness and the dreadful clicks of opening knives.

"That's right Jack!" Brother Poe shook his knife at Ludlam and the cops. Other voices joined him. "That's for sho baby . . . ain't nobody going nowhere! You hunkies better get the fuck off this ship!"

"This man," Ludlam pointed to Nelson again, "has broken the laws of a sovereign nation and caused bodily harm to one of its citizens."

"What about the little black citizen?" Nelson stood up. "It's more his country than them damn Dutchmen!" He pointed to the cops, then turned back to Ludlam. "I thought you got enough on the quarterdeck. If you stick your finger in my face again, I'm gonna break it off and put it up your ass!"

There was a brief rippling of laughter.

"Now, any of you whities draw back a club," Brother Poe waves his knife, "or reach for a gun, gonna get fucked up!"

"And that goes especially for you!" Nelson pointed to the sergeant, "you little cockeyed son-of-a-bitch!"

The officer had been getting angrier by the moment and could take no more. He reached for Nelson. "Let's go, you bloody ... " Before he spoke another word, Nelson slammed a hammy fist into his mid-section with a sickening thud. The sergeant's cap flew off as he belched, grabbed his stomach and dropped to his knees. The crowd cheered threateningly at the vastly out-numbered cops, who meekly cradled their clubs. Before he could fully catch his breath, or clear his head, the sergeant was searching for his pistol. Nelson started to kick him in the face when someone yelled, "Here come the Captain!"

Boatswain Mate Phillips blew his whistle, and Nelson stopped his foot in midair.

"Make way for the Captain!" Phillips shouted and blew the whistle again.

The seamen parted a path for their tall, two hundred pound, hurriedly dressed, unshaven Captain.

"What the hell's going on here?" he asked when he got to the scene. Ludlam was the first to speak.

"Nelson attacked this man," he motioned to the cop who had finally struggled to his feet, "and he hit me too!"

"I just pushed him when he tried to hold me for them," Nelson said. "If I had hit him, he would be in Sick Bay."

"Go and help your leader," the Captain told the cops.

For the first time since they came aboard, the policemen felt a sense of security, as three of them rushed to help the sergeant gather his composure. They admired the Captain's cool and demanding manner, and with the cold blue eyes, crew-cut hair, and hard jaws covered with gray stubble, he could so easily pass for one of them.

"Nelson also attacked a civilian with a knife!" Ludlam added, but that wasn't the Captain's main concern.

"How did these people get aboard!" he asked Ludlam. "You have the watch."

"Well Nelson had . . . "

"Right now I don't want to know about Nelson. I want to know why you let South Africans aboard my ship to arrest an American without consulting me?"

Ludlam was lost for words as the seamen began laughing, until the Captain waved his hand for silence. Everybody waited for Ludlam to answer. The Captain had tucked his shirttail into his short pants and buttoned his shirt, before Ludlam finally spoke.

"It . . . it all happened so doggone fast," he lied, "that I thought Nelson was African!"

Everyone in the messhall laughed, except Ludlam, the police and the Captain, who just shook his head.

"Ain't that a bitch!" Nelson said. "You know me . . . you know all the Stewards."

"Besides . . . " Brother Poe added, "Africans don't call people motherfuckers!"

"Sho' don't" Nelson stuck out his palm and Brother Poe slapped it as the laughter grew, "an' I called him a whole sack of 'em!"

"The foreigners on American property!" came a voice from the crowd. "We ought-a-kick all they ass . . . including Ludlam."

"That's enough!" the Captain shouted at the top of his heavy voice, and the Boatswain blew the whistle again. When the noise subsided the Captain lowered his voice.

"In the first place," he said, "there will be no more fighting aboard this vessel. and no one is going to be arrested."

32

The crewmen clapped until he raised his hand.

"Now I want these men to leave ... quickly and quietly."

The sergeant, who had put on his cap and straightened his uniform, saluted and led his men through a narrow wedge of mumbled obscenities.

"Okay! Let's quiet it down!" the skipper ordered. "I want this hall cleared so the cooks and messmen can get back to work. Everyone else go about their duties. I'll talk to you later," he told Nelson, then turned to Ludlam.

"I want to see you in my stateroom, right now! Get the Third to relieve you!"

The crewmen parted another path as Ludlam meekly followed the Captain and Boatswain Mate. When he got to the hatch, one of the crewmen kicked the print of a right shoe sole in the seat of his starched white pants. Ludlam didn't look back or tell the Captain.

By noon, the crispness in the air was gone, leaving the weather warm and humid. The Ghost had become a beehive of activity from the bridge to the bilges. Her overcrowded gangplank bounced constantly from the up and down trampling by Americans, Africans and Afrikanders.

White work foremen and port officials tried their best to keep from rubbing shoulders on the narrow plank with the black laborers in floppy, wide-leg trousers and dirty undershirts, or the black Yankees, who rushed back and forth between their duties and their women.

First Mate Ludlam cursed and slammed down the quarterdeck phone. He blew a speck of dust from the sleeve of his fresh uniform and stared at Boatswain Phillips, who turned his back. But Ludlam could tell he was laughing by the movement of his shoulders. Since that incident in the messhall, every black that passed him either giggled or laughed right in his face.

"I'm gonna find out who kicked me," he said to himself, "'cause niggers can't keep secrets. And when I do by God, I'm gonna find a way to sling his hash if it's the last thing I do!" To add insult to injury, he thought about that thorough chewing out the Old Man gave him. He had to bite his lip and shake his head to hold back tears of anger.

"I hate every black spear-chucking sonofabitch that ever breathed!" he mumbled, then pulled himself together.

"That was some drunkin' ape on the phone, probably calling from a whorehouse," he said, trying to insult Phillips, "wanting to know if the ship was leaving on time."

Phillips just leaned against the bulkhead and smiled with contempt.

"Well I hope he miss the departure an' get thrown in jail." Ludlam turned his back, walked to the lifeline, spat, and watched it fall slowly to the water. "'Cause I told that nigger we would be an hour late." He tried to smile as he peered down the dock and whispered: "Look at 'em . . . black savages all. If it wasn't for the clothes you couldn't tell one knotty head bimbo from another. By God, I hoped we'd get more white people this time. But we got more niggers than we got rid of . . . Niggers from everywhere! . . . Cuba, Puerto Rico, West Indies, Jamaica, Honduras. As if one kind of nigger ain't enough pain in the ass, this fuckin' ship's seventy percent nigger from the whole globe. But by God, it won't be too many more years before I retire, an' when I do, it's gonna be right here in good ole South Africa. Lot a great opportunity here for white folk. Best damn country in the world, 'cause they sho know how to keep a coon in his place!"

The ship's horn let out a long ear piercing blast, indicating it would soon be getting underway. A short stocky colored woman broke from her crowd and staggered along the dock.

"Eddie! Eddie! . . . my Eddie's gone!" She stumbled and fell. A seaman tried to help her, but when she cursed him, he turned away. She got up, made it to the edge of the pier and sat down near the gangplank, her legs dangling dangerously over the dock. Clean and sober, she might have been a fair-looking woman, but with her hair scattered over her head, and tears running down her pale dusty face, she resembled a witch. Some of the girls came over and tried to calm her down, but she got hysterical.

"Leave me alone!" she screamed, threatening to jump until they backed off. "My Eddie's gone. He's gone ... but my Eddie's coming back, you son-of-a-bitches ... you better believe it. I know my Eddie's coming back!"

This was the type of incident the cross-eyed sergeant that Nelson had hit in the messhall that morning was hoping for. He now had twice as many men, and he ordered them to move in on the coloreds.

"Clear the dock! ... Clear the dock!" he shouted. His men prodded the women with their clubs. "Clear the dock! ... all of you!" they shouted, echoing the sergeant.

"What the hell you mean, clear the dock!" a handful of seamen protested. "How come? They ain't bothering nobody!"

"They don't belong here!" the sergeant snarled, "and look at this!" He pointed at the drunken woman.

One of the crewmen dashed up the gangplank to sound the alert, while the cops and seamen cursed and argued with each other.

"We're going! ... we're going!" the women screamed when they saw the policemen preparing to attack the sailors. But that wasn't enough for the revenge-hungry sergeant, who provoked the Americans more by jabbing one of the girls in the rectum with his club.

Four cabs returning from the airport rolled up, slid to a halt, and sixteen more blacks piled out.

"What the fuck's going on here?" Johnson demanded, while Brother Poe halted the retreating women.

"This is my order!" The sergeant recognized a few of them and searched for Nelson in the bunch. But he wasn't there.

"He's trying to use wine-o Nellie as an excuse to pull this shit," one of the arguing sailors told Johnson. Without saying a word, Johnson walked over, snatched her up by the armpits, and practically threw her into a cab.

"Now stay there!" He slammed the door and walked back to the cops as black seamen swarmed from the ship.

"Now!" Johnson frowned to the sergeant. "These girls ain't leaving until you tell them bitches down there," he pointed at the white girls, "to leave."

The cross-eyed cop's temper got the best of him again. He started to raise his club, but a corporal grabbed him. When the other cops saw all those blacks coming towards them, they sensed sudden peril and reached for their guns.

Four shrieking blasts from the ship's horn ended what would have certainly been a deadly confrontation.

"All ashore that's going ashore!" the Boatswain's voice came over the loudspeaker. He blew a long, high note on his whistle and the horn sounded again. Most of the crew hurried back aboard, as the men coming from the Teahouse ran past the police and up the gangplank. The cross-eyed cop was still furious, and wanted his men to light in on the colored girls still standing near the gangway, and the Africans who had run with their boyfriends from the Teahouse.

"Why risk an incident with America," the corporal said. "In a few moments those bloody-blacks will be gone. Then no one will know the better how we treat these kiffers."

"The horn blasted again, and the voice repeated, "All ashore that's going ashore!"

The laborers finished their final tasks and their overseers hurried them off, while the white sailors, who were the last to scramble aboard, paused on the quarterdeck to throw kisses at their girls.

At thirteen fifty, the sailor that Ludlam had lied to jumped out of a taxi that was still rolling and streaked for the ship.

"You told me we was gonna be late!" the small dark skinned man said when he reached the quarterdeck, "but it's a good thing I don't trust yo' lying hill-billy ass."

Ludlam ignored him and ordered the tired squeaking gangplank to be hoisted and secured. The USNS *General Mitchell* gave a long bellowing howl, signaling the African dock hands, whose sweating brown and black bodies glistened in the sun, to untie the huge forward and aft lines. The whites on shore stood in awe of the countless dark

36

faces lining the decks of that American ship. But the policemen concentrated on the shouting and waving colored and African women.

"A damn sight more than I can stand!" the cross-eyed cop snarled, "I wish that stinking junk would stay in the Congo!"

"Or better, sink somewhere!" the corporal added.

At fourteen ten, the *Gray Ghost,* with her giant screw churning the water white, gave a final wail and inched away from the dock.

The cross-eyed sergeant gently patted the palm of his hand with his long heavy club, waiting for the ship to vanish around Table Mountain.

"Then he would make good use of it to chase the bloody-bitches away from the pier," he told himself.

Chapter Four

"THIS IS the Captain speaking!" came a booming voice over the loudspeaker. Everyone aboard stopped to listen, including the men handling the lines and winches under the eight mammoth lifeboats.

"Men ... " the voice sighed, "there isn't but one thing I can say about this drill. The only way to numerically evaluate it is X! ZIP! SHIT!" There was slight shuffling of the feet, hidden grins, and muffled laughter.

"Yesterday," the voice grew angry, "not half of the crew knew where their fire stations were. It took twenty-nine minutes to get the right gear in the proper place. It's been thirty-four minutes since I sounded abandon ship and now the First Mate tells me number five boat's flooded and they can't start the winch to lower number six ... What the hell kind of a ship are we running? If we're going to come eight thousand miles just to goof off, we might as well turn around and go home."

The sun was gone from the gray misty sky, as the bow of the *Mitchell* sliced a northward path through the rolling sea, leaving a long foamy trail.

"I realize a lot of you just arrived, but any seaman worth his salt knows the first thing you do after signing aboard a vessel is to learn your Watch, Quarter and Station Bill. We've been at sea for two days . . . two whole days!"

The Captain cleared his throat. "I know they had to scrape the bottom of the barrel to get men to ship out of Africa for six months. I also know this Congo voyage is considered a bastard cruise by most of the Military Sea Transportation Service. But to the United States this mission is the most important of any merchant ship at sea . . . by transporting thousands of United Nation's troops we're not only serving America but the whole free world. If there's a fire and we take twenty-nine minutes before starting to put it out, plus thirty-four minutes to abandon ship, all of us will end up in Davy Jones'locker. But gentlemen, throw that out of your minds. We have plenty time left before we reach the Congo . . . there will be drills, drills and more drills . . . morning noon and night, without overtime pay, until I am thoroughly convinced that every man on this ship knows where to go on every drill, the fastest way to get there, what equipment to carry, and how to use it! When we reach our destination, the *Mitchell* will be run by sailors in the fine tradition of American seamanship!" He cleared his throat again.

"I have just received a wire from Capetown about an incident at the airport the day we left. Add that to what happened in our messhall, and I've just about had it with this crew. If I ever again learn that one of my sailors insulted a member of the American embassy *anywhere,* all hell's going to break loose, and you'll never go ashore in that port!"

The seamen around lifeboat number three looked at a little dark pop-eyed man and giggled.

"How the hell was we to know he was American?" the pop-eyed man said as they secured the lines on the boat. He didn't identify himself . . . an' even if he did, who the fuck did he think he was, to tell us to cut out the noise?"

"He was just another jive-ass hunkey to me," Brother Poe said, and they all slapped each other in the palms.

"There will be no liberty in the Congo!" the Captain pledged. "The situation has become too tense and uncertain; it could explode anytime. Our mission is just to pick up Malayan troops and get the hell out of there as soon as possible ... I want all heads of departments and junior officers to assemble in the officer's mess at once ... That is all!"

The men who had been relieved from watch hurried back; others rushed for the recreation room to scramble for seats; while some, a little disheartened over the day's events, wandered around the weatherdecks in their bright-orange lifejackets, gazing out at the fading blue line on the horizon that separated the sea from the sky.

Three days and eight drills later, the old hands knew they were approaching the Congo river. Her overpowering current snaked a pale murky-brown color out into the hazy-green Atlantic, along with debris and vegetation washed downstream by territorial rains. The closer they got to the mouth of the river, the darker the water became, until even the whitecaps turned an oily tan.

A Portuguese destroyer suddenly appeared over the starboard bow, followed a few minutes later by another. The destroyers maneuvered close enough to identify the American flag, then slowly disappeared on the southwest horizon.

When the *Mitchell* started up the turbulent winding waterway separating Angola from the Congo, her decks were crowded. Excited voices filled the air; eager fingers pointed as cameras clicked and buzzed away trying to capture the essence of darkest Africa. The river itself was almost black and seemed motionless. But the maddening pace in which the Africans poled and paddled their long narrow carved-out boats around the huge swirling hunks of brush gave clear evidence of the river's swift defiant current.

Although the *Mitchell* was big and powerful, those extra drills to which the crew had been subjected paid off, because it took good seamanship to keep her from running aground. When she reached Matadi, long lines of Malayan soldiers, dressed in camouflage and wearing blue United Nations berets, were waiting and sweating in the hundred

40

degree heat. The moment the gangplank was secured, five officers rushed aboard and presented their identification to First Mate Ludlam. After a careless check he motioned the officers to Chief Steward Sullivan, who stood near the hatch with a group of stewards assigned to guide them to their living quarters. The commanding officer, a British Colonel, stationed two of his men at the foot of the gangplank with checkoff sheets and told the others to assist the guides. He gave an order and the lines began to move, slowly at first, then faster, the Malayan soldiers trying to get aboard before the daily one o'clock downpour that came during the rainy season.

Ludlam soon became annoyed with the jabbering, giggling faces filing past. Some looked like Indians, some Chinese, others like brown Chinese, all grinning and glad to be going home. He fixed his eyes on the once marvelous Belgian-owned hotel standing like a castle atop a large green hill. *"By God, I'm gonna take leave as soon as I get off watch."* He spat in the water. *"Live like people with people, away from these spooks and gooks."*

With his binoculars he could see sections of the thick rope in front of the hotel, patrolled day and night to keep whites from going to the village where they might be harmed. But personally, he wanted to believe the rope was to keep Africans out of the hotel. He took off his cap, wiped his face with a handkerchief and daydreamed of sipping tall drinks in plush surroundings ornamented by white women in pretty dresses.

A small African boy carrying a basket of mangoes and a stem of green bananas almost slipped past him. "What's your business?" he shouted, snatching the youth by the seat of his short flappy trousers. "Get off this ship!"

"Mangoes wana! Good mangoes, bananas! You buy wana?"

"I said get off!" Ludlam pushed the kid making him drop some of his fruit. When the lad stooped to retrieve it, Boatswain Phillips stepped between them.

"Let the boy pick up his stuff," Phillips said.

41

"I'm running this goddamn quarterdeck!" Ludlam snarled, kicking a mango into the water.

"You come Congo, okay!" the boy told Phillips. "You black like me, no trouble." Then he pointed to Ludlam. "You white man!" he shouted. "You come Congo you die!" The boy took an index finger and made the gesture of cutting his own throat, then ran down the gangplank bumping into oncoming soldiers. He paused at the bottom to shake his tiny fist at the tall white man in the long white suit.

Rinco lay on his back half asleep and half awake, the strength oozing from his body in perspiration that clung him to the moist sheets. He listened to the small fans mourn as they blew hot air around and around the compartment. From the grinding hum of the unbearable engine room below he could hear the distant whistle of the main air ejector screaming like a hysterical woman.

"Wake up man! You gonna miss chow!" Chitown came in dripping sweat and turned on the light. Rinco swung out of his rack.

"Why didn't the fireman call me to relieve the watch?" he asked, reaching for his socks. The heat from the engine room made the deck hot enough for him to hurry into his shoes.

"I secured the vaps at ten-thirty," Chitown said, running water into the face bowl. "The feed tanks are topped off, but the fresh water looks bad. We gotta get out of this harbor and soon."

"That stupid-ass chief engineer," Rinco complained. "With all those troops coming aboard, we should have been on water hours from the first day."

"Damn right," Chitown agreed. He finished washing, grabbed a towel and stepped aside. "This is the third day, we gotta be loaded. I can't hardly get to the vaps for those funny-talking motherfuckers."

Rinco laughed as he rinsed his face and mouth in lukewarm water from the cold water spout. "Don't worry, we'll be leaving tomorrow or the next day."

The ship's bell signaled the last call for dinner and they rushed out the hatch.

There were only six people left in the messhall. They joined Big Shot who sat alone eating ice cream. The tall, dark, lanky messman in a sweat-soaked tee shirt mumbled about people who wait till the last minute to eat, while he wiped his brow with a small towel. Rinco and Chitown ignored him and studied the menu. "Well dudes," Big Shot smiled, "what we gonna do ... shit or get off the pot?" They ignored him too and gave their orders. Big Shot ordered more ice cream. The messman grumbled again as he headed for the kitchen.

"What do you mean, shit or get off the pot?" Rinco asked.

"You know what I mean!"

"Here we go again," Chitown sighed.

"Damn right!" Big Shot said, "I know you secured the vaps, an' I know something else."

"What?"

"I know this pig-iron son-of-a-bitch is gettin' underway tomorrow night."

He smiled with them for a second, then got serious. "You dudes gonna have to run them shells night an' day, all the way to Malaya. This the last chance to hit the beach ... That hillbilly Ludlam is on the beach."

"He's on leave," Rinco admitted, "but he's confined to that hotel just as we are to this ship."

"Damn that!" Big Shot complained. "This is Africa, he's a red neck-hillbilly an' been livin' it up for three days ... we niggers gotta stay on the ship ... ain't that a bitch?"

The messman hurried back with their food, slapped it on the table and retreated to a far stool under a fan. They ate in silence until Big Shot finished his ice cream.

"It's been a long time since we been on the beach." He took a swallow of water and lit a cigarette. "I know you had a ball dry-docked in Capetown all that time, but me an' Chi ain't had no liberty since we left New York, except for them few hours. Hell, we just want a chance to look

43

around; see what's happening. It's gonna take a long time to get to Malaya."

"Don't speak for me," Chitown said. "We know what you want."

"Yeah," Rinco agreed, "don't give us that 'look around to see what's happening' bullshit."

"Damn right! I want some Congo action," Big Shot conceded. "When I get back to the city them cats gonna ask me 'bout these Congo broads. If I dummy up I'd lose my rep."

Four crewmen got up and left, leaving only the three of them and a drunken red-faced plumber who ate slowly, dripping perspiration into his food.

"How about you guys giving me a play?" the messman said, checking his watch.

"Alright dude," Big Shot answered, "we gonna make it in a minute, now how 'bout giving us a play an' let us rap."

Chitown and Rinco each ordered a bowl of ice cream to take with them. The messman shook his head in disgust and went back to the kitchen.

"If you want to hit the beach so bad," Rinco said, "why don't you try Johnson and Brother Poe? They're hip to the village and do practically anything they want to."

"I tried 'em already, they ain't interested."

"Huh," Rinco grunted, "they've got more sense than I thought. Ain't shit there, and it can be dangerous. You never know how these Congolese are thinking, or who they're fighting for."

"Aw, excuses! excuses!" Big Shot slammed his hand on the table. "What you mean ain't shit there? Women are everywhere. Ludlam's probably laying on a bitch right now , . . . right here in our grand-daddy's hometown, an' you dudes scared to go ashore in broad daylight. You ain't got a hair in yo' ass."

Rinco and Chitown looked at each other.

"You want to go to town with this clown Chi?"

"I don't give a damn!"

"Mellow!" Big Shot smiled. "I can sneak away from the engine room. They got me workin' on the upper level.

Ain't nobody coming up in that filthy ass inferno. What about you dudes?"

"If we hit the beach," Rinco said, "it's gonna be my way."

"What you mean?" Big Shot asked.

"I mean no sharp rags ... no flashing money, and you better leave your fancy watch and ring here, if you want to come back with your arm. We wear work clothes and try to blend in."

"Dungarees?" Big Shot frowned, then looked at Chi-town.

"Don't look at me, I ain't going pussy hunting."

"Naw ... but you sho' blend in."

"So do you, nigger."

"Yeah ... but they might string Rinco up."

The drunken plumber rose slowly and eased his way out.

"We'll go about five o'clock," Rinco said after they finished laughing. "Give some of that rain a chance to dry up. With Ludlam gone, it'll be easy to fake a work sign off."

"We leave together?" Big Shot asked.

"No, one at a time."

The messman returned, gave Rinco and Chitown their ice cream and headed for the plumber's dishes. When he started back their way, they got up and left.

Chapter Five

BIG SHOT and Chitown squirmed nervously in the rear seat of the car, looking out the windows as the car sped down the narrow winding road through thick, dark green jungle that shut out the sun. They were worried about the strange sounds within the brush, but more about the straining sound of the motor.

We'll make it fellows!" Rinco turned in the front seat and laughed.

When they reached the village, all three had the inclination to turn back but wouldn't tell the others. The houses looked battle-marked and the shops appeared looted. The streets were crowded, but Big Shot didn't see a woman. He spotted a man with a load of cameras and told the driver to stop. Before Rinco could caution, Big Shot jumped out and darted through the crowd.

"Wait here driver!" Rinco said. "Come on Chi!" They got out of the car and followed.

"How much for the whole bunch?" Big Shot was asking the dumbfounded African with the cameras when they caught up.

"Cool it, Shot," Rinco whispered.

"You cool it dude, I can clean up on this shit." He turned back to the African. "I'll give you fifty American dollars for everything, an' won't ask you where you got 'em from." When he reached into his pocket, Rinco grabbed his wrist.

"Dig!" Chitown pointed.

They looked and saw five ragged but well-armed soldiers approaching from across the street.

"Let's go!" Rinco ordered. "Walk, don't run!"

Cut off from the cab, they headed in the opposite direction. When the soldiers reached their side, they crossed over to the other, glancing to see if the Africans would follow. They did.

"Ignore them, don't look back," Rinco said, stopping in front of a short shifty-eyed man squatting beside a row of polished wood carvings. The man's folded arms failed to hide the handle of a knife stuck in his belt. When he recognized Rinco, he got up and shook hands. He was cleanly dressed in white but wrinkled and barefoot. Rinco told him of the oncoming soldiers. The man nodded and rushed to meet the soldiers with outstretched arms and a worried smile.

"Wait for a chance to make a break," Rinco whispered, appearing to look over the carvings, as Big Shot and Chitown gazed at the taxi a half-block away. At first, the man in white and the soldiers argued, then they started pushing him around. The Americans signaled each other and began easing slowly away. A bunch of half-naked children ran among the Africans and started playing around their legs.

"Now!" Rinco shouted. They made a frantic dash for the cab. hurdling and side-stepping like a trio of flashy halfbacks.

"Get the hell outta here!" Big Shot yelled as they all piled into the rear seat. Rinco and Chitown peered anxiously at the soldiers who were having trouble moving through the crowd.

"Come on man! Let's make it!" Big Shot shouted again. The curious driver finally started the car. When it pulled off, the soldiers stopped. One of them fired two pistol shots. The first missed, but the second thudded into the trunk. The driver speeded up as Rinco, Chitown and Big Shot hit the floor.

"Damn! that was close!" Big Shot wiped his brow, as they got up from the floor. "Who was that dude in white? Yo' long-lost cousin?"

"It's a good thing I bought a lot of stuff from him on the last trip." Rinco said.

"Damn right!" Chitown agreed, "because those cats would have robbed and wasted us right on the street . . . in broad daylight!"

Big Shot reached for his whiskey flask. "This a dog-eat-dog motherfuckin' town," he said.

"They probably haven't been paid in months," Rinco theorized, "and hungry men armed to the teeth are the most dangerous in the world."

Big Shot and Chitown lit cigarettes and passed the whiskey around. Rinco started to offer the driver a drink, but Big Shot objected.

"Naw dude, these niggers nutty 'nough already!"

"Me no nigger!" the driver took a hand off the wheel to turn and point at Big Shot. "Me Bakonga! . . . free! . . . independence!"

"Now you've done it, Shot." Rinco pulled out a cigar and unwrapped it.

"My country!" The driver pounded the finger into his own chest. His long narrow mouth snarled between his strong jaws and over his short smooth chin.

"You nigger!" His deep set eyes burned into Big Shot. "Me no nigger! . . . You nigger! . . . Me African . . . Bakonga! . . . freedom . . . independence!"

Rinco shook his head and lit the cigar.

"Man, turn around and watch where the hell you going," Chitown shouted, "before you run into a rhinoceros or something!"

The driver turned just in time. He was into a curve and had to fight the wheel to stay on the road.

"Me African, Bakonga," he repeated.

48

"An' watch out for them elephants too," Big Shot laughed. "They ain't got no bumpers on they ass."

"You a bitch with your shit." Rinco shook his head. "These Congolese fighting like cats and dogs, and you over here calling people niggers and motherfuckers."

Big Shot just laughed again. Chitown passed him the flask and he emptied it.

"Hey driver!" Big Shot yelled. "Where can we get some more booze?" There was no answer.

Rinco leaned over the seat and spoke politely. "We would like to go some place and have a few drinks. Do you know where to take us?"

The driver looked at Rinco, nodded yes, then frowned at Big Shot before making a turn onto an even smaller road. After a long bumpy ride, they pulled up in front of a large square-shaped cafe with bamboo curtains in the glassless windows. There was no music, dancing or laughter, only muffled chatter that ceased abruptly when the strangers entered. It was crowded, with nearly every table occupied and all eyes on them were hostile, including those of the two bartenders, who snarled from behind the long, empty, stool-less bar lining the right wall. The Americans stopped in their tracks and looked around. The silence was frightening; even the fluttering bamboo curtains were muffled by mosquito nets. Then came the sound of shuffling feet as they backed out the door and ran to the car. This time the driver saw them coming and started the motor.

"Damn!" Chitown said. "Everybody in this fuckin' country got a chip on their shoulder." Rinco started to suggest the driver accompany them but Big Shot cut him off. "Hell! I wouldn't go back in there with Superman!"

Chitown and Rinco were eager to return to the ship but not Big Shot.

"Dig dudes," he said when they were well away from the cafe, "after going through all this shit, I know we ain't never coming back, so while we here, let's all cop a broad." His shipmates shook their heads no.

49

"Well, ya'll know why I hit the beach ... Hey driver," he leaned over the seat, "we wanna see some women!"

"You waited too late man," Rinco said. "It'll soon be dark, and we don't want to be caught out here."

"Amen," Chitown seconded.

"I just want a little Congo trim," Big Shot pleaded. "I ain't gonna try an' make no home ... dig driver! You know the kinda girls I mean, the ones who like ta make money!"

The word money turned the driver's head.

"Oh!" he answered. "You want Pum-Pum!" He released the wheel and made a pumping motion with his hands, then looked in the mirror at his passengers as if seeing them for the first time. A wide grin spread across his face.

"That's right, dad." Big Shot winked at Rinco and Chitown. "You know what's happening ... this dude ain't nutty as I thought," he whispered.

For fifteen minutes the car raced past small scattered huts, until it reached a steep bumpy incline. At the top the driver made a near U-turn and coasted to a stop in front of a large fenced-in mud hut. He got out, went through the gate, returned in a few seconds and beckoned to them.

"Coming fellows?" Big Shot asked. He felt a little leery and wanted company.

"No thanks!" they answered. Big Shot got out and lit a pipe of hashish. "I won't be long."

"I sure the hell hope not." Rinco glanced up at the fading daylight.

"If we hear drums and see smoke coming up," Chitown yelled, "we're getting outta here!" Big Shot let out a nervous laugh and followed the driver through the small wooden gate.

"You know," Chitown lit a cigarette, "I believe Big Shot would fuck a rattlesnake if somebody held its head."

"Maybe so, if he was sure it was female," Rinco laughed and pulled out a cigar. "I see he still hasn't gotten over Pam."

"Who's Pam?" Chitown asked.

"His ex-wife."

"Damn!" Chitown was surprised. "I didn't think Big Shot was the type to even consider marriage. Did they have any kids?"

"No, but only because she didn't want any." Rinco pondered a moment, and then said, "I guess it's okay to tell you, because he would do it himself if the subject ever came up. He's not so squeamish about it anymore. Let's stretch our legs!"

They got out of the car and walked over to the shade of the tall bamboo fence.

"Man you never saw a finer looking chick than Pam." Rinco flicked an ash. "Slim and sleek, with beautiful long legs, curly black hair, and carmel-colored skin as smooth as a baby's ass. She dressed sharp and kept plenty money."

"She sound just right for Big Shot," Chitown said. "What could have happened?"

"He worshiped her," Rinco agreed, "and didn't mess around at all, the whole three years they were married. But one of the many nights she was supposed to be out of town, he let a few of his buddies talk him into going to this after-hour joint. They were sitting there watching stag movies, and guess who came on the screen?"

"Pam?"

"You said it. Man that tore him apart."

"I'll bet!"

"He ran out while his good buddies stayed to watch the action."

In a fleeting moment of compassion for Big Shot, Chitown grunted and shook his head as the air began to cool and they walked back into the sunlight.

"We made a Mediterranean cruise together shortly afterward. Man, that cat drank, doped and brooded so bad he had me worried as hell, for over a month. When he finally snapped out of it he went woman wild, and has been that way ever since. I guess it's some kind of obsession to out-Pam, Pam."

Suddenly they heard noise from behind the wall, but it

51

was only the chatter of women and the laughter of little children.

"Kids are wonderful," Chitown flipped away his cigarette butt. "The world can be falling apart all around them, but if they're not scared, sick or hungry, they will find time to play."

"Yeah," Rinco stomped his cigar into the dust, "and it's a damn shame when they have to grow up in a war."

"Say man!" Chitown had an afterthought as they climbed back into the car, "You never did tell me what the hell this war is all about. I mean African against African."

"There is no way I can make this story short," Rinco said, "so I'll break it down as best I can. After the long and bloody regime of King Leopold, when each village was forced to send so many men to work in the mines and on the plantations ... I mean they had to enslave themselves to pay the head tax the Belgians imposed on them ... Anyway, after King Leo, the Belgians built a few schools, hospitals and houses for the blacks. By letting the miners bring their wives and families to live with them, instead of leaving them in the rural tribal areas like they do in Rhodesia and South Africa, they figured they had the best-run colony on the continent and would rule the Congo forever. That little shit they did for the African was no more than you would do for a pet. The black man had no rights at all ... no political power ... no freedom of speech, assembly or press. They couldn't even form their own cultural societies."

Ain't that a bitch," Chitown said. "When you read the white books and papers, or listen to the media, you get all this crap about the so-called good things the Europeans have done ... abolished slavery ... stopped tribal wars ... constructed railroads, highways, dams, hospitals ... "

"For who?" Rinco cut him off ... "Everybody need hospitals, and the whites got the best ones. Sure they attempted to stop tribal warfare. How could they get enough men to mine for gold, diamonds, copper and uranium if the tribes were at war? ... Or operate their plantations if their workers were being kidnaped? They didn't build those roads to help the African, only to transport loot to the seaports for Europe. It was the same story all over Africa."

"You sure know a lot about African history." Chitown was impressed.

"Well I read everything about Africa I can get my hands on," Rinco said, "plus I've been over here long enough to see a lot for myself. But back to the war. The black man got tired of that bullshit throughout Africa. The Congo was no exception. In January of fifty-nine, Leopoldville had the biggest riot in Congo history. Hundreds were killed, and the whites were pinned down for over a week, until Belgium promised the Congolese their independence. Man, political parties sprang up all over the Congo, at least sixty of them. Damn near every tribe formed their own party. Lumumba's National Congolese Movement was the oldest and largest, so he became Prime Minister. Kasavubu's Bakonga tribe formed the Abkao party, and he became President. Those two at the top didn't dig each other, and that's the way it was all down the line.

When independence came there was no unity anywhere. It was all one big mess. Only sixteen out of thirty million Congolese had a college education. So there were no skills to run a country. Bloody fights broke out between tribes and between political parties. Underpaid soldiers rebelled and took out their frustrations on helpless blacks and the whites who were running over each other to get out. When Uncle Tshombe, with the help of Belgium hired mercenaries, set up a separate government in Kantanga to keep the copper mines, civil war developed. Lumumba asked the United Nations for troops to put down the seccessionist governments in Kantanga and Kasai. But it seems the U.N. only came to keep the fighting from spreading, thus avoiding conflict between the super powers."

He paused to reach for a cigar as Chitown lit another cigarette.

"Since Lumumba couldn't get the help he wanted from the U.N., he went to the Communist for arms and tried to unify the country. Then this Army leader named Mobutu, with help from the CIA, arrested him, and turned him over to Uncle Tshombe who had him killed."

"Damn." Chitown shook his head. "This situation is as fucked up as all those strange names you been shooting at me."

Rinco lit the cigar and went on.

"The remaining leaders finally got together and united behind this cat named Adoula. All except Uncle Tshombe, and he's the one we're fighting now."

As Rinco spoke, Chitown looked up at the darkening sky and felt uneasy.

"I wish Big Shot would bring his ass on," he said, then apologized for the interruption.

"That's alright," Rinco said and thumped an ash. "But there's one important lesson every black man who visits Africa should learn, especially Americans."

"What's that?"

Rinco threw away the cigar. "Do you know how many Belgians lived in the Congo? One hundred and fifteen thousand. And do you know how much the average one made a year? Over four thousand dollars, for each member of the family!" He stuck up a finger to emphasize the point. "And the poor African ... in his own land ... only made about forty dollars a year."

"So what's the lesson?" Chitown flipped away his butt. "The African is getting screwed worse than we are? We don't have to come all the way over here to know that."

"The lesson is," Rinco stuck his finger in the air again, "no sacrifice is too great for the white man to preserve his myth of racial superiority. Here, with your own eyes you can see his abandonment of a virtual paradise, where wealth abounds, rather than give the black man a fair shake. If he's willing to leave a land where his family earns fifty percent more than the average American family, just because he can no longer play the big boss, how in the hell can the American boot ever expect equality where he's out-numbered, out-gunned, and out-smarted. That's why I'm staying in Africa. Tanganyika should be getting its independence any day now. Then it won't be long before Kenya is free. We'll be going to East Africa later, and you can check them out. Because slowly but surely, the black man is inching his freedom all the way down from the Horn to the gates of South Africa itself. And believe me brother, if you want freedom, justice and equality, it's got to start right here where you came from . . . Africa!"

"Maybe so, but from what you've told me about Capetown, and what I've seen of Matadi, I'd just as soon be in Mississippi."

They both laughed, then Rinco said, "I haven't rapped to anyone this way since the CIA hawked me about a year ago."

"What?"

"Well, back then I was really into my black bag. I was trying to recruit black shipmates to stay in Africa, and even started group Swahili lessons."

"No shit?"

"I would get maybe a dozen cats, when the recreation room was overcrowded, or the movie wasn't shit. All of a sudden this two-man salt and pepper team started hanging around."

"Did they ever fuck with you?"

"Naw . . . I guess they were in route somewhere and didn't want their hole card peeped. So they backed off, and disappeared when we docked in Kenya. I started keeping a low profile because I wasn't getting anywhere with our crew anyway. Those cats would be attentive as hell while we were at sea. But as soon as we hit the beach, all they thought about was dope, booze and broads. I talk to you like this because I don't think you're a plant. I figure you for an average guy, trying to use the skills you learned in the service to improve the lives of your family."

"Right on both counts," Chitown agreed. "That's the reason I took this year long cruise. Added to my naval sea time, I hope to have enough to take the exam for Second Engineer. Then we can live pretty good."

55

"It'll work out if you both pull together."

"I sure hope so, because I'm beginning to have second thoughts."

Chapter Six

IT WAS almost dark when Big Shot and the driver returned to the cab. The African wheeled the car around, making a U turn, and sped down the slope.

"How did you like the Congolese action?" Rinco joked.

"It was hot an' tight," Big Shot smiled, "I whaled my ass off, but she didn't say a word. I didn't even get a grunt in Congolese."

"She just hasn't learned the fine, age-old art of bullshit," Chitown remarked.

"Yeah! maybe you right," Big Shot pondered, "but I wish I had a sack ta put over her god-damn head. That bitch looked like Kid Gavilan."

"Well you stayed long enough to go fifteen rounds," Rinco said, and Chitown burst out laughing. Big Shot joined him, and then Rinco, but their laughter was short-lived.

Complete darkness fell almost as suddenly as the afternoon rains, bringing an eerie stillness that silenced everything but the hum of the car motor, and the increasing sound of active insects.

"Do we have to go back through Matadi?" Chitown asked, almost in a whisper.

"Yeah!" Big Shot added, "Can't we take a short cut or something? I don't wanna go back through that bad motherfucker!"

"It's the only way," Rinco said, "unless you want to hack your way through the bush."

"Forget that shit!" Big Shot answered quickly as the headlights of the cab knifed the blackness.

When they got to the village it was a ghost town. Even the insects were stilled. The only light anywhere was the headlamps of the taxi, silhouetting the deserted buildings.

Suddenly the driver dimmed his lights, gunned the motor, and drove with reckless speed.

"Hey dude!" Big Shot shouted, "what the hell's the matter with you? Slow down before you hit something. An' turn on them damn lights!"

"No lights ... no lights." The driver drove faster. "Night," he said, "Congo bad ... no lights!"

"Night's when you need lights, you dumb" ... Big Shot turned to Chitown. "What the hell kind a country is this?"

"My country!" the driver shouted. "Bakonga country ... freedom ... independence!"

Once out of the village, the driver slowed down, but did not brighten the headlights. For about a mile, they rode in dark, nervous silence, then the taxi pulled to the side of the road and stopped.

Big Shot tapped the driver on the back. "What the hell's going on dude?"

"Shut up!" Rinco snapped.

"I fix! I fix!" The driver got a flashlight from the glove compartment, jumped out, went to the front, and lifted the hood.

"Something's fishy about this shit," Chitown said.

"It may be a stick-up!" Rinco whispered, "Get out of the car!"

"That's all the fuck we need." Big Shot patted the razor in his pocket.

When they caught the driver under the hood signaling with the light, he turned it on them and demanded money.

"We ain't gonna give you shit, till you get us back to our ship." Big Shot eased out the razor.

"How much do we owe you?" Rinco asked, trying to avoid a fight.

"All money!" the driver shouted, "Give me all money!" He signaled again, darting the light down a nearly hidden path, as sounds of movement came from the thick bush.

Chitown smashed his big right fist in the driver's jaw, knocking him to his knees.

"Get his car keys!" Rinco ordered. He picked up the dropped flashlight and shined it on four charging Africans. Chitown snatched the dazed driver up by the shoulders, and ran his hand through the African's pockets.

"I got em!" he said.

"Look out!" Rinco yelled as the other Africans were upon them.

The first one lunged at the light. Rinco side-stepped and the African went head first under the open hood. Two of them leaped on Chitown and rode him to the ground. The other one grabbed at Big Shot, but let out an ear bursting scream when the razor split his palm.

There was another, more muffled scream, as Rinco slammed the hood down on the back of the first attacker.

"Help! . . . Give me some help!" Big Shot's voice cried out in the darkness.

Rinco shined the light to see Big Shot on the ground trying to ward off the one-handed blows from a big powerful African, who had knocked him down and now straddled him. He then shined the light on Chitown, struggling to his feet, while exchanging punches with a tall tough man, and doing his best to shake another one off his back.

Rinco figured Big Shot needed the most help. He ran over and clubbed the African on the head with the long light, knocking him cold.

"Where my razor?" Big Shot rubbed the ground frantically, "I'm gonna kill this motherfucker!"

"Damn that razor!" Rinco snapped, "let's help Chitown!" He shined the light again. Chitown was now wrestling with the tall African. The other one was still draped over his back, and the driver was hugging his left leg.

"Let's go!" Rinco shouted, as Chitown was about to fall.

Big Shot got up, dashed over and kicked the driver in the ribs. He stiffened, grunted and flopped face down as Big Shot turned and ran for the car.

"Bring the keys! . . . bring the keys!" . . . he yelled, not noticing the badly scarred man who had finally raised the hood off his back, and was busy removing the cover from the carburetor to fight with.

Using the handle of the flashlight like a dagger, Rinco stabbed into the back of the man riding Chitown. He yelled, let go, and turned around. Rinco smacked him in the face with the globe, breaking the glass and plunging them into total darkness.

Chitown stooped and grabbed the legs of the man he was scuffling with, lifted him high in the air, then dropped him. When he landed on his back, Chitown pounded a big right fist down into the African's stomach like a hammer. He let out a hollow grunt, and rolled over on his side.

"You still got the keys?" Rinco asked while their attackers were temporarily disabled.

"Yeah!" Chitown answered, "but let's get that cat out from under the hood," he pointed to the car silhouetted in the moonlight. The African had just removed the cover when they snatched him from behind and threw him to the ground.

"Come on! . . . come on!" Big Shot squirmed nervously as they jumped into the front and back seats. It seemed like an eternity before Chitown got the right key in the ignition. He turned it again and again, but nothing happened.

"Let's make a run for it!" Rinco suggested when they heard the Africans calling to each other.

"Okay!" Chitown said, "I'll turn on the lights so we can see down the road."

But what they saw froze them. The huge black African stood only a few feet from the front bumper in a war-like pose, with the carburetor cover drawn back like a spear.

A long nasty gash in his forehead poured bright red blood down between two bulging, hate filled eyes, and dripped from the tip of his nose into his snarling lips. He let out a scream and threw the cover into the windshield with all his might.

"Let's go!" Chitown whispered as the enraged African leaped up on the hood and started stomping the web-like crack in the windshield, showering Big Shot and Chitown with glass as they crawled out the doors. He screamed again, and dove at Big Shot when they ran past him.

"Come on cats!" Big Shot yelled when he felt the tips of the out-stretched fingers on his back. He passed Rinco and Chitown without breaking stride.

The wounded African took up the chase for about fifty yards, but saw the gap widening and decided to go back and start the car.

The Americans didn't slow down until they rounded a curve, out of the beam of the headlights. Then they paused to catch their breath and listen for the sound of the car. Every time the engine started, their hearts jumped into their throats, but every time it sputtered and died they relaxed.

"I'm bleeding!" Big Shot gasped.

"Shut up dammit!" Chitown snapped.

Rinco pulled out his cigarette lighter and struck it. "Let's take a look," he said.

Big Shot unbuttoned the bloody shirt and opened it wide.

"I don't see nothing man," Rinco said. "Do you Chi?"

"Naw, ain't nothing wrong with that nigger, or he'd feel it. I'm the one hurting. That was a hard-hitting mother-fucker I duked with. And the one on my back almost choked me to death."

"The dude I was fighting wasn't no short-stop either." Big Shot felt his face. "My jaw so swollen I can hardly open my mouth."

"Good!" Rinco said, but Big Shot talked on. "This blood must be his . . . from when I whacked his ass."

The cab engine started again, and they held their breath. It whined for a few seconds and died.

"Let's get the hell out of here," Rinco said, "before they decide to jog down the road after us."

But they couldn't see their hands in front of their faces, and almost panicked until Rinco took over.

"This is the way we'll do it," he said. "One of you grab the back of my belt, and the other grab his, so we won't get separated. I'll lead, since I've been down this road before in daylight."

For over an hour they crept slowly, in single file, behind Rinco's out-stretched arms clawing the cool still blackness. Their eyes wandered in search of some reflection, or guiding light. There was nothing. The moon had disappeared, and there wasn't a star in the low-hanging sky.

Suddenly a noise ahead stiffened them. The sound of motors grew closer and louder. A convoy of trucks traveling by lantern light, turned from another road and headed their way.

Rinco tried to ease toward the brush, but his right foot dropped from under him, and he fell sideways down a sunken shoulder. Big Shot tried to grab him, Chitown tried to hang on to Big Shot, and all three tumbled down a four-foot slope, filled with dead leaves and painful twigs.

The rumbling trucks, loaded with loud-talking Africans, awakened the jungle, as they came closer and closer. Big Shot, Rinco and Chitown lay still where they had fallen, shuddering from the sound of strange voices and mysterious noises in the brush. It was over ten minutes after the convoy passed before they moved or spoke.

"Everybody okay?" Rinco asked, concealing his pain.

"Okay!" they answered, despite their aches and bruises.

"You guys seen how those trucks came at us?"

"Yeah . . . so what?" Big Shot answered.

"That's the road we take to get back."

"Well let's hit it!" Chitown said, and they climbed out of the ditch.

"It won't be much slower if we crawl." Rinco took a deep breath. "And it might keep us from falling into another hole." They all agreed, and stayed in single file by touching each other's heels while Rinco patted the road in front of them.

By the time they reached the spot where the trucks turned, they were aching all over. Their clothes were torn and filthy, and their knees felt numb. When they stopped to rest their weary bodies, and remove the gooey mud stuck between their fingers, Big Shot flopped out.

"Hey!" ... Rinco noticed a distant glow. "Look ... look over there!"

"Aw, they just probably pot-boiling some po' son-a-bitch, that's all." Big Shot grumbled.

"I don't know," Rinco said, "but I think it's in the direction of the dock."

"It is!" Chitown exclaimed as he and Rinco stood up to get a better look. Big Shot rose to his elbows and flopped back down. Rinco and Chitown let out a cheer when they recognized the small red beacon as the single mast light of the *Gray Ghost*.

"I don't see what the hell ya'll hollering about," Big Shot said, "we still got a damn long way ta go ... an' I'm beat dad."

"Ain't that a bitch Chi!" Rinco shook his head. "All the shit we went through, and he's got the nerve to complain about being pussy whipped."

"Well ... let his black-ass lay here and wait for the subway," Chitown said.

"Aw, get-up off me dudes." Big Shot struggled to his feet.

"Fuck you!" Chitown turned angry. "We've been shot at, jumped on, run off the road by a whole damn army, and crawled through ten miles of shit ... just because you *had* to dip your wick. Well I certainly hope you don't get offended Mr. Big Shot. I just hope like hell the bitch burned you. I hope your nuts swell to the size of grapefruit, and you look like a chimpanzee about the ass."

They both relaxed when Rinco fell back to his knees and rolled over laughing.

Chapter Seven

FIRST MATE Ludlam, dressed in a green short sleeve shirt that hung over the waist of his starched khaki pants, scanned the crowded dock in search of the Canadian Captain who had given him a lift to the hotel the first day of his leave. The Captain wasn't around.

Placing his right hand over his bare head to shield his eyes from the sun, Ludlam glanced back at the hotel. It was too far and too damn hot to lug water. But he had promised an old Belgian widow, who them black bastards burned out about a month ago and killed her husband, that he would bring some fresh water, "'cause she's in a bad way," he told her lovely, well-stacked daughter. The daughter was the real reason he was going through all this shit in the first place.

Boy ... I sho' want to lay her before we get underway, he told himself, but he could tell by how low the *Mitchell* sat in the water that she was good and loaded. He cursed under his breath and scampered up the gangway.

Chief Steward Sullivan, a short, stout Irishman who had the watch, saw him coming through tiny blue eyes that were magnified by thick glasses, and grinned.

"How's everything at the hotel?"

"All fucked up!" Ludlam grunted. "I came to get a couple gallons of water."

"Water?" Sullivan looked at him quizzically.

"Like I said, all fucked up. They ain't got much water at the hotel."

"I'll be damned!" Sullivan said. "How the hell do the people live?"

"On the little they got. They have to ration it out. Not many people there either, an' they leaving as soon as they can get transportation."

"What about the train? Isn't it running?"

"Yeah, but it's waiting for more whites to come from the outlying provinces, so they can have enough passengers for a U.N. escort. I think they'll be leaving soon as they get a bunch of nuns trapped up there in Kivi. That three-day ride to Leopoldville is dangerous as hell."

"That hotel may be dangerous as hell, too!" Sullivan warned.

"It ain't for me." Ludlam glanced down at the slight bulge from the forty-five automatic tucked in his belt.

Sullivan appeared not to notice. "I can't see for the hell of me why you waste your leave days up there," he said.

"I ain't wasting my leave by a long shot!" Ludlam winked.

"Not anymore," Sullivan smiled, "because we get underway tonight."

"You full-a-shit!"

"No I'm not ... twenty-one hundred. You saved us the trouble of a phone call. If I were you, I wouldn't go back up there."

"Why not?"

"Rumors have it that Congolese troops, deserters, or maybe just loyal to Kasavubu, are massing to attack the village. They might hit the hotel."

"They wouldn't dare! Not while an American ship is here." Ludlam scanned the dock again.

"I don't know." Sullivan took off his glasses and wiped

them. "The Canadians and Sudanese aren't taking it lightly. They wired Leopoldville for reinforcements."

"Hell, they need reinforcements anyway. It's only forty of them, an' I wouldn't trust a Sudanese as far as I could spit." He glanced around to see if any blacks were within ear shot, then went on. "These Congo son-of-a-bitches sure fucked up a good country. Look at that beautiful hotel. When the whites leave it won't even function at all. I hope all these niggers blow each other to hell!"

Sullivan just shook his head. Ludlam was disappointed by the indifferent response and hurried through the passageway. He soon returned with two gallon cans of cool fresh water. Without saying another word, he started down the gangway.

"You better try and be back before dark." Sullivan's warning fell on deaf ears as Ludlam gave a final glance for the Canadian, then headed toward the hotel.

"I wish those woolly head bastards would come," he thought. "I got a carbine, two hundred rounds and another forty-five in my room just waiting on them." He became completely unaware of the surroundings as he imagined himself blasting down a multitude of frenzied black Africans with the widow's daughter clinging desperately to him for survival. "I bet she ain't had a man in a long time. . ."

He had no idea he was being followed by a half-dozen armed irregulars, as he visualized the girl's long brown hair scattered over fluffy white pillows. He could almost feel her soft skin sweating under his. He started to hasten his pace when he envisioned her whimpering and clawing at his flesh. By then the Africans had caught up. One stepped in his path and held out a rifle.

"What!" Ludlam was appalled. His first impulse was to grab the rifle, but when he realized the situation, fear leaped into him. The gun in his belt suddenly felt heavier than the water he carried in his trembling hands. Except for one, apparently the leader, the Africans were well-armed with European automatic and semi-automatic rifles. The leader stood back with his hands on two forty-four pistols worn western style.

"Look here!" Ludlam shouted at him. "I'm American an—"

"Hands up!" the leader shouted back.

"But you can't . . . "

"Hands up!" repeated one of the soldiers as he pointed his rifle at Ludlam. Ludlam dropped the cans and raised his arms slowly. The leader stepped forward and started patting him down. Ludlam looked around for a white, or sympathetic face in the crowd that had gathered. There was neither.

The leader froze for a split second when he felt Ludlam's gun, then quickly raised the shirt and snatched the gun out. A murmur went through the crowd, and the soldiers put their fingers on the triggers of their weapons. The leader waved the forty-five in the air, cursed in Congolese, and slapped Ludlam across the face with his other hand.

"White man!" Ludlam heard the voice of a kid just as an overripe banana splattered on his chest. He looked down into the dark, sneering face of the boy peddler he had put off the ship when they arrived.

"Come Congo, you die . . . I tell you monkey man!" The peddler gave the gesture of slitting the throat with the finger, as one of the soldiers pushed him back.

All the atrocities described by the widow's daughter flashed through Ludlam's mind. He sweated, trembled, and his face grew pale, but he tried his utmost not to appear frightened. He knew he had to talk, and talk fast, but didn't know what to say. He glanced back at the ship. It seemed miles away.

Not a damn soul paying any attention to what's going on, he told himself, but it's just as well. The whites sho' as hell ain't gonna come down here, and the niggers would only laugh.

Ludlam kept his hands high as the leader continued the search, dropping the contents from his pockets into the hat of one of his men. They examined everything then gave it all back except his money and hotel key. When he asked for them the leader pointed and yelled. "You CIA . . . spend money to corrupt . . . We take in name of Congolese Government!"

"What damn Congolese Government?" Ludlam was surprised by the firmness of his own voice.

"What government you fight for white man?" the boy threw another banana that missed, and a soldier pushed him back again.

"Get out Congo!" the leader shouted at Ludlam.

"Get out! . . . Get out!" the others repeated, and the crowd took up the chant.

"Get out Congo! . . . Get out!"

Ludlam started to turn and run, but thought about the weapons and ammunition still locked in his hotel room. Somehow he had to get them back to the ship's armory, or pay for them out of his own pocket.

"I'm leaving . . . I'm leaving!" he said. "Just give me my key so I can get my luggage. You can keep the damn money!"

"We keep damn money anyway," one of the soldiers said and all of the Africans laughed.

"An' . . . an' . . . this water," Ludlam's voice began to crack, "I must get it to the hotel. An old woman is very, very sick."

"Get out Congo!" The leader checked his watch. "Five minutes . . . no out of Congo . . . die!"

Ludlam could hardly believe his ears.

"But I can't even get to the hotel in five minutes," he pleaded. "I just wanna give this water to the sick old woman an' get my bags. Then I'll gladly get the hell away from here."

"You want hotel . . . Go!" The leader threw him the key that bounced off his chest and fell to the ground. "Five minutes . . . no out of Congo . . . we kill!"

"The hell with the water," Ludlam said, "I just . . . "

"Four minutes." The boss pulled and cocked the hammer on the forty-five he had taken. The crowd spread out. The other soldiers started unlocking their safeties as the boy begged them to shoot.

68

"I'm leaving, I'm leaving!" Ludlam spun and ran for the ship. Hate and anger built with every stride. Over his shoulder, he saw one of the Africans drop and aim a rifle. His heart pounded as he zigzagged and picked up speed. He didn't look again until he reached the gangway, out of breath. The Africans were shouting, dancing, drinking his water, and sharing it with the crowd.

Ludlam spat and cursed while laboring up the gangplank, then cursed again when he saw Sullivan and the Boatswain laughing.

At twenty-three sixteen that night, with one thousand Malayan troops and her full crew aboard, the USNS Mitchell tucked her weary gangplank securely to her side, and edged out into the black hostile river. The ship made a hard, hundred and eighty degree starboard turn, then steamed full ahead downstream.

The radioman received a message from the UN garrison guarding Matadi to be forward to Leopoldville: CONGOLESE TROOPS OF UNDETERMINED ALLEGIANCE HAVE DISRUPTED COMMUNICATIONS AND ARE ATTACKING THE VILLAGE. IN URGENT NEED OF REINFORCEMENTS ...

The Captain slowed to one third, relayed the message, and asked Leopoldville if he could assist. Leopoldville replied: AIR SUPPORT IMMINENT ... PARATROOPERS LESS THAN ONE HOUR AWAY ... HIGH COMMAND ORDERS UN FORCES TO HOLD ... HIGH COMMAND ORDERS USNS GENERAL MITCHELL TO CONTINUE HER MISSION WITH ALL DELIBERATE SPEED ...

As the vessel approached the Atlantic, the men still lingering topside could see light from distant fires and hear the roar of aircraft and the sound of cannon.

Chapter Eight

ON CHRISTMAS Eve, as the *Mitchell* rounded the choppy Cape of Good Hope out of the South Atlantic into the Indian Ocean, parties among the many cliques, ranks and races were being held throughout the ship.

The "black engineer's compartment," where Big Shot, Chitown and Rinco slept, was the favorite spot for the crap shooters, boozers and dope heads. It was the hangout of the hipsters, where they could do their thing without being squealed on. The "set" started about eight o'clock that evening. Everyone brought his own high. Johnson and Brother Poe, in rare spirit, contributed three fifths of gin and a half-ounce of pot, while Nelson and Party-Time brought ham, bread, salad and kool-aid from the galley.

They laughed, lied and signified as they drank, snorted and smoked. The longer the party lasted the louder it got, as the pot-heads turned up Nelson's portable phonograph to drown out the boozers who wanted to joke and clown, while the snorters just wanted "to be left the hell alone."

Rinco left the party and relieved Chitown for the midnight to four watch. When he got off duty, the party was still going strong, but the late hours had caused them to soften their voices and cut off the music. The food was long gone, so they sat around talking about old times, past adventures and women. They talked about Africa, politics, history and more about women. When the pot was gone, everybody hit the remaining booze bottles and told dirty jokes until daybreak.

There wasn't a single gripe during the Christmas meal. No one could find fault with baked ham, roast turkey with all the trimmings, shrimp and crabmeat cocktails, three kinds of pie, plus cake and ice cream.

A large shoe-box-shaped present from a seaman's mission in New York was placed on each man's bunk by the compartment cleaners. Every box contained the same things given every year: a calendar, diary, prayer book, wool cap and scarf, five cigars, a wallet-size frame with the picture of a female movie star and a fishing line complete with sinker and hooks.

At fifteen hundred an announcement came over the speaker that a special matinee movie, "The Robe," would be shown. After the movie an inter-faith Christmas service was held. For the first time during the voyage, the chapel was almost filled. And there were moments when each lonely man found himself somberly thinking of the people he loved, and the many Christmases gone by.

The farther they sailed into the Indian Ocean, the hotter it got. The crew renewed their number one gripe. It had started in Capetown when they had tried, but failed to get their living quarters air conditioned while the ship was in drydock.

"Why should we have to sleep in hundred degree heat, while the officers and Malayans sleep nice and cool?" the angry sailors demanded.

The officers were hard pressed in explaining that a thousand men, crowded into four troop compartments, sleeping seven high, make air conditioning a necessity.

"Bull shit!" was the sailors' response. "If cool air was just a necessity for officers and troops, the unlicensed men don't count for shit. And we are the ones that really make this god-damn ship run."

The officers argued. "Every man had to sign articles in order to be aboard. And those articles clearly stated that they were going to Africa. So heat was to be expected. This wasn't a luxury cruise. The *General Mitchell* wasn't the *Queen Mary,* or the USS *United States.* This was a working ship. Everyone here was getting well paid to do a job. And since officers always have the last word, the last word on the subject was "stop your bitching and turn-to."

On New Year's Eve, all deliberate speed was cut in half when the number two boiler malfunctioned and had to be shut down for repairs. This dampened what little was left of the holiday spirit.

The loss of power at sea did not only effect the fire and engine rooms that moved the vessel, but every department aboard the ship. The Evaporator Flat, where Rinco, Chitown and Smitty made fresh water by boiling and condensing salt water, received a great amount of the ship's auxiliary steam. This steam was also used to run the turbine powered generators, the deck machinery, refrigeration plants and cook the food.

Although the Chief Engineer made an announcement that the problem was minor, and the boiler would soon be back in operation, there were fewer parties, and "Auld Lang Syne" was sung on a somber note as the disgruntled crew steamed East by North-East on the lonely, swirling Indian Ocean.

Morale was low. The crew had had no liberty or mail since they left Capetown. The morning following the loss of power, eight-and-a-half-by-fourteen-inch sheets of paper with news compounded via RCA/New York were placed in the messhall. It was the nearest thing to a newspaper they had seen in weeks, and some of them read every word. It was a strange comfort to know that snow, icy winds and wintry downpours engulfed much of the U.S ... that it was 22 below at Minot, North Dakota, and a freezing line stretched from Southern New England, across Northern Texas into the Southern Rockies.

They learned that UN troops, planes, and armored cars appeared to have broken the back of organized Katangan resistance in Elizabethville ... that UN jets had also attacked the headquarters of the Belgian operated Union Miniere Mining Company, and that troops had dropped mortar shells around Hotel Leopoldville.

Edmund Gullion, United States ambassador to the Congo, had arrived at Ndola, Northern Rhodesia, where he planned to meet with Tshombe and take him to a truce meeting with Adoula at the Congo coastal town of Kitona.

Turban wearing Sikh warriors and other Indian soldiers, supported by Navy and Air Force units, had smashed into Goa, Damaq and Diu in an apparently successful lightening campaign and seized the three tiny possessions, ending four-hundred-fifty-year-old Portuguese colonies in India.

There was also a short financial synopsis, as well as a report on temperature highs in New York, Boston, Chicago, Los Angeles, Montreal, New Orleans, Seattle, Paris, London and Berlin.

As soon as the sailors got to the sports, the bets were on between the Giants and the Green Bay Packers for the NFL championship. In the AFL it was Houston and San Diego.

A week passed and the boiler still wasn't fixed. The ship slowed down to 11 knots. The crew said the ship was cursed, as the long hard-working days, with the burning sun pounding down like the hot breath of satan, dragged into longer nights; nights when men schemed and scampered for topside spots to lay carts, beach chairs, and small folding beds to try and escape the smoldering heat.

The only haven was a much-too-small, air conditioned dayroom, that stayed over-populated after working hours. There was always a crowd of sailors around the three tables, watching the whist and rummy games. Others cooled off while reading, rapping, writing letters, checking the bulletin boards, or just trying to hear the radio. The radio was bolted to the forward bulkhead above the old Coke machine, that was either broke or empty one hour after it was fixed or filled.

This crossing seemed to take forever. The supplies got low and the chow got lousy. Despite the abundance of nuts, canned fruit and hard candy placed on the messhall tables, crewmen from every department blamed the stinking, no-good food for their stomach trouble. The Chief Steward was forced to make periodic on-the-spot inspections to assure, among other things, that the bakers sifted the worms from the flour and checked the crackers for ants.

The heat also began to take its toll. Three deckhands were in sick bay from sunstroke and five engineers from heat exhaustion. The engineers suffered more because their quarters were directly above the Fire and Engine rooms. They worked, bathed and slept in seething, unmerciful heat.

After sixteen weary days and nights, the brilliant green shoreline of Malaya loomed. It was a resplendent sight. The loud brass band was barely audible above the noise of the hundreds of jubilant people lining the docks of Port Swettenham. They yelled and waved, while countless white gulls filled the air with their barking as they glided gracefully along the waves and hovered over the fantail in search of discarded refuse.

An hour after the *Mitchell* docked, people were still coming. Black, brown and yellow they came, down the long dusty road that weaved between bright vegetation and large stilted houses. In small cars, on scooters and bicycles they came, past the busy warehouses where men and women labored side by side.

Native males came in snowy white, drab gray; in short and long trousers; shirted, undershirted, barechested and barefooted. Chinese women in gay luminous split dresses came with Indian and Malayan women strutting in their festive colored saris and shawls. The big brass band, playing under fluttering birds to a background of glittering greenery and smiling people dressed in sparkling colors, seemed to lift a tinted globe from the sun, making that morning just a little brighter than most.

At eleven-thirty mail call was announced. Chitown left Rinco and Smitty working in the evaporators and rushed up to the Purser's office. He returned with three letters from his wife Jean, a package for Smitty, and four newspapers for Rinco. They all stopped work and sat on the long wooden bench to read their mail.

Chitown's hand trembled as he opened the letter with the earliest postmark. It told of how she cried upon receiving and answering his letters and how she loved and missed him so much. As he read the second letter, a sad sickly feeling crept into his stomach. She told him the very thought of being separated for a year tore her up inside, and the lonely nights were ripping her heart to pieces. She wondered why in the hell he had to go so far and stay so long?

The answer made him sicker. It had not been necessary for him to take the first ship the Military Sea Transportation Service offered. He could have waited for one of the shorter European cruises. All his life it seemed that people were always warning him against impatience to no avail. He took that first ship because he wanted to get the necessary sea time as quick as possible, then take the examination for Third Engineer. But the last letter not only shattered that dream temporarily, it made him realize he had to end this Congo voyage, and maybe never become a Merchant Marine officer.

"Do you think I could call Chicago from here?" he asked Rinco.

"I doubt it, you may have to wait until we hit Bombay. What's the matter?"

"It's my wife man." He almost choked as he waved the letter. "She wrote this from the hospital."

"What!" Rinco was shocked.

"How is she?" Smitty asked.

"I don't know for sure. She was in a auto accident. I've got to find out if she's home or still in the hospital. All I know now is her collar bone is broken."

Rinco pondered a moment, then said, "Maybe they can reach her from the ship when we get to sea. It's a long

75

shot," he cautioned when Chitown smiled, "but it's been done before."

"How?" Chitown asked anxiously.

Rinco nodded toward Smitty, who often hung out in the radio shack.

"First," Smitty said, "the radioman has to pick up a ham operator in New York who can put the call through to Chicago. And all it would cost is the price of a long distance call between the two cities. They'll put it on your phone bill."

"Hey! ... that's a good deal!" Chitown was enthusiastic. "I sure hope it works!" He sat down, stared at the letter in his hand, then asked Smitty, "How long have you been married?"

"Eleven years."

"Wow!" Chitown said. "Eleven years! ... How long have you been sailing?"

"Fifteen years. I did eight in the Navy before I got fed up with that bullshit."

"Your wife ... " Chitown put his letters away, "she don't give you any trouble about going to sea all the time?"

"Hell no! In fact, if it wasn't for the sea, I don't think me and the old lady would still be together."

"What do you mean?"

"I mean that absence makes the heart grow fonder in our case. When I first get back from a voyage, life couldn't be sweeter. Everybody's so glad I'm home. But by the time I'm ready to leave again, we're at each others' throats like cats and dogs. Plus, I've got four kids that drive me bug fuck."

"I guess a married sailor can have a pretty decent life after all," Chitown said.

"Hell yeah!" Rinco slapped him on the back.

"That's right!" Smitty agreed. "My family's been places I couldn't dream of taking them on a regular job ... Europe, the Med, the Caribbean, not to mention the things I've purchased from around the world at bargain prices."

"That's the kind of life I had envisioned for me and Jean." Chitown tried to smile. "Only I wanted the money and prestige of being an officer. It would have been beautiful, but it's all over now." He shook then dropped his head.

"I'll bet Big Shot's griping his ass off inside that hot sooty boiler," Rinco said, trying to get Chitown out of his insalubrious mood, "while Johnson and Brother Poe are flying to Singapore."

"Yeah!" Smitty laughed. "Did you see Big Shot's face this morning when the Second told him there would be no liberty for boiler-room personnel until number two was ready to go back on the line?"

"I sure did," Rinco said, "and he was still bitching ten minutes after muster was over because the rest of the crew's getting early liberty."

The ship's horn blew for early chow, so they rushed up the ladder to eat, shower and hit the beach.

Port Swettenham's business section consisted of three blocks lined with pale green, two story wooden houses. The top floors all extended out over Hindu, Moslem, Chinese and English stores, restaurants and shops. It was late afternoon, and most of the people crowded the shady sides of the streets.

Rinco was still trying to take Chitown's mind off his troubles by carrying the conversation as their small hot taxi moved slowly through the thick traffic of bicycles, scooters and little European cars, down the wide dusty street. He talked about the Chinese, who ruled the economy, while the Malayans held the political power. "And the British," he said, "really fucked up the country when they came. Then they brought in the stinking-ass Indian."

"You sure got a hard-on for Indians, haven't you?" Chitown finally said.

"Damn right!" Rinco nodded. "We'll be picking them up in Bombay, so I'll let you judge them for yourself. Wait until you see them spit and wash their feet in the drinking fountains."

They turned their attention to an old man dressed in white and wearing a huge dragon-head mask, hobbling down the sunny side of the street, beating a piece of tin with a stick. He stopped in front of a Chinese restaurant and started chanting.

"He'll be there until someone comes out and gives him a coin to stop the evil spirits," Rinco said.

"I guess some people all over the world have to find a hustle in order to make it." Chitown grunted as his eyes followed a Malayan woman peddling a bike. "How much farther?" he asked, more anxious than ever for a drink.

"Not much," Rinco answered.

The Seaman's Club was crowded with Mitchell crewmen eating, drinking, talking loud and playing pocket billiards on the extra large English tables. Rinco and Chitown both had two drinks while waiting for their steak dinners, then tried to throw darts until they could get an empty pool table. But it wasn't until the sun had begun to set, cooling the air, and most of the sailors had headed for Kaula Lumpur, that they got one. Rinco stayed to talk with Chitown, who was trying to drown his sorrows in alcohol.

They drank, shot pool, ate again and shot more pool. The evening wore on and whenever Chitown made one of his frequent trips to the bar, Rinco would think about his predecessor, a seaman named Sims, that disturbing letters had also driven to heavy drink.

But unlike Chitown, Sims wouldn't confide in anyone. He would just sit and stare into space until it reached the point he had to be called several times before answering. He finally cracked and had to be sent back to the States under escort, along with two other crewmen who were up on criminal charges. However he figured that Chitown would be all right as soon as he knew he was going home.

At twenty three thirty Big Shot entered the club, dressed in brown silk slacks, a white on white short-sleeve shirt, white bucks and a tan straw hat.

"Look who they let out of the bilges!" Rinco laughed. "You get that boiler fixed?"

"Yeah!" We got that son-of-a-bitch ready." He wiped his face with a fresh folded handkerchief. "Now look out Kuala Lumper, here I come . . . let's go cats!"

"Not me," Chitown said, "I don't feel like it."

"You never do . . . what about you Rinco? I got a couple joints we can puff on the way."

"Naw! I'm gonna stick with my man Chi. He's got a problem we're trying to iron out."

"What's the matter man?"

"My wife was in an accident. I'm trying to figure out the quickest way to get sent home."

"Damn!" Big Shot muttered. "Sorry to hear that. Is she hurt bad?"

"She tries to sound like it's not too bad, but a broken collar bone is nothing to play with, not to mention the cuts and bruises. Hell!" he croaked, "I don't even know if she's out of the hospital."

"Damn, I see why you want to get home. Did you show the letter to the Captain?"

"He will tomorrow," Rinco said, "but I don't think it'll do any good until she contacts the Red Cross . . . and *they* notify the ship."

"Well . . . maybe so," Big Shot agreed. "What ya'll playing, eight ball? I got the winner."

Rinco looked at his watch. "You don't have time to play pool. Kuala Lumpur's almost fifty miles from here, and they roll up the sidewalk at one o'clock."

"Huh!" Big Shot grunted. "How long do you think it take for me to beat you dudes? First I'm going an' fill my flask."

It didn't take long. Chitown got four shots, and Rinco three.

"Well chumps," Big Shot grinned, hanging up his cuestick, I'm gonna blind ya'll with ass."

Rinco racked the balls as Chitown went for another drink.

Chapter Nine

BIG SHOT leaned back in the rear seat of the taxi, took a long slow swig of scotch, and shook his head violently as the whiskey burned its way down his stomach. These were the moments he regretted; the quiet lonely moments when he had to drink by himself. They always brought back thoughts of Pam; thoughts of the wonderful years and how much fun they had together; how beautiful she was, and how she treated him as if he were her only lover.

Then, just as suddenly he would think of that fatal night at that after-hour joint in Manhattan.

"How come you charge so much to go ta Kuala Lumpur?" he asked sarcastically, trying to take his feelings out on the driver.

"Kuala Lumpur long way ... road dark soon ... velly bad."

The car was speeding out of Port Swettenham, down a wide road that had abruptly narrowed from four to two lanes.

"How long will it take to get there?"

"Hour ... maybe hour-half!"

"Damn!" Big Shot muttered, looking at his watch. "It's after eleven now!" The two lanes, with traffic moving in opposite directions, split as if being peeled, forming a complete circle for no apparent reason, before rejoining.

Big Shot took another drink, shook his head, and recalled that fateful night he went to that damn after-hour joint. The night he saw the only woman he had made love to for over three years, undressing on the screen for another man. He knew damn well she wasn't always that way. But there were so many hurting "whys" that would never be answered, things he never bothered about when it all started. Why? She didn't need the money. She had everything . . . a nice crib, new ride . . . wall to wall rags and a husband who made all kinds of bread. Maybe that was part of the reason. But if she got bored and lonely when he was at sea why in the hell didn't she tell him? Why didn't she give him an ultimatum? It was the least she could have done if she had really loved him.

"I would have left the Merchant Marine for you baby," he whispered to himself, "'cause I can hustle just as good on the beach."

Then he thought about the agonizing months that had followed, after he rushed home, packed, left and never saw her again. Those were the months of drink and misery that he may not have survived if it had not been for Rinco.

"But that's okay bitch." He rolled down the rear windows and lit a joint. "I'm just glad I found you out for what you are. You did me a favor. You hipped me that marriage wasn't shit. Now I got world-wide hoes."

As he smoked he thought about Freda, and how that Capetown moonlight shining through the unshaded window glowed on her fine golden body and long black hair. It was so boss laying naked in that small partitioned room drinking, smoking pot and making love until daylight caught them sweaty and exhausted.

The driver grinned at him through the mirror as he smoked the reefer down until it burned his finger, then thumped it out the window. He stretched, then laid back to recall that foxy redhead Fraulein who Freda reminded him of. They looked almost alike, except for the hair and eyes, and Freda's slightly darker body. The Fraulein's name was Greta. They had met at a huge ballroom in Bremerhaven, with phones on every table and a number hanging overhead. He dug her, dialed her number and rang her bell.

He smiled again and closed his eyes as the swift warm air whipped through the car. His mind shifted to the gorgeous senoritas of Latin America, the exotic beauties of the Orient, the deep tan lovelies of the Caribbean, and countless other foxes throughout the sea lanes of the world.

Then there were the broads in the Apple, the flamboyant grays and high-stepping sisters in pale lipsticks who strutted through Showman's, Small's Paradise and Sugar Ray's. He'd had all types of women, from the bull-shit society kind to the shapely shadows in dark doorways on late lonely nights. But even after four years without Pam, there were still old love songs that could wipe the smile from his face if no one was looking.

A sharp turn and a bump in the road jarred him from his trance. He looked out into the dark towering jungle and his mind flashed back to that terrorizing night in the Congo.

"We better roll up these windows man, befo' a Bengal tiger jump outta them trees down on this little bitty motherfucker," he tried to joke with the driver as fear gripped his chest and throat. For a moment he was relieved to see a few scattered headlights approaching, but as they neared and passed on the dark narrow road, the marijuana made him think each one would be a head-on collision.

"Damn," he said and took a drink to calm himself, "how much longer we gotta ride man?"

"Kuala Lumpur! Kuala Lumpur!" The driver pointed to his right over rolling black, brush-covered hills. The lights of the town were still far off and looked like the first spark of daybreak crawling over a horizon of shadows.

"Hurry up, man!" Big Shot took another drink. It had been a long voyage and his body ached for a woman.

It was well after one o'clock when they arrived. The streets, like those in Port Swettenham, were bright and wide but nearly empty. All of the bars were closed. Because of the many ships in the harbor, the better brothels were filled and the girls occupied. The driver took him to three houses, all Chinese. The few girls they saw were left because of their looks, or their customers were either drunk or asleep. The girls peeped from behind dark curtains, sniggling like children, while bearded old men sat humped in huddles, glaring through opium puffed eyes.

"Say dude!" Big Shot snapped, following the driver back to the car. "You Malayan. I know you can take me ta some Malayan girls ... hell, I've had Chinese broads from Bangkok ta Taipei."

"We see! We see!" The driver hunched his shoulders.

They drove to a settlement of small shabby houses, got out and went on foot through narrow, stinking alleyways with hungry dogs barking at their heels. Again Big Shot became disgusted going from house to house. The girls were both Chinese and Malayan, but too young, lean and dirty looking.

"Man ... you the dumbest cab driver I ever seen," Big Shot scolded while the man was trying to explain to a Mama-san why the customer wouldn't comply. She had followed them to the door to throw out a pan of water, but couldn't understand why he didn't convince the John that the girls were young, pretty and very nice.

A tall curvy figure wearing a bright red-flowered, robe-like top and silk Arabian style pants, emerged from a doorway across the alley and started towards them. It came closer. Big Shot lit a cigarette and watched eagerly as it passed the squatting, chanting silhouettes. When the light from the open door fell on the smooth brown face, he saw an inviting smile.

"Just what I been waitin' on!" He crossed and threw his arm around her.

"You come with me?" She gave him a soft giggle.

"Damn right baby! Let's go! You wait there dude!" he yelled over his shoulder. The driver turned from Mama-san and came running.

"Stop! Stop!" The driver pulled at his arm.

"What the hell's the matter now?" Big Shot snatched away.

"Billy-Boy! He-she! He-she!"

"What the hell you talkin' 'bout man?"

"He-she! Boy-girl! Boy-girl!" the driver laughed.

The figure broke and ran back into the shadows. Mamasan roared and called to her girls. Every doorway within earshot was suddenly darkened by small giggling bodies. Big Shot stood stunned and silent biting his bottom lip as anger swelled.

"Let's get the hell away from here," he said, "befo' I start kickin' some motherfuckin' ass."

"Come! Come!" The driver led him on foot down another alley out into a crowded, brightly lit, open air restaurant. It resembled a huge round picnic area. They walked past the fast-talking multicolored people to a wide empty street.

After they had walked about a block, the driver said, "This way ... This way!" Nelson popped out of the doorway they were about to enter, then Party-Time came staggering after him.

"What's happening baby!" the three crewmen shouted at the same time.

"This place!" the driver pointed, "this pla ... !"

"Shut the fuck up!" Big Shot cut him off. "Any Malayan broads in there?" he asked Nelson.

"Yeah, nothing but."

"What they look like?"

"Not bad, not bad at all."

"Hey ... you a cab driver ain't you?" Party-Time blew his stinking breath in the man's face. "Take us back to the ship."

"That's my taxi," Big Shot snapped, an' I ain't payin' until *I* get back to the Ship."

"They might call you Big Shot, but you ain't big." Party-Time rolled his eyes at him. "Big Nelson here is the biggest dude on the Ghost. An' if we want to, we'll take the damn cab!"

Big Shot started to hit him but Big Nelson stepped between them. "Don't pay any attention to Party-Time," he said, "you know how he is when he's drunk. If it's alright with you, we can all go back together, 'cause ain't many cabs around this time a morning."

"Mellow by me," Big Shot agreed.

"We'll pay our part of the fare," Party-Time snarled, "so go on an' get yo' sloppy seconds."

"They're all seconds, you dumb, bug-eyed motherfucker!" Big Shot frowned as they entered the brothel. He tried to appear cool and selective in choosing one of the half-dozen brown skin women parading before him. But his mind was made up the instant he saw the third one. Meanwhile, Nelson and Party-Time ordered bottles of boot-leg Philippine beer and relaxed on a long understuffed green sofa.

It wasn't just his fear of the dark eerie jungle that made him glad to have company on the long ride back, Big Shot told himself when they were in the cab heading for the ship. He hoped Party-Time and Big Nelson could keep him from thinking about Pam again. Why had this obsession to make it with a Malayan led him into the arms of a woman who looked just like that dirty bitch. Except for the narrow eyes, they could be identical twins. She had the same height, the same hair, mouth and smooth brown skin.

"What kind of cruel fuckin' game is fate playing on me?" he mumbled, pulling out a handkerchief to wipe his sweating face and palms.

"You say something?" Big Nelson hunched him with his elbow.

"Nothing man!"

"That crazy motherfucker talkin' to his self," Party-Time giggled from the front seat.

"Why do you hang with this ignorant ass dude?" Big Shot asked Nelson.

"He may be ignorant," Nelson lit a joint, "but he ain't dumb. He's smart enough to owe me a lot a bread. Now I

85

gotta hang with him to keep somebody from killing his black ass before I collect." He passed the reefer. Big Shot took three pulls and laid back.

"Of all the women in Malaya, why did he have to end up with Angel?" he asked himself. But what bothered him even more was the fact that whenever the ship returned, he would be on the first thing smoking back to her. He took another pull on the joint and gave it back.

"Pass the shit up here man," Party-Time said, brushing the driver's temple as he threw his hand back over the seat.

"You fucked up enough," Big Nelson said between puffs.

"Bullshit!" Party-Time shouted, "you know the party ain't never over with me. Come on man, give me the shit!"

Big Nelson shook his head and passed it up. Party-Time took a long wet draw and tried to pass it to the driver, who waved it away.

"What's the matter baby? You can't drive high?"

The driver shook his head no.

"Well this Party-Time, goddamnit." He pushed the reefer under the driver's nose. "An' when you in my company, you party!"

Big Nelson reached up front, snatched the joint from him and threw it out of the open window. "Now stop fuckin' with the cat. He got to get us back to the *Ghost.*"

"And you call *me* crazy," Big Shot laughed.

"Fuck you, Mister Big Shot!" Party-Time snapped, then turned on the car radio without permission. "Ain't you got nothin' but Chinese shit on this motherfucker." He scanned a few stations then cut the radio off. "Ya'll need some blues over here, all you po' motherfuckers." He reached his palm back for someone to slap it, but Nelson and Big Shot just looked at each other in disgust.

"You hip to the blues ain't you driver?" Party-Time went on, "B.B. King, Muddy, John Lee ... all them bad cats."

"Why don't you shut the fuck up?" Big Shot said. "How

you expect these people to dig our sounds. They don't know nothin' 'bout us."

"Show's how much you know," Party-Time retorted, "they hip to us alright. This ain't *our* first time here, like you, mister know-it-all Big Shot. Hey driver!" he yelled as if the man was a half block away, "tell this mother-fucker ya'll hip to bloods!"

The driver said nothing. He just glued his eyes into the beams of his headlights, knifing into the blackness.

"We them boss cats off the Congo ship. We bring ya'lls' sons an' brothers back from Africa ... where they ain't got no god-damn business no way." He offered his palm again and Nelson slapped it extra hard.

"Damn!" he snatched it back, "you don't have ta be that damn mellow!" Nelson hunched Big Shot and they both giggled.

"What ya'll call us over here?" Party-Time turned his attention back to the driver.

"I no ... no ... " the man shook his head.

"Understand is the word, motherfucker. Don't you know the King's English?"

"Don't you know anything but motherfucker?" Big Shot said.

"Fuck you man," Party-Time mumbled, then turned his body toward the driver. "In America they call us niggers. I wanna know what ya'll call cats like me over here?"

The driver looked him in the face and grinned. "Same-same!" he said.

Everyone laughed but Party-Time.

"Well ... who's going to light-off?" Smitty asked, as he Chitown and Rinco ate breakfast together in the messhall.

"What time?" Chitown asked.

"Eight o'clock." Smitty took a sip of coffee. "The First wants all the feed water we can make before getting un-derway at nineteen-hundred."

They flipped coins and Chitown won the watch he wanted, the four to eight. It would give him the whole day to see the Captain and buy Jean a present.

"Since I got the eight to twelve, I better get on down and light-off." Smitty finished his coffee and headed for the evaporators.

"After I see the Captain, I'm going to the Seaman's Club for a couple bottles of Scotch. You want anything?" Chitown asked.

"Hell no!" Rinco felt his head. "Don't mention whiskey to me as bad as I feel. I don't see how you could hold so much."

"Man I couldn't get drunk, just sick." Chitown tried to force down some more food. "I had so many dreams for Jean and me, but now that she really needed me, where am I . . . A half a world away. Everything's gone to shit!"

"Dreams don't die that easy." Rinco slapped him on the back. "You can still make a good life for your family as a seaman. When you get back, move her to New York and sign up for one of those Atlantic ships, where you are only gone twenty days at a time."

Big Shot, tired and disgruntled, dragged up to the table and flopped down.

"What time did you get in?" Chitown asked.

"I don't know." Big Shot shook his head. "Must of been about four."

The messman came to their table and frowned at Big Shot. "You got just ten mo' minutes to order an' eat."

"You pricks sure think you're slick, don't you!" Chief Sullivan smiled when Johnson and Brother Poe strutted up the gangplank. "You were supposed to be back at nine o'clock . . . it's eighteen hundred."

"I'm hip we was supposed to be back," Brother Poe said, "so you could put us on that damn guide detail. You know we don't wanna be bothered with no Malayans."

"They all aboard?" Johnson asked.

"Don't try to bullshit me," Sullivan said. "We leave in an hour, so you know they're all aboard."

"What the fuck is this?" Brother Poe said when he stepped through the hatch and saw a soldier setting up a machine gun in the passageway. "Hey Sullivan, come here!"

"Take the quarterdeck!" Sullivan ordered the Boatswain and followed Johnson through the hatch.

"No! ... No! ... No!" All three of them shouted to the dumbfounded Malayan who didn't understand English.

"Get that out of here ... right now!" Sullivan waved his hands in the air. "One of you check the troop's wardroom and see if you can find an officer."

"I'll go," Brother Poe said.

"And if you happen to see Ludlam anywhere, tell him I would like to be relieved sometime today!"

"Mellow!"

When Brother Poe returned with the officer, Ludlam followed, more out of curiosity than any desire to relieve the watch. But the soldier had dismantled the weapon.

"Make damn sure your troops get the word that no arms are allowed outside their compartments," Sullivan snapped at the officer, who saluted and started chewing out the soldier in Malayan.

"That's right!" Johnson laughed, "or Ludlam will steal 'em to make up for that shit he ran off and left."

Sullivan departed, and Ludlam did a slow burn as Johnson and Brother Poe slapped skin.

"An' you gonna have plenty chance ta use that gun too!" Brother Poe pointed to the soldier. "'Cause Tshombe gonna put somethin' on ya'll's ass."

"Yeah!" Ludlam grunted to himself as he took over the quarterdeck, "with all these niggers aboard, the poor son-of-a-bitch probably thinks he's in the Congo now."

At nineteen hundred, the docks were again filled with colorful people waving, shouting and crying good-bys. Fifteen minutes before the *Mitchell* got underway, the big brass band started playing. It could still be heard well out into the harbor, as the troops lining the middle decks continued to wave back at the following boats.

The *Mitchell's* course was plotted northwest, up the Strait of Malacca, around the top of Sumatra and full ahead west, across the Bay of Bengal. After passing Ceylon, she turned northwest again and followed the coastline of India into the Arabian Sea. Four days out of Port Swettenham, she dropped anchor in the murky brown waters of Bombay harbor.

89

Chapter Ten

NO WHERE on earth had destitute people mastered the art of begging in a manner comparable to the beggars of Bombay. Every foreigner passing through the big iron gates behind the long gray warehouses lining the wharf was pounced upon with unreined audacity.

Dusty old shaggy haired women crying "Rupee! ... Rupee! ... Rupee for the baby daddy!" shoved starving, ragged infants in their faces. There were so many beggars that whatever compassion the sailors may have had soon turned to contempt, as they flinched and jerked away from natives who tried to read their palms, shine their shoes, or manicure their nails with weird, rusty instruments. Others peddled rings, knives, pornographic pictures, and everything from good merchandise to worthless junk. Countless out-stretched arms and cries of "Rupee! ... Rupee!" filled the air from thin tilted faces with filth-embedded skin and teeth turned black from chewing betel nut.

Walking became so difficult that the crewmen were forced into waiting taxis for a three block ride to the Prince of Wales Seaman's Club.

On arrival they were again confronted by hordes of beggars, with that pitiful chant of, "Rupee! ... Rupee!" The car doors were pried open by a tall, bearded turban-wearing doorman, who pushed and kicked a path for the Americans to get inside the massive lobby that looked like a shopping center.

Chitown was relieved to see Rinco near the front of the long line where seamen waited to change their currency at the glass enclosed money cage. Big Shot was right behind him, rapping to Johnson and Brother Poe.

"Hey ... What's happening baby?" The three of them shouted their ritual greetings as he approached, then continued their conversation about the availability of drugs in India. Johnson and Brother Poe looked like Africans in their usual khakis, mess jackets and skull caps. Big Shot, on the other hand, could easily be mistaken for a New York businessman in his light gray suit. Chitown walked up to Rinco.

"Do I have to change the bread I'm sending home?" he asked.

"Naw, just what you plan to spend in the streets. The Telegraph Office takes American money."

"Is that where I make my call, too?"

"You haven't got through yet?"

"Yeah, I got through last night, after sitting in that hot-ass radio shack for three hours. But nobody answered there. The letter I got today said she was out of the hospital and staying with her sister. But that was dated two weeks ago." He reached into his pocket and handed Rinco a stack of bills.

"Maybe she's still with her sister." Rinco moved up. "Do you have *her* number?"

"I didn't have it with me, but now I have. I'm gonna call them both until I get somebody. Because I'll crack up if I don't find out how she's doing."

"She was well enough to be released," Rinco said. "I know you are thankful for that."

"I sure am," Chitown sighed and shook his head. As the line inched forward, he gazed around at the flourishing souvenir stands. One of the displays was a wall full of knives behind a wooden counter. There was every type and size imaginable, from the wide-curving Gurkas to swords and daggers hidden in canes, umbrellas and swagger sticks. Other stands were loaded with jewelry, leather goods, rolls of silk, oil paintings, and rare Ebony wood carvings from East Africa.

The ship's gonna be here two days, he thought, *plenty of time to buy gifts, but not for the Red Cross to take action.*

"Where you two dudes going from here?" Big Shot asked, as Rinco stepped up and slid a bundle of money to the cashier.

"I'm going to the telegraph office with Chi," Rinco answered.

"Then we're going to find a nice quiet bar and get blasted," Chitown added.

"You mean ho-house," Brother Poe said, "'cause they ain't got no bars in India."

"Why not?"

"'Cause the whole country's been on prohibition since forty-nine. The Indians have to entertain at home."

"That's why it's so fuckin' many of them!" Johnson interjected and gave Brother Poe some skin.

"Bet I know where you three blind mice are going." Rinco turned from the window and handed Chitown his share of the money. "Straight to Papa-San's."

"You got that right, baby." Johnson patted the large leather bag strapped over his shoulder. "We ain't had a set with old Papa-San in a long time."

"Then we going ta fuck the farmer's wife," Big Shot cracked as the cashier counted out his Rupees, "I wanna see what's under them long Saris."

"Long legs, that's what!" Brother Poe said.

"We got to split," Rinco said. "Got to get my man here to a phone booth."

"Dig you cats later," Chitown waved.

"Later!" they waved back.

92

"Notice you don't see anybody taking pictures." Rinco started an idle conversation when he saw Chitown about to lose his temper, as they plowed through the multitudinous beggars behind the big doorman who used his huge arms like machetes as he hacked through the jungle of flesh toward the waiting taxis.

"Now that you mentioned it ... " Chitown gave him a puzzled look.

"It's against the law. Not just because of the beggars ... you'll see Bombay's got many more ghastly sights. The people don't dig it either ... if they see a foreigner with a camera, he's in trouble."

Chitown grunted and shook his head, as the doorman pushed them into a cab.

"Government building!" Rinco shouted to the driver. "You can't go wrong when you tell them government building. It's the railroad station, bus depot, telegraph office and phone company, all under one roof."

The car crept cautiously down the narrow side streets, picking up and losing beggars along the way. But when he reached the wide avenues, the driver, perhaps in anger, mashed his foot on the accelerator and drove as if the company paid a bonus for every pedestrian he ran down. There were plenty who barely escaped the deadly steel by jumping and darting at the last second.

Their destination was on a main thoroughfare lined with long, high-stretching palm trees, accentuating huge, magnificent onion and spear-shaped, multi-dome public buildings that looked like a mixture of Muslim and Southern European architecture.

The inside of the Government Building was jammed with people of all colors and descriptions, including tourists from Europe and other parts of Asia, all impatiently jumping from line to line, buying travel tickets, sending telegrams or making phone calls.

Rinco and Chitown had to get at the end of one such line. It was fifteen minutes before Chitown got a booth.

"I'm very sorry," the operator said in crisp, fluent English after trying for ten minutes to get his call through, "but we are having difficulty contacting the United States. If you wish to keep trying, it may take some time. Shall we ring you back?"

He looked out at the long line. "I'll try again later." He thanked her and hung up.

"You get through?" Rinco asked when Chitown exited the booth.

"Naw! They're having trouble. I may stick around a little. Right now I want to wire this bread off."

"Okay, follow me." Rinco led him across the post office lobby to the far side. After a much shorter wait he wired three hundred dollars with the message: CONTACT RED CROSS IMMEDIATELY. STOP. TELL THEM WHAT HAPPENED AND YOU NEED ME HOME. STOP. WILL BE HOME SOON REGARDLESS. STOP. ALL MY LOVE FOREVER. WILBER.

"That may reach her before I can get a call through," he said turning from the counter and folding his receipt.

"At the rate you're going, it sure may," Rinco agreed. "Let's take in some sights. You can come back and call later. They stay open until eleven."

"Okay," Chitown said, "let's go!"

Rinco made sure the next driver avoided the beseeching side streets, and cruised the wide picturesque boulevards. The heavy traffic consisted of big red, double-deck buses, black cabs with orange tops, and everything else from bicycles, motor scooters and pushcarts to horses and buggies. Bombay was a huge city. They rolled and bounced for miles on unused trolley tracks, under endlessly stretching wires and countless billboards.

Never before had Chitown witnessed such human contrast, as Rinco pointed out and tried to explain the many different conflicting castes and cultures dashing across the streets and weaving up and down the crowded sidewalks. There were Sheiks and Maharajahs, scholars and peasants, all religiously adhering to a strict code of dress and manners, and all keeping their distance from the lowly, untouchable Harijans.

94

It wasn't long, however, before Rinco's and Chitown's eyes and minds settled on the women from Kashmir. Those they saw were tall and olive-skinned, with shining black hair that dazzled in the sunlight, as they strolled in long silk saris flowing artistically in the soft dusty wind, with the graceful movement of their bodies.

"I know where we can get a few drinks," Rinco suggested. "It's high as hell, but I'm tired of riding."

"Me too. And a taste would be mellow!"

"Number twenty-two!" Rinco told the driver.

"Just like Capetown, huh?"

"Naw, not exactly. Here you give a driver a number, it can be practically any number, and I bet he'll find a cathouse to match."

After they had a long laugh, Chitown tapped Rinco on the shoulder and pointed. The car was passing à large public square with a fountain in the center, where groups of Indians sat smoking opium.

"See how backward these ass-holes are," Rinco said. "If they were drinking booze, the man would bust all of them."

Chitown shook his head in disbelief. "You mean to tell me that you can smoke all the shit you want, but if you break out a bottle you go to jail!"

Another sharp contrast awaited them when the taxi turned into a junky sidestreet, splattered with bright red spittle from betel nut, and stopped. They jumped out and rushed past a bunch of withering old addicts to a high wooden, vine-covered gate. A guard let them in.

They moved across a spacious lawn dotted with canopy-covered tables, down into a sunken, thickly carpeted, elaborately furnished waiting room.

The women were English, Indian, Chinese and Malayan, expensively dressed in the latest Western fashions. They all sat on couches and in secluded booths with Mitchell crewmen.

"Ali-Baba! Ali-Baba!" Mama-San shouted, getting up and coming across the room.

"Hi ya doing Mama-San?" Rinco gave her a hug. She was a short, fair-skinned Indian who could pass for a Mediterranean, if not for her native dress and a mouthful of gold.

"I go get Betty! Right now!" she winked.

"That's alright, Mama-San, no hurry. I know she's busy."

"Whatsamatter you?" She gave Rinco a light punch in the chest. "Betty not busy, all day she wait for you."

"Knock off the bullshit," he laughed, "and fix us a couple drinks. Scotch and water."

"Whatayamean, bullshit!" She frowned before leaving.

"Why she call you Ali-Baba?" Chitown scooted into an empty booth. "The beard?"

"Yeah!" Rinco laughed, taking a seat on the other side.

Mama-San returned with Chitown's drink, but Rinco's was brought by a dark, pretty Malayan girl who squeezed in beside him and laid her head on his shoulder.

"Chi, this is Betty . . . Betty, Chitown."

They spoke, smiled and nodded. Mama-San sat next to Chitown.

"Very soon now I get you a girl!" She gave him her golden smile.

"That's okay," he said, downing half of his drink. "Right now I'll just settle for another one of these." He finished it off.

"Very soon now!" She checked her watch and looked at one of the doors. "I get you a nice girl."

He pointed to his empty glass. She picked it up and left again.

"Why you just come Ali-Baba?" Betty asked Rinco. "I wait for you all day."

Chitown laughed.

"I was busy." Rinco took a drink.

"With another girl?"

"Hell no, baby! I just had other things to do, important things."

She looked at Chitown, who nodded, then back to

Rinco. "You not busy now!" she purred, running her hand under his shirt. Let's go!"

"You gonna cop a chick, Chi?" Rinco asked, stroking Betty's long silky hair.

"Naw, I'm just gonna have a few drinks."

"Well, I wouldn't advise it here ... these drinks cost over two dollars apiece ... in American money ... Dig! Johnson and Brother Poe know where to get booze for their black market operation."

"Yeah? I hope it ain't gin."

"I don't know what kind." Rinco looked at his watch. "They've left Papa-San's by now and should be at number fourteen."

"Number fourteen," Chitown repeated.

Mama-San returned, sat the drink on the table, and left for the third time. "I go now. Get you a girl."

"That's alright, Mama-San ... I ... " It was too late. She went through the door she had been timing.

"I don't want to go through no changes, so I'm gonna split." He downed the drink with a frown and shiver, then reached into his pocket.

"That's okay," Rinco said. "I got it. You better try and catch those dudes before they shack up or you're out of luck. I'll meet you there later." He kissed Betty on the forehead. "I'm gonna be here awhile."

Chapter Eleven

THE DRIVER moved leisurely through the crowded bazaars and winding sidestreets for fifteen minutes before Chitown realized he was deliberately running up the fare.

"Say man! Fourteen couldn't be that far from twenty-two, so how about getting the hell there, huh? With a little chop-chop."

The driver wheeled around a corner and blasted his horn at a bunch of jumping, cursing, fist-shaking people. He stopped near the end of the block and pointed to a big brown building with a tall narrow door.

"Fourteen! Fourteen!" he said. Chitown saw the number, paid the driver and got out. He followed the loud voices of Mitchell crewmen through the door of the building to the end of a long dark hallway, where he pushed through double doors into a huge, bright, crowded ballroom. Big Shot saw him and rushed over.

"Hey, baby! What's happening? Where's Rinco?"

"I know where he is," Brother Poe cut in, turning from the girl he was with. "With that black-ass Malayan at twenty-two, right?"

"That's right." Chitown lit a cigarette. "He said he would drop by here later."

"They got some boss bitches at twenty-two, but they want too much bread." Brother Poe put his arm around the girl and winked. "These chicks jus' as boss, an' all of em like ta get high."

"Speaking of high, you guys got anything to drink or know where to get it?" Chitown asked.

Big Shot and Brother Poe looked at each other, then laughed.

"We got a little wine," Big Shot answered. "Come on."

Chitown followed him across the floor full of Indian girls dancing with crewmen and Malayan soldiers.

"Make yo' call?" Big Shot asked.

"Naw, but I sent a telegram with some bread." He looked at his watch. It was a quarter to ten. "I'm going to try again tomorrow."

"That's mellow 'cause we'll be tied up at the dock. You can split anytime."

"Where you cats going?" Johnson came up to them on the other side of the floor.

"To my room . . . gonna give Chi a hit a grapes."

"He can pick up some lush on the way, we gotta get back to Papa-San's."

"Damn right!" Big Shot snapped his finger. "Dig, Chi, Papa-San wasn't home, so we gotta go back ta cop, come on with us."

"Ya'll coming back? I'm supposed to meet Rinco."

"Hell yeah! We got our broads all lined up."

They found Brother Poe and left.

Johnson gave the driver a store number. He took off blasting his horn until he reached a wide corner, then stopped the horn and started his mouth. They sat for five minutes listening to how nasty Calcutta was before Johnson interrupted.

"I've never been to Calcutta, but if it's any filthier than Bombay I hope I never do!"

"You no see Calcutta, you no like Bombay . . . why?"

"Because it's a grimy-ass, fucking city, that's why!"

The Americans all laughed.

"Bombay great city!" the driver argued. "You no like nothing . . . why you come to India? . . . Why?" There was a brief silence.

"To get you dumb motherfuckers to fight our wars for us." They laughed as Johnson passed his palm around for skin.

Not another word was passed between the angry driver and the seamen, until they stopped in front of a small, dingy store.

"We'll be right back." Johnson said.

The best Chitown could get under the counter was two half-pints of brandy. The other three bought large bags of white pistachios, and they all hurried back to the cab.

"Number fifty," Johnson snapped, "and no more yapping!"

When they reached the top floor of a ragged, pale gray building, they were met by a half dozen young giggling brown girls with long braided hair. The girls led them down the trash laden hallway into a wide spacious area, partitioned by half-pulled curtains to form a group of small junky rooms. In a far corner, by a small window, a short archaic woman squatted on a quilted pallet.

"Papa-San back yet?" Brother Poe asked.

She nodded, "Yes!", rose slowly, offered her seat, and went to the next room. The giggling girls crowded around jabbering in their native tongue. They all looked undernourished and wore soiled dingy saris with lots of cheap jewelry and small tattoos on their arms and foreheads.

"Papa-San! Papa-San!" Johnson and Brother Poe greeted a bent, toothless, white-haired old man who emerged carrying a black medicine bag.

"Duflamy One . . . Duflamy Two!" He gave them a big smile and warm handshake.

"Naw . . . you got it wrong again Papa-San," Brother Poe laughed. "I'm Duflamy One . . . see, I got on the blue cap. Get them girls outta here."

The old man gave an order and the girls hurried to another section of the room. The last one gave Big Shot a glance and giggle before pulling her curtain.

100

"Now let's get down to business." Johnson said after Brother Poe had introduced Big Shot and Chitown. Papa-San squatted and opened the bag.

"What you want? . . . Opium? . . . Hash-ish . . . Heroin?"

"You know damn well what we want!" Brother Poe said.

"Hash-ish . . . Hash-ish!" Papa-San clapped his bony hands and grinned. "I know! . . . I know!" He dug into the bag and took out a large oilcloth. He unfolded it slowly, exposing three ten-inch dark brown balls.

"Damn!" Johnson drew his switchblade, picked up a ball with it and smiled.

"Since it's four of us, let's chello. He pulled a hollow cone from the pocket of his mess jacket.

"Mellow with me!" Brother Poe said.

Using the switchblade, Johnson cut a piece from the ball, rounded it to the size of a quarter,and stuck it to the tip of the knife. Meanwhile, Brother Poe had begun splitting cigarettes and dropping the tobacco into Big Shot's cupped hands. Chitown opened his brandy as he watched Johnson light the ball and let it flame for a few seconds before blowing it out. Then Johnson dumped the ball, smelling and smoking, into Big Shot's hands and started mixing it with the tobacco. Brother Poe dropped a rock into the large end of the cone and waited. When the tobacco was almost black, they stuffed it into the cone on top of the rock. Johnson opened a clean handkerchief and covered the small end. Brother Poe lit the other end, then he and Big Shot got their handkerchiefs ready. Chitown took a burning swig of booze while Johnson took three long, slow draws and gave the chello to Big Shot, who took two draws, strangled, and passed it to Brother Poe. Brother Poe let the air out of his lungs, took a three second pull on the chello and held his breath. Chitown shook his head no when it was offered to him.

"Hide whiskey! Hide whiskey!" Mama-San rushed in, grabbed the bag beside Chitown and held her hand for the other bottle. "Police! Police!" she whispered. Chitown quickly gave the bottle to her, and she vanished behind a

101

curtain. Chitown and Big Shot got nervous because Johnson kept smoking.

"Any liquor? ... spirits?" came a deep, heavy voice. The huge size of the cop barely permitted him to clear the height and width of the door. He wore a dark blue, long-sleeve coat, short pants, a thick black beard, turban, and knee length socks.

"No spirits baby!" Johnson passed the chello to Brother Poe. "But we sho' gaining altitude."

"I see!" the policeman stooped and took the chello. They were still and silent as he examined the unusual pipe, and burst into laughter when he smiled and handed it back.

"Well, cheerio!" The policeman waved and headed for the door. He turned suddenly and asked again. "No liquor?"

"No whiskey!" Papa-San shook his head.

"Cheerio!"

"Cheerio!" they all answered.

"Ain't that a bitch!" Big Shot laughed. "I never seen no shit like this before."

Chitown took a deep breath. "I sure don't wanna drink here anymore ... how about a hit of that hash?" He took out his handkerchief. Brother Poe passed him the chello.

"It's getting late, Papa-San," Johnson said. "Let's go and take care business."

The old man flashed a bare mouth smile and got up. Johnson grabbed his own bag and followed him toward the room he came out of.

"Don't forget the coke," Brother Poe said.

"I got good coke!" Papa-San laughed.

"I know damn well you have."

Chitown wondered what Johnson had in his bag for Papa-San, but knew better than to ask. They had finished that mixture, dumped the ashes, and were re-filling the cone when Johnson and the old man returned.

"Here you go, baby!" Johnson threw Brother Poe a small plastic package of cocaine, then sat down, holding his leather bag as if it contained a fortune.

102

"You sho' a mellow dude Papa-San." Brother Poe passed the chello to Big Shot and opened the package. Using a knife with a small spoon on it, he scooped out and took a deep snort of the white crystal powder in each nostril, handed the package back to Johnson who did the same.

"You no break rocks!" Papa-San laughed as they choked and coughed with tears running down their faces.

"Didn't have time!" Brother Poe said and Johnson slapped his palm.

Big Shot and Chitown decided to just stick with the pipe. After the third round, Chitown declined everything. He laid back on his elbows and ran his tongue over his lips. The effect of the hash was somewhat like the effect of strong marijuana, so far as the dry mouth and nervous relaxation were concerned, but this high was frightfully more dimensional than any pot he had ever smoked. Everything seemed over-focused, and sounds rolled at him like waves smashing against a seawall.

Mama-San emerged with the brandy he had completely forgotten, followed by the giggling girls.

"Be careful with whiskey," she cautioned, then quickly changed the subject.

"Why you no catch girls?" She pointed to each of them. "You? ... You? ... You? ... You?"

They looked at each other, then back to her. The girls just giggled.

"Dig Mama-San, we gotta get back to the ship and go on watch!" Johnson lied. "We be back to see you and these pretty chicks later."

"When?" she asked with her hands on her hips.

"Tomorrow or the next day maybe ... we'll be here a long time!"

"Let's go!" Brother Poe glanced at his watch, "or we gonna be late!"

They shook hands with Mama and Papa-San, then waved goodby to the girls.

103

Rinco wasn't at Number Fourteen when they returned and floated across the floor to the cushioned benches that lined the far wall. The crowd had thinned considerably, but three waiting girls ran to Johnson, Big Shot and Brother Poe, who immediately headed for their reserved rooms.

"These some boss broads," Big Shot winked over his shoulder at Chitown. "You better cop one befo' it's too late dude!"

"Maybe I will." Chitown sat down and re-opened his bottle.

"Be careful with whiskey!" came a soft whisper from a short, round face girl with Chinese eyes, who came from a side door and slid down beside him. "You want to drink, come my room."

He was so high off the dope and brandy, that it was a few seconds before he could focus her clearly.

"I'd prefer to drink out here right now, if you don't mind."

"Okay!" she smiled, "but hide bottle. I get you glass."

"Bring a glass for yourself!" he said.

"Thank you!"

When she returned, they quickly finished the first bottle. The girl snuggled close, telling him all about her younger brother she was sending to college. Chitown only pretended to listen while watching the small groups of seamen scattered along the walls and out on the dance floor. They were all joking and signifying, while trying to bargain with the remaining girls to lower their prices. But the only sound that captured him was that weird record with the strange beat and garbled lyrics that played over and over. He started to get hot. He removed his jacket and wiped his brow with a handkerchief.

"You stay with me tonight ... okay?" The girl opened the other bottle and poured them another drink. "I have nice room."

He ignored her, took another burning swallow, lay back, closed his eyes and thought about his wife. He yearned for the sound of her voice and wished he had tried again to get his call through. There was so much he wanted to say. It would have meant the world to tell her he was on his way home. He finished the drink in two gulps, then jumped up shaking in anger and self condemnation.

"I'm going back to the ship!" he handed the girl his glass and started weaving along the wall. She grabbed the half full bottle, caught up with him near the record player, and pleaded for him to spend the night. He ignored her by trying to catch the English words to that strange music that had been bugging him. He bent his ear to the speaker, and when he straightened up he was furious.

"This 'Old Black Joe'!" He snatched off the record and held it over his head. "How much did this thing cost?"

The room became silent as all eyes shifted to him.

"Four rupees!" the frightened girl answered, reaching for the record.

He calmly dug into his pocket for some coins, threw them across the floor, then smashed the record on his knee.

"What the matter you, mon!" Boatswain Phillips walked over to him. "Why you break these people music?"

"Fuck you!" Chitown snapped.

"Fuck you too, mon!" The fact that Chitown was high gave Phillips courage. "You Stewards and bilge rats think you own everything; think you can take other people's property anytime you want!"

"They playing 'Old Black Joe'!" Chitown shouted, expecting some response from the other crewmen gathering around. When he got none he shouted again. "They dancing to 'Old Black Joe' and laughing at you stupid-ass niggers!"

"Don't call me nigger!" Phillips growled and butted Chitown between the eyes.

Chitown saw stars, his knees buckled but he stayed on his feet. Phillips swung a right fist that caught him flush on the jaw, spinning him like a top into the crowd. He heard voices cheering, choosing sides and making bets.

"Get that motherfucker Boats!" someone yelled and

105

pushed Chitown back towards his adversary. "Teach him not ta take yo' bitch!"

Chitown could barely see as he stumbled from the shove. The crowd had formed a circle around him and Phillips. He wiped his watering eyes and tried to appear more groggy than he really was as he slowly backed away from the West Indian, who inched closer, crouched like a boxer looking for another good shot.

Suddenly, he drew back and threw a round-house right. Chitown blocked it with his left forearm, and at almost the same time, drove a ferocious right hook into Phillip's mid-section that made the crowd gasp. Before Phillips could fall Chitown grabbed his wrist with both hands and started spinning him around and around, faster and faster until he was stretched out waist high. Phillip's whirling feet knocked over chairs, shattered glass from table tops, and bounced off fleeing bodies.

Centrifugal force rendered Phillips helpless, and when Chitown released him like a hammer-thrower, his scream joined those of the women when he felt himself flying through the air. He crashed a thin plaster wall and belly-flopped beside a small bed where Big Shot and a girl, both naked, were annihilating the springs. Big Shot jumped up off the equally terrified girl and dashed from the room out into the crowd, generating uncontrolled laughter.

Chapter Twelve

CHITOWN RAN from the house and headed in no general direction, turning corners on impulse. The lights, people and buildings spun slowly like a huge haunting carousel. He stumbled over a woven basket and a live Cobra hissed at him. He yelled and broke across the street, pursued by curses from a haggard old man shaking a wooden flute.

Bombay seemed like another city. The side streets were nearly bare of vehicles, but filled with carts and cattle, as the people took to the edge of the curbs in grim respect for the countless homeless sleeping bodies that littered the narrow sidewalks. Chitown ran and ran, trying to escape that horrible hissing sound that grew louder and louder with his every step. He ran until the streets were suddenly empty of sleepers, but the hissing persisted, coming from all directions.

"Damn! I must be losing my mind!" He stopped and leaned against a building to catch his breath and press his hands to his ears in a vain effort to drown out that now deafening sound. He screamed when a bony hand with long black fingernails reached through a barred window and grabbed his shoulder. He snatched away and ran back into the street, shocked by the sudden knowledge that he had wandered into the dreaded "Cages."

They were more frightening than Rinco had described, and worse than any nightmare because it was real. That terrifying hissing which started with the snake now came from old four-story buildings on both sides of the street, stretching for blocks.

Every visible window and door was barred and jammed with prostitutes, waving their arms through the bars as if clawing for the wind, while making that eerie, hissing sound through their teeth. All were Indians of various shades and manners of dress. Most wore tattoos and some sort of jewelry, including colored stones embedded in foreheads and rings in noses.

Chitown stood momentarily spellbound by the bedlam, then hastened his search for a cab. The sounds grew louder, completely engulfing him. The stretching, clawing hands seemed to move closer and closer. He stopped and almost panicked, not knowing which way to go when a taxi turned the corner and headed his way. He ran to meet it, but stopped short when he saw a passenger.

"Hey Chi!" ... Rinco shouted from the rear window, "get in!"

"Goddamn man, am I glad to see you!" Chitown sighed after he had closed and locked the door. "I thought I was cracking up. I've never, never seen any shit like this before!"

"Some of the cats at fourteen think you've already cracked, the way you tore up that joint with Phillips." Rinco laughed and pulled out a cigar.

"Is he hurt bad?"

"Naw, but maybe now he'll leave you alone."

"I don't know." Chitown's trembling hands fumbled for a cigarette. "I guess he'll always believe I shacked up with Janet that night."

"The nigger's crazy." Rinco blew a puff of smoke. "I've told him a thousand times that you left with me and went back to the ship."

"Well ... " Chitown lit the smoke. "He just might get up off me. I hope I didn't really fuck him up."

Rinco laughed again. "Aw that hard-head's all right. But I sure wish I could have seen him flying through the air. They say you threw him right on top of Big Shot."

Until Rinco told him about Big Shot running out into the crowd buck naked with his wet dong flapping, then rushing back and hurting his bare foot while trying to kick the ailing Phillips in the ass, Chitown had almost forgotten what a truly good laugh felt like.

Once away from the "Cages", virtually every inch of the sidewalk again became covered with prone people. They slept between filthy old rags, sacks and blankets, not squirming or moving as the car roared by scattering dust and debris, while fat slimy rats scampered around and bounced over them. It was hard for Chitown to take. He reached for his bottle, then realized that he had left it at number fourteen.

"Have you eaten since this morning?" Rinco asked.

"I haven't even thought about it."

"What say we stop and have chow?"

"Good idea, I'm hungry as hell!"

"Hey driver!" Rinco said, "Prince of Wales Seamen's Club!"

At the club, Rinco had fish and chips with a large soda, while Chitown downed two steaks and three cups of coffee.

Exiting the club, they noticed that the night was pleasant and the beggars inactive, so they decided to walk to the dock.

"Damn!" Chitown whispered, frowning down at the still, silent bodies. "They look like they're dead."

"You can bet a lot of them are," Rinco said.

"What!" Chitown stopped in his tracks.

"That's right. It would be safe to say five percent of these people will never wake up, but the sidewalks stay full because there's always someone to take their place."

For the first time Chitown began to appreciate the agony around him. He felt ashamed of all the self-pity he harbored when the only emotions he had shown those poor, suffering people were impatience and disgust.

"You mean to tell me human beings die by the droves? Every night? On the street?" He hurried the pace.

"Yep! In front of homes, gardens, movies, restaurants, anywhere ... mostly from disease, malnutrition and exposure."

"Malnutrition? With all these short ribs and sirloins walking around? Are these people crazy!"

"Those cows are sacred." Rinco laughed and pulled out a cigar. "They wander unmolested."

"Ain't nothing sacred as chow!" Chitown said. They showed their identification to the guard at the only open gate and made their way down to the dock.

"Now we're gonna catch hell getting a boat." Rinco looked up and down.

"I can't get over those dying people," Chitown persisted. "You mean a cat come to open his shop gotta step over a dead body?"

"That's right." Rinco thumped the cigar butt into the water.

"How the hell do they bury 'em ... throw 'em in the ocean?"

"Naw! The Hindus are cremated, the rest they feed to the buzzards."

"Aw come on man, you gotta be bullshitin'."

"Okay, I'll show you tomorrow."

"No thanks! But seriously, you don't mean the public can watch people burned and eaten?"

"Only friends, relatives, and officials ... it's done everyday, outdoors, behind high walls."

"It's still hard to believe." Chitown shook his head. "I don't believe it!"

"See those lights?" Rinco pointed to the left.

"Yeah!"

"Let's go that way, maybe we can get some of those lazy ass Indians to take us to the ship. Probably cost a fortune."

"You know, Chi." Rinco lit another cigar as they sat at the open rear end of a small, smelly, loud-putting boat that rolled and dipped it's way through the choppy water. "I don't give a damn about Indians in general, not just because they're a bunch of phonies acting like God's gift to the world when they're just global flunkies for the British. I hate them for the way they live in East Africa. You'll see when we get there." He paused for a second. "But it still rips me up inside whenever I see that rolling red flame and dark smoke climbing behind those pale gray walls, or that flock of black vultures gliding down from the sky."

Chitown was quiet for awhile. "Oh, I don't know," he said. "Everybody's got to die. And I guess their way of disposing of the bodies is as good as any. 'Specially when you consider how crowded India is."

Rinco looked sharply at Chitown, then sighed. "I suppose you might be right," he said.

They were both silent all the way back to the ship.

The morning sun gave a deep golden glow to the dirty brown harbor as the *Mitchell* churned slowly towards the dock.

"Now all hands! ... Quarters for muster at zero eight hundred!" the boatswain blasted over the speaker. "Deck department on starboard side of number three hatch, engine department in machine shop, stewards department in officer's messhall ... quarters for muster at zero eight hundred!"

As soon as she tied up and lowered her gangway, over a dozen crewmen who had stayed in town all night rushed aboard and dashed for the chow-hall. At muster the men were bored and angry as the officers re-read the bulletin sheet that had been placed throughout the ship.

The U.N. command was preparing a new offensive. Replacements were urgently in need. The departure time was advanced twenty-four hours. The workday for the steward and deck departments would be twelve hours until all six hundred troops and their equipment were loaded.

111

To be sure the crew would be intact at twenty-one hundred when the ship got underway, liberty was canceled.

This brought on most of the grumbling. There was also a severe storm developing, the officers argued, and additional time was essential to try and avoid it.

Chitown, who was burning more than anyone because of his shattered hope of heading home from Bombay, really got mad at the look on the First Engineer's face as he read his request for eight hours annual leave. The officer shook his head no and started quoting the bulletin, but Chitown cut him off. "Wait a minute, man, that's for annual, not liberty. You know my wife's been in an accident and I'm trying to call her. We don't have a thing to do with loading troops."

"The evaporators have to be cold shocked," the officer argued, "and two condensate pumps are on the bum."

"I believe Smitty and I can handle that," Rinco intervened. "The cold shocking's no problem, and I know what's wrong with the pumps."

After deciding it wasn't worth the trouble to invoke a technicality, the First Engineer signed the request and gave it to the Engine Yeoman.

"If I get my call through early, I'll come straight back and help out."

"I don't give a damn about that," the officer said. "Just make sure you're back when your time's up."

"I'll be back, but what I've got to do is more urgent to me than anything in the Congo or on this damn ship!"

At zero eight-fifty the first truckloads of Indian troops began arriving in their drab olive uniforms and black berets. By the time Rinco and Smitty came topside for their morning coffee break the scene was all too familiar. Gear-laden soldiers in long, slow lines crowded the dock easing towards the forward gangplank. Their uniforms were all the same dull color, but instead of berets, the Hindus rolled their hair under bright turbans and many sported thick, black beards. Gurkas from the extreme north, who looked more Chinese than Indian, wore large red patches on their sleeves and wide brim hats folded up on one side, similar to the Australians.

Ragged Gunga-Din-type peasants labored under heavy burdens, in and out of the warehouses, and up and down the dock and gangway. They moved like ants, back and forth between the troops and the giant cranes that rolled noisily along the narrow tracks.

A long stream of cabs bringing friends, relatives and newsmen were allowed through the gates. This flooded the dock with civilians who had to be kept out of the way by only a handful of dashing and darting blue-coated policemen.

The evening meal was almost over when Chitown got back with Big Shot, Johnson and Brother Poe who were not only late as usual, but were not even aboard for muster and had just learned about the early departure from Chitown. A bright red bus was unloading a big brass band, as they pushed their way through the mass of organized confusion to the gangplank.

Clutching his cherished package, Chitown rushed back to the messhall. After ordering, he lost his appetite, pecked at his food for a few minutes, then got up and went to the fantail in search of Rinco.

"You guys get those pumps finished?" he asked when he saw Rinco watching the proceeding from the fantail.

"Hell yeah! We were through before noon. That jive-ass first was just trying to make something out of nothing, all they needed was repacking."

"I'm hip . . . thanks."

"You get your call through?"

"Yeah man!" Chitown smiled. The connection was lousy, but it was sure great to hear her voice. I brought her some gifts." He showed the package. "She's doing fine, much better than when she wrote, but she ain't got that bread I sent yet."

"Don't worry! It usually takes a couple days."

"Well the main thing is, she knows I'm coming home.

Nothing in the world's more important than that. I could tell by the way she sounded."

The band struck up amid a thunderous ovation while a speaker's platform was being erected. They listened until politicians started arriving in long, shiny cars, then went below to the compartment.

At twenty-one fifteen, grimy hands untied the huge lines that vanished beneath the water until the looped ends crawled up the pale gray side of the *Mitchell* like giant nooses to the grinding sound of her winches. Her belly loaded with three hundred Malayan and six hundred Indian soldiers, the *Mitchell* belched black smoke from her stack and eased out into the harbor.

For over an hour Chitown stood alone on the fantail watching the fading lights of Bombay. "Bombay, India," he whispered. "Two oceans and three continents away from you, baby, at the very time you need me most." He put the coffee cup to his lips and took another burning swallow of whiskey. He heard her trembling voice in the rumble of the ship's shaft and the splashing waves illuminated by the full moon. "Don't worry, baby," he promised that faint glow on the black horizon where he had last talked to her, "each turn of this screw is cutting the distance between us, and believe me, Jean, I'll never leave you again." He drained the cup and threw it over the side.

Chapter Thirteen

THE *GRAY Ghost* was running true to form as a cursed ship. Changing course three times in four days couldn't take her out of the path of a circling storm. For most of the troops it was their first time at sea and their compartments reeked with the stench of vomit.

Each day the weather got rougher, until hot food could not be prepared. It slid off the grills and spilled from the kettles. The result was cold sandwiches, fruit, cookies and small cartons of milk. Everything movable had to be tied down, and many men slept strapped in their bunks. Anxiety filled the vessel and tempers were short. The miserable heat they had endured coming over, would have been a blessing compared to this fear of being stalked by a typhoon.

It was the third time during this particular watch that Rinco had to switch discharge from the badly needed feed tanks back to the nearly overflowing fresh water tanks. The furious sea made it impossible to maintain steady levels in the evaporator shells. Therefore, seventy percent of the water they made was too salty for the boilers, and had to be discharged into the tanks for crew's consumption, or dumped into the bilges.

Rinco staggered back and forth, checking the sea water boiling around the steam filled tubes, through the thick glass portholes of the loud, cylindrical shaped, asbestos-covered monsters. The tubes sat three on each side of a long steel walkway, like giant squids, sprouting white insulated pipe in all directions, decorated with black stencil and bright red valve wheels.

Topside, the *Gray Ghost* rose and fell with the heavy waves as violent winds blasted their tips across her weatherdecks, washing away everything that wasn't tightly secured.

As the ship dipped, the deck dropped from under Rinco, and on her slow rise, seemed to drive his ankles into his knees.

Just twenty more minutes in this hole, he thought, glancing up at the clock surrounded by gauges in the middle of the big black panel board, *then it's Chitown's baby.* He cursed when the salinity indicator climbed to point eight grains of salt per gallon. Number two port shell was full again, submerging the tubes. He reached under it and opened the discharge another turn. Now the first starboard shell was dry, with steam fogging the porthole. When he stooped to cut off its discharge, the ship took a fifty-degree roll, sliding him back against the railing of the port shells.

He hung on tight as the ship righted. Then she took a sixty-degree roll that begun throwing the evaporators into turmoil. The needles on the gauges danced wildly to the grunts and groans of the pumps below. The indicator held at all the red, while the port and starboard shells filled and emptied with the roll of the ship.

He struggled to the board and dialed the engine room.

"Engine room! Third Mate Ross!"

"Say, Third! . . . This is Styles! . . . Request permission to secure the vaps!"

"Why?"

"Why the hell you think, man? I can't make nothing but

116

sea water. The whole plant's salted up. I can't hold the levels anymore!"

"Okay! . . . I'll check with the First."

"Well make it fast . . . this joint's gone haywire!"

After what he felt was much too long, permission was granted. He flipped open the top of the metal desk welded to a beam and got a long monkey wrench. Squeezing halfway around number one port shell, he used it for leverage to close the hard auxiliary steam valve.

It was a rough, sweaty job under normal circumstances. Now he could use only one hand; with the other he held the railing to keep from being slung into the hot, bare flanges. He finished wringing wet, replaced the wrench, pushed the cut-off buttons for the pumps, then went below to close the main circulating valve.

The *Mitchell* reared like a stallion, dived bow first into the sea, rose slowly like a giant whale, and dived again. Throughout the ship people were bounced back and forth against the hard steel, some tearing flesh and breaking bones. The ship's loudspeaker barked damage control crews into action. The wind grew fiercer, ripping away two lifeboats on the starboard side. One went overboard and the other dangled dangerously from a single line. The ship was slapped around by the angry, mountainous sea like a handball while the engineers flooded all empty tanks for ballast and the Captain tried every combination of engine and rudder to keep her bow into the wind. The ship took a slow, sixty-five degree roll and everybody figured, *This is it*. But their prayers were answered when the ship righted.

Rinco was hanging desperately to the bottom of the ladder on the lower level when he heard the steam explode from a crack in the line. Within minutes, the upper level was completely fogged, and the saturating cloud crept downward. With the heavy bobbing and weaving of the ship, it took all of his strength to climb the ladder.

When he reached the upper level, it was hard to breathe. Visibility was zero and water poured from his body. He tried to struggle to his feet, but kept slipping and

117

sliding on the hot, moist deck until he lay exhausted with his arms wrapped around the bottom of a railing post to keep from being thrown back to the lower level.

Chitown sensed Rinco was in trouble when he opened the hatch and saw steam pouring into the troops' compartment.

"Is there an officer here?" he shouted, making his way through the noisy, frightened soldiers crowded around the evaporator door.

"Captain Bhalla ... " a tall, dark Indian stepped forward and gave Chitown a salute ... "can I be of any help?"

"Yeah! there's a man trapped below. I need a long rope and some men to handle it."

The officer turned and started giving orders in Hindu while Chitown opened the door and shouted into the steam for Rinco.

"You guys hang on to the other end!" he said when a soldier gave him the rope. He tied one end around his chest as four men stretched it out.

"When I give two yanks," he demonstrated, "pull me up fast!"

"Very well!" The officer repeated the instruction to the rope handlers, and ordered everyone else back out of the way. Chitown took a deep breath and started down. When he reached the middle landing, where the long, fire escape type ladder turned, he paused for a second to listen. The leak came from somewhere near the forward bulkhead, far enough from the working area to keep workers from being scalded. Unable to see, he tried to call again. The strong hot vapors choked, but failed to turn him back. Instead, he hurried, praying Rinco had not suffocated.

He sank to his knees on the upper level and crawled blindly for the telephone.

"Engine room! This is Kane! Cut off the steam to the vaps right now! The line's busted and Style's trapped down here somewhere ... get the doctor fast, he's got to be in bad shape!"

Chitown left the receiver hanging and went sliding on all four, skinburning his hands and knees. He saw stars when his forehead hit a railing post, and flopped on his side in a daze. It was getting harder to breath by the second and he felt himself growing weaker. He heard a cough and groan near the lower ladder and quickly got back to his knees. With his head throbbing, he crawled for the sound.

"Rinco!" The word exploded out of him when he reached the sweat-soaked body. He shook the body. It was Rinco, all right. Relieved to hear another cough, Chitown grabbed Rinco around the waist and gave two jerks on the rope. Then he let go the rope, got Rinco under both armpits, and started backing up the ladder. The rope tore at his chest, making breathing even more difficult, but he held fast. When he tried to turn on the middle landing, he slipped, crashing his back into the steel stairway.

When the hell they gonna cut off that steam? he wondered before passing out.

The Indian Captain knew something was wrong when the rope became harder for them to pull. As the roaring hiss of the steam began to subside, he led his men down the ladder and brought Chitown and Rinco out. The medical team arrived with portable oxygen, and carried them to sick bay on stretchers. The bay was loaded with casualties. So many soldiers were injured that one of their compartments had to be converted into another sick bay.

After being revived, Rinco was given first aid and released in a temporary no-duty status. Chitown was kept in sick bay because of bruises on his head and back.

Slowly, the wind died down, and by morning the rain had stopped. The once raging sea turned calm, smooth, and glassy green. Listing ten degrees to starboard, a long black cloud streaming from her stack and her speed cut in half, the *Gray Ghost* leaned her way towards Africa.

One crewman, a Filipino cook, and two Malayan soldiers were missing, never to be seen again. The Captain wired Leopoldville, reported the casualties, and gave a first estimate of damage. Beside sixteen crewman, nearly a hundred soldiers were injured. Medical supplies would soon be low. The refrigeration plant was knocked out, endangering perishables. Leopoldville immediately shortened their destination from the Congo to Capetown.

The crew soon dismissed the tragedy of the storm because of its elation over going to Capetown. Back to modern, jazzy Capetown at last. Capetown, where passions ran wild with broads, booze, and the beat of drums, despite the danger lurking the streets. The anticipation kept them from being bored as long, hard hours were needed for the monumental task of cleaning up and repairing the ship. Within two days both Rinco and Chitown were back in the evaporators helping Smitty with the busted steam line. Everyone was concerned with getting the vessel upright, watertight, and fully functional. There was always the possibility of another storm, and a weakened ship could quickly become a coffin.

However, their long weeks of anticipation were bitterly shattered by the orders they received thirty-six hours from Capetown. The ship would only be there twenty-four hours. She was to take on vital parts, fresh food and medical supplies, then get underway for her newly assigned home port, Dar Es Salaam, Tanganyika. From there the troops would be flown back and forth to the Congo. This would give future voyages a direct route across the Indian Ocean, saving nearly five thousand miles by not having to sail around the Cape of Good Hope to West Africa. It was no consolation to the disgusted crew. The sea time saved was no compensation for abandoning Capetown.

The next day was payday, and the traditional crapgame had been going on for hours when Rinco got off watch at twenty-hundred. He gave the code knock to get in the compartment. Ten half-dressed crewmen, all holding money, were standing, kneeling, squatting, and sweating around a blanket while four small fans circulated the hot smoke and musk.

"Hey, baby!" Big Shot waved a thick wad of bills and winked. Johnson and Brother Poe, who always ran the games, also had their usual three hundred dollar anchor pool ready, so that players could gamble on the time the ship would dock. The pool was represented by a white sheet of paper with sixty neatly ruled squares numbered to represent the minutes in an hour and taped on a piece of cardboard. For five dollars a square the player could pick any or as many that were not sold and sign his name across it. The number that matched the exact minute they docked according to the ship's log won two hundred and fifty dollars. Johnson and Brother Poe split the other fifty.

Rinco peeled off his work clothes and started to his locker for soap and towel.

"Just three more left, baby," Johnson shouted, "better come on."

"Okay!" Rinco took the board and pen. Numbers four, forty-nine, and seventeen were open. He took forty-nine and gave Johnson the money.

"Thanks, baby, everybody here copped one but Big Shot."

"Fifty-nine ta one too much odds for me," Big Shot looked up. "I don't bet on no clocks, no horses, no ballplayers, jus' me. I put my bread on Big Shot."

Rinco locked up his watch and wallet, then went to shower. Even under the sputting water he could still hear cursing and finger snapping as the dice bounced off the bulkhead.

"Haa dice! Nine, baby ... quinine, bitter dose ... Now ... nine! Read 'em an' weep."

"How much?"

"Shoot it all, baby!"

"Better watch dis nigger, he lucky 'nough ta shit in a swinging jug."

"Gimme a natural, baby ... Haw!"

"I got these, nigger, shoot again."

"Got these too!"

"I don't give a fuck ... but if you wanna play baseball I bet another ten. Catch that!"

"You on!"

"Okay, juice 'em Lucy ... Haa!"

121

"Six the point!"
"He make it for ten!"
"Ten he don't!"
"Bet!"
"Six dice ... Haw!"
'C.I.X. sweet dice, Haw!"
"Seven an' out!"
"Motherfuckers!"
"Next shooter!"
"Shoot twenty!"
"Twenty dollars he shoot!"
"Back man got him!"
"I hit for ten!"
"Got that too! ... shoot!"
"Eleven the winner!"
"Gotdamnit!"
"Shoot the forty!"
"I got twenty!"
"Twenty open!"
"Got it!"
"Pot right ... shoot!"
"Four!"
"Little Joe ... Haw! Joe dice!"
"Bar it for ten!"
"I'll take five!"
"Ain't dat a bitch, I take the other five ... shoot!"
"What the fuck you catching dice for? You ain't fading, you five dollar motherfucker!"
"Leave the dice alone man, go ahead shooter!"
"This is that jinx-ass praying motherfucker, he burn candles an' shit on ya."
"Double duce! Joe the winner!"
"See! What I tell ya!"
"How much you shoot?"
"Twenty!"
"That all! Gimme a chance, baby."
"I'll give you a chance, you jive motherfucker, the chance of a one leg man in a ass kickin' contest!"

"Shoot!"

Rinco barely heard the movie call and couldn't make out what picture was announced, but anything was better than that hot, funky compartment. He finished showering, rushed into his clothes, and left.

After the movie, he stopped by the dayroom. It was packed to the hilt and roaring with laughter. A portable phonograph blasted South African jazz records as the crowd clapped along with a bunch of crewmen doing their interpretations of the Puti-Puti.

When he returned to the compartment, the winners were counting their money, while the losers drank free gin and waited to borrow. One of them tried to tease him by asking, "You going to Seapoint to see Madam Zulu tomorrow?"

"Damn right!" he retorted. "Those women respect their men. It's better than getting your head busted over a bunch of skunky-ass bitches that fuck every scroungy sailor that hit port!"

The compartment got quiet, as the perils of Capetown suddenly outweighed the joy.

"That cat walkin' round with the split I put cross his mug know better then ta fuck with me again," Big Shot bragged as he pocketed his winnings.

"I wouldn't be too sure." Johnson held up his scarred hand. "I had shattered the Skully's snot box who gave me this."

"Well I ain't worried." Big Shot reached into his locker and came out with a ten-inch switchblade. "With this, an' my razor, me an' them mothers can get it on."

This prompted other guys to rush out and get the weapons they had bought in Bombay.

"What the hell's going on? ... A mutiny?" Chitown quipped when he came in from his watch, and saw all the different knives, blackjacks, cleavers and knuckles.

"Hell naw!" Johnson answered. "We're just pulling into Capetown ... you still got that shank I gave you?"

"Yeah!"

123

"Then you better sharpen it up . . . and get something to go with it . . . you might have had a easy time kicking Phillip's ass, but you ain't rumbled with Brother Skully yet. When you meet him, you better have both hands and feet working at the same time. That's why I got a pair of knucks," he waved them in the air, "to replace that shank."

"Alright!" Rinco shouted, "I got the four to eight watch. Let's un-ass the compartment!"

He started to undress. The crowd pocketed their weapons and began to leave.

"Say, Chi!" Brother Poe showed him the card, "you might as well take this last chance on the anchor pool. Only two more left, an' I got one sold."

Chitown signed in square number seventeen and gave Brother Poe five dollars.

"Thanks, baby." He took back the board and hurried out to get high with Johnson and Big Shot.

When the room emptied, Rinco brushed his teeth, and climbed into his bunk, as Chitown prepared to shower.

"Man . . . I can hardly wait till tomorrow," he sighed. "I sure hope the Red Cross came through so I can get home where I belong."

"Me too, Chi," Rinco said, "but I'm beginning to have my doubts about the Red Cross."

"What do you mean?"

"Well . . . it seems to me, that if they were going to do anything, they would have notified the ship by now."

"Yeah! I thought about that too. But if they don't, I'm going anyway!"

"What?!" Rinco sat up. He wanted to, however, just couldn't discourage Chitown farther by explaining the difficulties he would encounter trying to travel from Capetown.

"How about covering for me while I sneak off early to buy a ticket!"

"Sure thing . . . how much money you got?"

"Five hundred dollars. I took everything off the books."

"You'll need more. I can let you have a few hundred."

"Thanks a lot man! You'll have it back as soon as I get home."

"No sweat, Chi ... you saved my life. I just hope you make it."

Chitown became embarrassed and changed the subject. "All those dudes with their weapons kind of shook me up. Is Capetown really that bad?"

"Hell yes! Those Skullys will cut your throat for a crummy shilling."

"Damn!" Chitown shook his head. "Now I wish I had got me something in Bombay. I'm going to be carrying a lot of bread. And all I've got is this lousy shank."

"You probably won't run into any Skullys just going to the airport." Rinco got up, went to his locker, and gave Chitown a long blackjack-type weapon.

Chitown examined it closely. Two welding rods were driven into a file handle and soldered to the metal tip, along with two bed springs made into one by welding, and fitted over the rods.

"A cat named Sims made that before he cracked up," Rinco said.

On the loop end of the spring, which extended a half inch, hung a lead sinker. Chitown swung the weapon around and marveled at the power and flexibility derived from wrist action. "What's this tape on the sinker for?"

"That's covering a fish hook he soldered on. In case somebody grab it, they let go in a hurry! There's also a hole drilled in the handle for a wrist strap."

"Man that Sims must have had a hell of an imagination ... this thing is something else!" Chitown shook his head.

"Yeah!" Rinco climbed back into his bunk. "He made it from that fishing gear they give us every Christmas. When he started staying aboard, he let me have it. I carried it all the time, until I stopped hanging in the colored section. Take it with you ... who knows ... if you can't get away, you might want to hit the beach."

"I doubt it, but just in case ... "

125

"This is the Captain speaking!" came that familiar voice, booming over the loudspeaker ... "As you are all aware, we will dock at Capetown between zero eight, and zero nine hundred tomorrow morning. Except for those who work nights, liberty will not commence until noon ... More important ... liberty will definitely expire at zero seven hundred day after tomorrow. We will get underway at zero eight hundred ... sharp ... I repeat, so there will be no doubt. Liberty expires at zero seven hundred ... we depart at eight ... This ship will leave on time ... Anyone remaining in Capetown, will be treated by the South African government as a deserter, and undesirable alien ... That is all!"

"Well that shit don't concern me." Chitown put the weapon in his locker and went to shower.

BOOK TWO

Take me away. God, Take me away
Away to see love smile again on
A sunny day. Away from hate, fear
Sin and scorn, this repressive man-made
Hell below the horn.

Chapter Fourteen

THE SOUND of human voices filled the warm brisk air, rising over the crackle of high gliding doves, as the *General Mitchell* sliced slowly through the glittering waters of Table Bay. Both officers and crewmen, some who began crowding the decks as early as seven A.M., waved, shouted and whistled at the girls that cluttered the dock, while workers, spectators, cab drivers and policemen looked on.

The scene was almost identical to the day the ship left. The harbor had the same tint of blue, and it looked like the same snow-white clouds clung in serene beauty to the top of Table Mountain.

It was nine o'clock when Chitown secured the evaporators. Keeping an ear open for mail call, he rushed to the compartment, showered, changed into a brown sport outfit and went topside.

"Hey man! You won the anchor pool!" Brother Poe met him in the passageway and counted out two hundred and fifty dollars.

"Damn!" Chitown grinned, "I can't believe it. Out of all the pools I've played, this is the first time I ever won."

"Well you sho' got this one, baby. We tied up at eight seventeen. Congratulations!"

"Thanks, man!" They slapped skin. "You seen Rinco?" Chitown asked.

"Naw, but I guess he down on the dock with the rest of 'em. Dig you later!"

It was like a dream come true. Not the first dream of profitable adventure, but the realization that now he certainly had enough, with what Rinco loaned him, to get home.

The ship rocked lazily between a French and a British vessel as Chitown shaded his eyes from the sun and scanned the crowded dock. Rinco was with a small bunch of seamen talking to four neatly dressed Zulu girls. Then he saw Big Shot with his arm around Freda, and Janet holding hands with Phillips. Janet's head was lifted and her large brown eyes combed the decks. When she spotted him, he turned away.

"Mail call! ... Mail call!" came a voice over the ship's speaker. "All department yeomen lay up to Engine Yeoman's office to pick up your department's mail!"

Smitty had beat him to the Yeoman's office, and was sorting letters on their bunks when he rushed into the compartment.

"You and Rinco got three apiece," Smitty said, "and Big Shot his usual bunch of pretty, sweet smelling ones."

"I see!" Chitown laughed. "What you got there?"

"Fruit cake." Smitty Sniffed the can. Heavy on the brandy."

"Oh yeah?"

"From the old lady. Have a piece."

"Naw thanks."

"Okay ... by the way, congratulations on the anchor pool."

"Thanks, you just don't know how bad I need it."

"I see you fixin' to hit the beach and blow some of it." Smitty winked.

"Yeah, I hope to blow a lot of it."

130

"I'm going to get ready, too. With one lousy-ass day in Capetown I'm sure as hell not working in those vaps! See you later?"

"Okay!"

Chitown ripped open the first letter. It told him how thankful she was to get that money from India, and how good it was to hear his voice. She told how the money was spent, but the end of the letter burst his balloon. She had bad news from the Red Cross. They could not help him because he wasn't in the Armed Service. The other letters told, even more emphatically than the earlier ones, how sick, lonely, and depressed she was. She cursed the Merchant Marine and wondered why he couldn't write more often. If he still loved her he would find a way home under these trying circumstances. The last letter was the saddest. She loved and missed him so, that hardly a night passed that she didn't cry herself to sleep.

Don't worry, baby! he looked at his watch. *I'm gonna be home sooner than you think. Damn! it's after ten o'clock, better get this show on the road. Maybe I can call and give her the good news.*

Rinco was still chatting with the Zulu girls when Chitown approached and told him he was ready to go to town.

"I heard about the anchor pool," Rinco smiled, "I see your luck's beginning to change for the better."

"Except for the Red Cross." Chitown lit a cigarette. "They turned me down because I'm not in the service."

"I knew it would be some jive reason." Rinco took him by the arm and introduced him to the women.

"I'm very pleased to meet you delightful, ladies." He quickly noticed their statuesque features, long waistlines and shapely figures, then checked his watch again. "I hate to leave, but I've got to make it to town."

Rinco excused himself and walked with him to a taxi.

"Look!" he said, "don't be too disappointed if you're not able to leave from Capetown, with that anchor pool money you'll have more than enough to make it from Dar Es Salaam."

"I'll try not to be." He managed a feeble smile.

"You want the address where we'll be in Seapoint, in case you can't leave and want to hit the beach? I'm sure you'll have a nice time." Rinco nodded towards the women.

Chitown looked and pondered. "Naw! that's alright. The next time I leave the ship I'm gonna have my gear an' be headed for home. Thanks anyway."

"Good luck!" They shook hands, and Chitown got in the cab.

"To the airport!"

As the car passed Janet and Phillips, she waved and threw him a kiss. He thumped his cigarette out the window.

Big Shot was getting dressed for the beach when Chitown made his disheartened return late that evening.

"What you doing back so soon, dad?"

"The real mystery is why you're still aboard? This is Capetown." Chitown didn't bother to try and explain his mission, or its failure.

"That funny talkin', motherfuckin' Chief Engineer! That's why. Sonofabitch had me workin' on them goddamn boilers again." Through the mirror Big Shot studied Chitown's sad expression as he grunted and flopped down on his bunk.

"Dig, man, why don't you hit the beach with me? Freda's throwing a party, booze, broads, chow, everything . . . it's better than sittin' by yourself on this big iron motherfucker."

"Naw, I'm gonna cool it." He got up and went to his locker.

"Janet wanna see you, dad, you oughta catch-up with that fox."

"Damn Janet!" He took out a bottle. "Want a drink?"

"No thanks, dad, ain't got time, gotta blind ya with ass." He put his knife and razor in different pockets, then gave himself a final check in the mirror. "Gonna be a boss set, dad . . . sho' you don't wanna come?"

"Naw! I've had enough of South Africa."

"Okay! suit yourself . . . later!" Big Shot went out and closed the hatch.

Filled with loneliness and depression, Chitown mixed a drink, gathered his stationery and sat down at the desk. He began a long letter to his wife, describing how he also loved and missed her. He told of winning the anchor pool and his plans to jump ship in Tanganyika. Explaining the slowness of the mail, he informed her that he might be home before she received the letter. When he finished the glass was empty. He poured another and went to the sink for water. The whiskey caused his stomach to groan and burn, making him realize he had missed all three meals.

Immediately, he thought about the Teahouse. There he could not only get food, but also newspapers and magazines to fight the boredom. He quickly prepared the letter for mailing and left the compartment. After dropping it through the slot in the Purser's office, he peeped in the dayroom while on his way to the Quarterdeck. It was empty, except for the drunken, red-faced plumber who lay stretched out, fast asleep. The only other people aboard were the watch standers, and Indian troops who were not allowed ashore. He hurried off the ship and down the deserted docks to the Teahouse, but it was closed.

"Damn," he sighed. "Now I wish I had got that address from Rinco." Darkness crept with him back into the shadow of the Mitchell.

Maybe Big Shot's set's still going, he hoped, pausing at the foot of the gangway to watch for an approaching taxi. Parties mean food. He tried not to think about the music, dancing and women, especially Janet. Big Shot and Phillips had kept Janet on his mind too much already. They were responsible for that hot annoying night when he lay sweating in his bunk. He could hear the Puti-Puti in the rumble from the engine room, and see her shapely body grinding with her full breast bouncing as she spun around the dance floor.

He noticed a car driving swiftly up to the dock. When

it stopped, Nelson staggered out, his processed hair scattered, and lipstick on his shirt collar.

"I sure hate ta hav'ta come back ta this stinkin' pig-iron bitch!" he said as he passed Chitown and started up the gangplank, "'cause they sho' swinging at Thirty Four Burke Lane."

"Hey driver!" Chitown yelled, "wait here! I'm going to town . . . be right back!"

Enroute to the compartment he had second thoughts about taking all his money ashore, but sneak thieves roamed skeleton crewed ships. Something cautioned him about going ashore at all. It was only one day; he could rough the gloom and hunger.

But why the hell should I sit around starving with all this bread in my pocket? he reasoned. After separating what he figured to spend from the rest, he took off his sport coat, slipped into the leather jacket and held the knife, and reached for the weapon.

Big Shot answered the door at Thirty Four Burke Lane, and grinned, "I told you ta hit the beach with me dad, now you done missed Janet. She done cut out with that lame-ass Phillips."

"Who cares, I just came to get some chow." Chitown glanced disgustedly at the empty-bottle-littered table. What was once food had long been reduced to bones and crumbs.

"You missed that too . . . but dig, we going to the Zambesi. You can cop a grease there."

"Mellow!" Chitown flopped down in a large overstuffed chair. "Where is everybody?"

"Where the hell you think? We ain't got but one night. Which remind me, I ain't seen you with a broad this whole cruise."

"Well let me remind you to mind your own business."

Freda emerged from behind the long green curtains that led back to the partitioned rooms. She was wearing a stunning red dress that molded her smooth, golden body.

"Hello, Freda," he rose to shake hands.

"Hello Chitown, so glad you decided to join us. Have you met Margo?" She pointed toward the elegantly dressed woman that followed her. Margo almost took him off his feet.

"No, I've never had the pleasure." He scanned her glowing coffee-brown complexion, crowned by silky auburn hair cropped at the earlobes.

"The pleasure's mine," she smiled back with her full red lips and pale gray eyes, as they shook hands warmly.

"That's the chick who gave the other party!" Big Shot wrapped his arm around Freda.

"Yeah!" Chitown said, "now I remember. I only saw you from a distance, and had no idea you were so gorgeous."

She thanked him very much, but withdrew her hand when Jake came through the back door with Johnson, Brother Poe and the two girls in darkglasses, floating on the smell of hashish.

"Hey, baby!" Brother Poe gave him some skin. "You splittin' to the Besi with us?"

"Yeah!" I could use some chow and a couple drinks."

"Why don't you come too, Margo?" Big Shot winked at Chitown who quickly seconded.

"Oh, I would love to," she looked at Jake, "but I've got to do something about cleaning this messy flat. Perhaps I'll join you later."

"I hope so," Chitown said. "Now if the rest of you are ready, let's make it. 'Cause I'm hungry as a dog."

Chapter Fifteen

JAKE PULLED up in front of the Zambesi Club and waited impatiently for them to pile out.

"Make damn sho' you pick us up 'round eleven-thirty," Brother Poe told him.

"Verry well," Jake nodded, then made a U-turn and headed back to Thirty Four Burke Lane.

Freda led the way through the swinging doors, down two steps, and past a smoky, glass-enclosed kitchen, with the smell of highly spiced food.

"This is far as I go for now!" Chitown slid into the first Bamboo frame eating booth, while the rest of them went through a narrow door on the right. In the faint glow from a large red globe hanging over a raised bandstand, they made their way along the edge of the noisy, crowded dance floor. The only other lights were single candles at each of the staggered tables along the walls. The ceiling was high and plain, ornamented by three huge low-hanging, slow-moving fans. They were near the rear of the club before they found an empty table. A tall olive-skinned waiter lit the candle, took their orders, and went for the six scotch and waters.

There were no strange decorations or exotic paintings as the name of the club would imply. The walls were covered only by vertical strips of bamboo bound by cord. The stage had no microphone or other sound carrying equipment, so the four piece African combo and their female vocalist could barely be heard from where they sat. With the exception of a few scattered crewmen, most of the patrons were hardly distinguishable between white and colored.

When the waiter returned with their drinks, Big Shot proposed a toast to the joys of Capetown, but suddenly froze.

"Pen that boss action!" He pointed to an exceptionally attractive woman in a dazzling blue evening dress at a near table. "Is she colored?"

"Hell, yes!" Freda scowled, "biggest whore in town!"

"Fuck these shots!" Johnson was saying when Chitown, finished with dinner, found them. "Let's chip in and get some whiskey."

The sailors all agreed and bought three fifths of scotch. The waiter made a quick trip bringing plenty of ice and water. They gave him a five dollar tip, and he backed away bowing and grinning.

Chitown was surprised, and a little uneasy, when he saw Phillips and Janet approaching the table. Phillips didn't want to stay but she insisted, so they called the waiter and joined the party.

"Just get some glasses," Big Shot said as his eyes fixed on her wide swaying hips and big hairy yellow legs. Then he pointed to Phillips, "you can buy the next one!"

Phillips frowned and grunted as everyone else laughed.

Janet turned to Chitown and asked, "Are you happy to be back in Capetown?"

"Sure, why shouldn't I be?"

"Oh! ... I was just wondering." She removed her sweater and let it hang over the back of the chair. "You left without a girl before ... you don't have one now. So I have my doubts."

137

"Well you know what you can do with your doubts, but I wish you'd tell this dumb motherfucker I didn't shack-up with you that night."

"Put-up!" Brother Poe shouted,and they all laughed again.

Phillips did a slow burn. Not only because they were laughing at him, but he wanted to know, just *who* did she sleep with that night? Her strapless low cut dress was nearly as short at the top as it was at the bottom, and she relished the way Chitown's eyes lingered on the visible parts of her plump breast. He caught himself when Johnson passed him a burning pipe filled with hash. Two of the pipes were being circulated around the table. When Phillips declined, they all laughed at him again.

"I wish they had some damn mikes!" Big Shot nodded toward the dark sweating vocalist, "or these lames would shut up so we can hear that chick sing again. She knocked me out the last time we was here."

"Oh, she's great!" Freda said with a bit of envy, "toast of the Coons' Carnival!"

"The what!" Big Shot and Chitown said at the same time, then looked at each other while the other sailors laughed.

"It's a Gala we hold every New Year's Eve," Freda explained. "I'm sorry the *Gray Ghost* missed this one."

"We sho' didn't miss the one before that," Brother Poe gave Johnson some skin, "an' it was a mellow mother-fucker!"

"But this was the best by far!" Janet closed her eyes and snapped her fingers. "We danced, sang, stayed high, and just had one hell-of-a-three-day party."

"And three nights too, huh baby!" Phillips tried to kiss her, but she jerked her head and winked at Chitown, who pretended not to notice.

"What I wanna know," he turned to Freda, "is where this coon shit come in?"

"Well ... a long time ago," she finished her drink and Big Shot poured another, "some Negro minstrels came here from America ... "

138

"Negroes?" Chitown interrupted. "I thought only white people could get visas to travel in South Africa."

"But my dear!" she continued, a bit annoyed, "that was a hundred years ago, long before apartheid."

"The minstrels were so sensational," Johnson's girl finally spoke, "we adopted their costumes and dances . . . that's how it all started."

"Coons' Carnival! Ain't that a bitch." Big Shot said. "That hunkey a motherfucker, got these niggers over here callin' us coons for a hundred years."

The seamen all laughed, but it wasn't funny to the women. The word "nigger" burned like the whiskey going down their throats.

Big Shot apologized and asked Freda to dance. Johnson and Brother Poe sent their girls back to the washroom to mix more hash for the pipes. Janet was getting drunk.

"What yer say we dance, Chitown?" She ran her fingers through her hair.

He took a nervous drink and glanced at his watch.

"Tell me who yer waiting on, honey," she giggled.

"Who the hell you suppose to be with!" Phillips snatched her around.

"You, damnit!" she snarled. Johnson and Brother Poe burst out laughing just to farther antagonize Phillips.

"Well, act like it! You wanna talk, talk to me!" He pounded his finger in his chest. "You wanna dance, dance with me." He jumped up and jerked her from her chair.

She looked back at the table and laughed as he pulled her onto the floor.

"That broad ain't got it all." Chitown's eyes followed her short, awesome body that had had him squirming and sweating for many nights, ever since he saw her do the Puti-Puti.

"You should go on an' pull her," Johnson said. "She been shooting at you ever since you hit Capetown. And these chicks for real, they ain't jive like those stateside broads."

"Damn right!" Brother Poe added. "We ain't got but one night an' you can forget about Margo."

"And since you've already kicked Phillips' ass, you can forget about him too!" Johnson laughed and gave Brother Poe some skin.

The girls returned, and the five of them smoked hash while Phillips, Janet, Big Shot and Freda danced. Chitown began to feel hot and dizzy after the third draw. He peeled off his jacket and loosened his belt to adjust the uncomfortable weapon hidden under his shirt.

"What's the matter?" Johnson saw the beads of perspiration forming on his brow. Brother Poe and the girls giggled.

"I shouldn't have fucked with that last pipe," Chitown said. "But I'll be all right." He pulled out a handkerchief and wiped his face. "Where's the head?"

"To the left of the bandstand," Johnson pointed.

"Watch my coat!"

"Okay!"

I just can't smoke that shit when I'm drinking, Chitown admitted, recalling Bombay as the dancers he passed seemed to lean and wobble.

The stench of the small toilet made him sicker. He bent over the commode and tried to throw up. Nothing came out but sweat as he strained to catch his breath.

Sticking his finger down his throat didn't help, so he folded his collar under and went to the facebowl. He let the water run cold, then started washing his face and neck. Suddenly there was a churn in his stomach and a lump in his throat. He rushed back to the commode and threw up practically everything he had eaten, while hoping no one came in and saw him. When he finished, he went back to the facebowl, gargled, washed out his mouth and felt a bit better. He wiped his face, checked himself in the mirror and blew his nose.

The music stopped amidst a round of applause and people came storming through the door. He checked to see if the weapon was still hidden, then hurried out. Feeling much better, he paused by the empty bandstand to take a deep breath.

"Good evening," a small, soft arm slipped around his.

He looked down into the smiling face of the singer.

"My name is Reba. We met this morning on the dock."

"Oh yeah!" he remembered.

"Do you like my singing?" She reached up to straighten his collar.

"I couldn't hear," he apologized. "We're sitting all the way back."

"I know, I've been watching—are you with one of those girls?"

"No, I'm not," he studied her with interest. The dim red glow made her face alluring without the aid of makeup; her short, bushy hair fitted like a cap and smelled of scented soap.

"Do you like jazz?" she asked.

"Sure, I love it."

"I sing jazz and blues. You come my house tonight, I have many records: Count Basie, Billie Holiday, Sarah Vaughn, Hamp, many many more." She spread her arms. "You come my house."

Before he could answer, she took his hand and led him to a nearby table. Two tall dark men rose slowly.

"This is Etobi," she pointed to the stoutest one, who extended his hand.

"Chitown!" he smiled and shook, "Glad to meet you."

"And this is my cousin, Ihetu."

Chitown started to shake, but recognized him and didn't. "You the guy I saw at the Post Office this morning, the one that wouldn't speak when I asked a simple question?"

"I'm sorry," the African recalled. "Please be seated and allow me to explain."

Reba sat down with him. "You see, my friend," Ihetu took a drink, "although I'm only a porter, my job is Civil Service and a government rule prohibits Africans on duty from talking to Non-Europeans."

"What?" Chitown was flabbergasted.

"We have no alternative but to abide by these horrible laws if we wish to work. I do hope you were able to send off your money."

"Naw!" Chitown paused, embarrassed by not realizing the man's position. "They just let me know I couldn't send more than twenty dollars."

Etobi offered him a drink.

"No thanks," he got up and extended his hand, "I've had too much already."

"Very well." The African shook it warmly.

"Glad I met you, fellows, but I've got to get back."

"Is it all right if I go?" Reba asked.

He looked down at the Africans, who smiled approval.

"Okay, you might as well meet some of my friends."

Janet's angry, unblinking eyes burned into him as they approached the table. The men rose courteously when introduced, but the women just smiled half-heartedly. He gave her his seat and went for another. When he returned, the table was silent.

"How long you been singing here?" he asked, glancing around at the cold, snobbish coloreds.

"Nearly a year." She sounded nervous. "But only on Saturdays and nights when they expect a crowd."

Johnson, Phillips, and Brother Poe had heard her many times and all gave compliments. This inflated her ego and she opened up. For the first time Chitown realized she was pretty high by the way she raved about this being her country and the pride of her people. All of the girls giggled but Janet.

"Is that who you were waiting on?" she sneered.

Chitown ignored her. "Look, baby," he tapped Reba on the arm, "have you got to sing again?"

"Yes," she said, "two more songs."

"Then you need something to help straighten you up." He signaled the waiter and ordered a cup of black coffee.

"I can't see what you want with her!" Janet leaned back in the chair with her hands on her hips, "when you can get me."

This infuriated Phillips. "That's enough!" he jumped up, knocking over his seat. "What the fuck you think you're doing . . . I blew a lot a' dough on your stinking ass today!"

142

"Go to hell!" she took another drink. He gritted his teeth and slapped the glass out of her hand. Then, figuring she wasn't worth the chance of tangling with Chitown again, he backed away patting his pockets.

"I'm still loaded goddamnit!" he sneered, "and you sure not the only bitch in Capetown!" When he turned to leave he bumped into Jake and the waiter.

Chitown paid for the coffee while Jake took the empty seat and poured himself a drink.

Big Shot kissed Freda on the jaw. "You ready to go baby?" he whispered, "'cause I've had enough a' this kind a entertainment."

"Anytime you are." She emptied her glass as the drummer came back to get Reba.

"What you gonna do, Chi?" Big Shot winked, looking from him to Janet as he slipped Freda's coat over her shoulders. Johnson and Brother Poe's women had to put on their own.

"He's certainly not going to Thirty Four Burke Lane." Janet took the seat abandoned by Reba and poured them both a drink. "Or Seapoint either!" She shouted loud enough for Reba to hear.

"You damn right, baby!" he smiled to himself. Jake finished his drink and got up.

"Let's make it!" Johnson said as he and Brother Poe put their pipes away. "And Chi ... you be cool, and remember ... eight o'clock we leave!"

"You can bet I'll be on that ship," Chitown said.

"Later!" They all waved and departed.

"We're going to have a hell-of-a-good-time at Number Nine," Janet promised, scooting her chair closer until their legs touched. To Chitown she looked like a beautiful, beckoning Gypsy.

"Why not?" He felt the spot where Phillips had butted him. *The dues are already paid.* He wanted to grab and kiss her, but Reba's sultry singing voice drifted back through the now thinning crowd, and he knew she was watching.

143

"Let's go!" Janet divided the last of the whiskey. "It's getting late." He hated to walk out on Reba but Janet had him spellbound. They hurried their drinks and he began to feel dizzy again. It gave him an idea.

"Look!" he said as they rose to leave the Zambesi, "let's act like I'm sick and going out for air."

"Why pretend anything to that ugly . . . "

"Listen!" he pointed his finger in her face, "you knock that shit off right now!"

"Well who do you want?" She stepped back and put her hands on her hips. "If yer so damn concerned about Reba, take yer ass to Seapoint!"

"I don't want her. I want you," he softened his voice, "but this isn't Phillips, so watch your mouth!"

After staring at each other for almost a minute, she said, "Oh very well," and slipped into her sweater.

"As Reba's eyes followed them past the bandstand and out the door, she felt as if another passport to the good life outside South Africa was leaving her.

Janet and Chitown walked over a block before spotting an empty cab. He shouted and signaled, but the white driver ignored him.

"First class!' she grunted, then stopped beneath the canopy of a closed gift shop. "Let's walk. Number Nine isn't very far."

Her words fell on deaf ears as he backed her into the doorway, squeezing and pawing her breasts. After a tight embrace, he crashed his lips on her's. Their mouths opened wide, and their tongues fought wildly as the two heads ground into each other. He ran his fingers through her long curly hair as he kissed her eyes, cheeks, the tip of her nose, then sank his mouth softly into the bend of her neck.

"Let's hurry, baby," she whimpered, "it's almost curfew." She grabbed his hand and they scampered across the street. Something made him pause to look around when they reached the bottom of a long, dim, upgraded alley.

"This is the fast way," she whispered. "Are you coming or not?"

"Okay ... Okay!" He reluctantly followed her into the darkness.

From the time they left the club, four sulking Skullys had trailed Chitown and Janet. On a hand signal from the leader, who wore Big Shot's long blistered razor scar across the front of his angry face, they drew their knives and crept up the alley in silent pursuit.

To the dismay of the combo, Reba speeded the tempo, and cut her last number short. She jumped from the bandstand, told Etobi and Ihetu she would be right back, then rushed out into the street. At first, she didn't know which way to go. Her eyes searched up and down until she saw Janet leading Chitown into the alley.

Reba took off her shoes, dashed across the street, and peered up the alley. She saw the figures of Chitown and Janet silhouetted against the dim light of the street above. The four bobbing heads of the creepers were nearly hidden in the shadows of the darkened buildings with step-down doorways.

"Chitown! Look behind you! Behind you!" Reba shouted before turning and streaking for the Zambesi.

"Skullys!" Janet gasped.

A cold bolt of fear shot from the pit of Chitown's stomach and lumped in his throat as he ripped buttons from his shirt, snatching out the weapon.

Seeing no one behind them, the Skullys spread out across the alley with their long, glittering knives and continued stalking. Janet walked toward them, pleading in Afrikaans. Chitown glanced back over his shoulder and started to make a run for it.

Too far! he changed his mind. *Uphill he would be a slow moving target if they decided to throw their knives.*

A crisp sound echoed when the leader slapped Janet off her feet. The Skullys paused briefly to kick and curse her as she sat weeping. Chitown made a dash for the level running room at the top of the alley, but when they came at him, he tightened the strap of the weapon around his wrist, popped open the switchblade, and turned to face them.

"Come on, you sons-of-bitches!" he yelled, trying to build courage. He turned sideways, offering a smaller target while feinting and jabbing the knife forward like a boxer's left, with the weapon drawn to strike.

Got to keep 'em in front of me! he thought, darting back and forth across the narrow alley, trying to edge toward the top. The leader charged. Chitown swung the weapon. The leader fell back just in time and it missed his head. Another sprang from the right. Chitown swung backhanded. The Skully yelled and dropped his knife as the lead sinker caught his plunging wrist. When he stooped to retrieve the knife, Chitown kicked him in the face. He rolled on his side with a groan. The two Skullys on the left tried to sneak past, but Chitown headed them off, cursing and swinging the weapon. Speaking Afrikaans, the leader ordered the attackers to spread out. He bent to scoop a handful of dirt, spotted the knife and flipped it back to the man on the ground holding his bleeding nose, with the broken wrist cradled in his lap. On a whispered command the wounded man grabbed the knife with his good hand and crawled into the nearest doorway.

"Janet! Get some help!" Chitown called, but she just sat sobbing. He took another glance back over his shoulder and wished he had run.

The leader charged again, throwing the dirt at Chitown's face and reaching for his legs. Too cautious to get within range, the windblown dust missed its mark and the man's outstretched fingertips slid off Chitown's eluding knees. Chitown crashed the weapon down in the base of the leader's neck and he dropped to the ground screaming.

While Chitown faked back and forth at the other two who inched closer, the one with the battered wrist sneaked past and hid in the shadows to await his chance. The leader, squeezing his swollen, aching flesh, barked new orders from a safe distance. The two men facing Chitown fingered their knives by the blades to throw, as the one

146

who sneaked behind held his tightly by the handle for an underhand stab.

"Help! Help!" Chitown shouted to the dark windows. In spite of the loud cursing and screaming, not one of the windows had lit up. Not one door had cracked a curious inch.

Chitown dropped to his knees as the men threw high and low. The high knife missed, but the low one caught him in the upper left arm. He grunted and dropped his knife as pain shot down his arm and up the side of his neck. Still undetected, the man hiding in the shadows hastened his pace. Chitown snatched the knife from his arm and threw it at the two charging Skullys. They ducked and looked back to their leader. The man behind Chitown crept deathly downward.

On the presumption his enemies were now without knives, Chitown attacked. His move caught them off-guard, especially the rear one who was almost in striking distance. The Skully on the left threw up his hand too late to ward off the blow that landed on the side of his face, shattering teeth and breaking his jaw. He spun and ran blindly downhill, holding his throbbing, bleeding mouth. The leader also retreated to seek aid for his broken shoulder. The other one lunged and grabbed the end of the weapon as the one behind drew back his knife and closed the gap. Three spine-chilling screams filled the air. First, the Skully on the end of the weapon when Chitown whirled, jerking the handle with all his might, ripping the embedded fish hook across the palm, plowing up flesh and veins; Janet; then Chitown, when the man behind him plunged the knife into his body. The Skullys took off in opposite directions. One ran uphill in terror, squeezing his mutilated palm and biting the fingertips to fight the pain. The stabber started downhill, but tripped over Janet.

"You son-of-a-bitch!" Chitown went after him. The man had almost scrambled to his feet when the weapon pounded down into his head. It made a frightful thud, like breaking ice under a thick cloth. He jerked upward, then collapsed, still and silent. His knife had stuck deep in Chi-

147

town's back at a right angle, just missing the spine, and extending outward below the rib cage. Chitown tried to remove it, but when he touched the handle his whole body stiffened with pain. His head began to spin. Suddenly his knees buckled, and he flopped face down in the dirt.

"Janet!" he coughed. "Help me ... Help me, please," he begged before passing out. But Janet had vanished into the night.

Chapter Sixteen

IHETU'S SMALL car turned up the alley in a cloud of dust and stopped ten feet from the two figures lying side by side. Reba was the first out. She took a quick glance at the Skully with his face to the sky, then hurried to Chitown. Ihetu and Etobi studied the fallen colored under the beam of the headlights.

"It's the American! He's hurt bad!" she called, turning Chitown's head to the side gently and ripping the sleeve off her blouse. "Get it out! Get it out!" Her heart pounded as Ihetu gripped the handle carefully and snatched out the knife. Chitown gave a short, soft groan. Reba pressed the cloth to the wound as Ihetu and Etobi lifted him slowly, one by the legs and the other under the armpits.

"Hurry!" she pleaded, stumbling over the legs of the Skully, but holding the rag in place. She looked back at the tight eyes and open, twisted mouth.

"We must get him to his ship." Ihetu backed the car out of the alley and sped up the street.

"No, no!" Reba shouted from her kneeling position in the rear, where Chitown lay crumpled on the seat with his head and feet touching the doors. "The first thing we must do is stop the bleeding!" She pressed the soggy, sticky

149

blood-soaked cloth harder to the wound. "Take him to my house, then get Anya!"

"No!" Etobi turned and looked back. "This is too dangerous for her . . . and the organization. Ihetu is right . . . he should be under his flag, where his own people can care for him . . . we should not be involved!"

"We are involved!" she argued. "And in danger each day of our lives . . . please let Anya help him . . . he's bleeding bad."

"It's past curfew now," Ihetu checked his watch as they approached a well-lit intersection, "how will we get him through customs to his ship?"

"Let *them* take him!" Etobi eagerly suggested.

"I'm ashamed of you," she said when the car stopped for a red light near a blazing, blinking neon sign. "We're his people also . . . by the time we're searched, questioned and possibly arrested, he will be as dead as the other man." She cleared her throat and wiped the tears from her cheeks.

"What would Anya think of you if she learned you wanted to leave a helpless, bleeding black man who had done us no harm at the mercy of the whites? . . . Please!" She wiped her face again. "It would not delay her escape to stop the bleeding."

Etobi took off his shirt and handed it back to her. "There's blood on his hand also," he noticed. Reba examined his hand, then worked up his arm. "My Lord!" she cried. "He's been stabbed in the shoulder too!"

The two men looked at each other and nodded. When the light changed, Ihetu wheeled around the corner onto a fluorescent-lined, four-lane boulevard and headed for Sea Point.

Chitown momentarily awakened to the strong smell of antiseptic and the beam of a light in his face. The blurred figure of a woman in orange stood over him. He tried to move but couldn't. His legs were pinned and a wet towel was being pressed against his forehead. She put a white cloth to his nose and he began to spin head over heels, faster and faster with every breath to a high, ear-piercing sound. The light snapped into two lights, then more and more all different colors coming closer and closer, spinning faster and louder, until everything blackened into a muffle of whispering voices.

When Chitown opened his eyes again, the lights were gone, taking with them the strange sounds and spinning sensations. He felt nauseated. His shoulder and side ached whenever he turned his head and gazed around the small, dim, silent room.

The woman in orange sat on the far side reading from the feeble beam of fading daylight that seeped through the curtain of the single window. He tried to speak as he felt the tape strapped tightly across his waist and shoulder, but only managed a groan.

"It's all right, it's all right!" she whispered, rising and hurrying to him. "You're safe here, but badly hurt, so move little as possible." She looked back at the door. "And please talk softly ... I will get you some water." She moved swiftly with the grace of a cat, and was back in an instant, sitting on the side of the bed. She placed her left hand under his neck and gently raised his head. He strangled a little when the cool moist liquid passed through his hard, chapped lips, down his dry throat into his growling stomach.

"That's enough for now," she withdrew the glass, set it on the floor, and felt his hot, damp forehead.

"I'll get you something for the fever and pain, then perhaps we can talk." His eyes followed her around the part of the room that served as the kitchen. Under the high window sat a table, two chairs, and a three-eyed hot plate. On the opposite side was a small sink and refrigerator. She was tall, but the neatness of her long, slim waistline made her seem taller. Golden, half-dollar size earrings dangled beneath short, even hair as she returned with a chair, shaking a thermometer in the other hand. After taking his temperature and checking his pulse, she gave him three pills and raised his head again.

"You can drink all of the water, but drink slowly."

151

"Where am I?" he asked when he finished. It hurt to cough and clear his throat.

"Sea Point."

"Sea Point?"

"Yes, you had a fight with a gang of toughs, do you remember?"

Fear temporarily replaced the nausea and pain as he bitterly recalled the screaming, cursing, cutting and clubbing. However, his subconscious mind hinted of something even more terrifying.

"How did I get here?" He realized he was naked except for his shorts and the tight, sticky bandages on the aching upper half of his body.

"Reba, Ihetu and Etobi brought you. This is her apartment."

"Of course." He tried to smile. "She's the one who warned me . . . and you patched me up."

"Yes, my name is Anya."

"Wilbur Kane . . . they call me Chitown." His feverish subconscious still held fast to that terrifying secret as he tried to put the pieces together.

"I know." She felt his head again. "Reba told me."

"There's no way I can ever repay you wonderful people for saving my life."

"Just get well for her sake, she likes you very much."

"Where is Reba?" . . . And why is it so dark and quiet?"

"At work. She should be in shortly. No one else is supposed to be here." She glanced back at the door, then leaned to him and whispered. "You killed a man last night."

"Killed a man!" he said, but no sound came from his lips. *So that's what's been bugging the back of my mind*. But his subconscious refused to rest. She sensed the uneasiness and was sorry to have told him.

"Please try and relax. You've had a pretty rough time of it."

"Is it okay if I smoke?"

"Sure." She went to the foot of the bed, took a cigarette from the pack in his shirt pocket, and placed it in his mouth. He could not help but notice how beautiful she was when he saw her face clearly in the light from the match.

"Thank you!" He took a long draw and let the smoke out slowly.

"You are a brave man and courageous fighter." She checked her watch with the flame before blowing it out. "There were four of them."

"That's right!" he remembered. "It *was* four. I lost count 'cause one of 'em sneaked behind me."

"Were you moving when you were stabbed in the back?"

"Yeah, struggling for my weapon—good thing he wasn't a pro."

"He wasn't trying to kill."

"What do you mean?"

"That knife was aimed at the base of your spine, to make you a paraplegic for life."

I'm glad I killed that son-of-a-bitch, he thought during the pause. "Just how bad am I hurt?"

"You've lost a lot of blood, but no arteries were lacerated. It could have been much worse." She pulled back the cover and checked his bandages. "The knives went clear through, fortunately they were clean. You may be able to move around in a few days. Meanwhile you must be careful or it will start bleeding again."

"A few days?" The words hit like the knife plunging into his back. The fact that he was still alive softened the blow and convinced him Lady Luck, however fickle, was still around.

Their heads jerked with the click of the lock. Reba hurried in and closed the door, bringing a large paper bag and a sigh of relief.

"How is he?" she asked, putting the bag on the table and taking off her coat.

"Filled with fever, but with the proper rest and care he should recover rapidly ... did you get everything?"

"Yes." Reba turned on the light. When their blinking

153

eyes met, he managed a faint smile. "I want to thank you, Reba."

"How do you feel?" She rushed to the chair and touched his hand.

"Not too bad," he lied.

"Chitown . . . " she said, biting her lip to hide the worried look on her face, "I must tell you this now . . . your ship . . . the *Mitchell* . . . is gone. It left this morning at eight o'clock for Dar es Salaam."

"No!" he tried to rise, but fell back screaming in anguish and sorrow. *The ship's gone!* That haunting horror finally broke from his subconscious. It echoed through his throbbing body, pounding with each accelerated heart-beat. "The ship's gone!"

"Hold him still!" Anya whispered. "Don't let him reinjure himself." She prepared a hypodermic. "I'll calm him down."

"I'm sorry, Chitown," Reba held his hand and stroked his brow as he shook his head from side to side. "We had no idea your ship was leaving so early. Please try and relax. It was nearly seven before you were out of danger. We couldn't risk breaking curfew again, so all fell asleep."

Anya grabbed his wrist and stuck the needle in his arm.

"I know Reba, and I'm grateful . . . if it wasn't for you I would have died in that alley." He gazed up at the ceiling and tasted the odor of morphine in his mouth. "But what the hell am I gonna do now?"

"Get well!" she answered. "Anya is leaving tonight for Tanganyika. She has to slip through three countries, but if your ship is still there she can notify Rinco. he will know what to do."

"Tell him to get in touch with the American embassy," he said as his mind drifted into another world.

"Very well," Anya promised. "In the meantime take it easy and regain your strength. Reba, Etobi, and Ihetu will help you decide what is best to do here."

There was a light tap on the door, and another wave of fear swept the small apartment. Anya froze as Reba eased toward the door with her ear tilted. The tap came again in signal form, and when Reba opened up, Etobi rushed in.

"Is Ihetu outside?" Reba asked, double locking the door.

"Yes," he answered slowly, "everything's ready. How is the patient?"

"Still bad off," Anya said, "but if he eats well, drinks plenty liquid, stirs little as possible, within the next few days he should begin a rapid recover."

Etobi looked at his watch. "It is late. We must hurry."

"Here are instructions for his medicine." Anya handed Reba a sheet of paper. Reba tore off a blank portion, took a pencil from her hair and started writing on it.

"His shipmate's name is Rinco Styles ... Engineering department. He's very smart and will know what to do!"

Anya nodded, folded the paper, and put it in her pocket. The two women paused silently to look at each other, then hugged as they broke into tears.

"We must go now without further delay." Etobi went to the kitchen and picked up Anya's suitcase. They said goodby to Chitown, but by then their voices were only distant echoes.

"When he's better," Etobi said, "notify Ihetu and we will drop in for a chat."

"I'm sure he will be all right," Anya whispered, "give him as few pills as possible, and be strict about him drinking plenty liquid."

"Very well." Reba's eyes filled again. "Anya!" she said, "we have been friends so very long ... I do hope we meet again someday!"

"I am sure we will!" Anya tried to smile through her tears as they gave each other a final embrace. "Please take care of yourself."

"I will. You do the same ... goodby and good luck!"

"Thank you ... goodby!"

Reba cracked the door to see if the coast was clear. When they left, she returned to the bed and felt Chitown's forehead.

"You must eat something soon."

155

His eyes were half opened and he managed a faint smile.

She turned on the radio, but he only heard a high-pitched ringing in his head. The realization of his awesome predicament supplanted the slowly returning pain with mental agony. He was a deserter and an undesirable alien, helplessly trapped in the most hostile country on earth for black people.

Chapter Seventeen

FOR THE weakened *Mitchell,* it was hazardous sailing around the choppy Cape of Good Hope. Then, listing heavy to starboard and still bellowing black smoke, the ship steamed north at less than half speed, along the east coast of Africa toward the turbulent Mozambique Channel.

She was in such bad need of repair that the crew worked day and night, with little time for rest and none for recreation. To them, the weary six-day voyage seemed more like three weeks, until the bright picturesque morning of March 9, when the ship finally dropped anchor in the calm sky blue harbor of Dar es Salaam, Tanganyika.

For the first time, the Captain was truly proud of his crew. He told them over the speaker that they had repaired over sixty percent of the storm damage, and praised them for their efforts. Since it was Friday, he gave every man the ship could spare the weekend off, to begin immediately. Only the special Sea and Anchor detail had to be back the next morning, because at zero nine hundred the vessel would move in and tie up to the main dock.

Those aboard the first liberty boat were in a festive mood as it putted toward the curving beaches, fluttering

157

palms and modern sandstone buildings, topped with orange and pink mango tile.

After leaping from the launch onto the long floating pier, and passing unchecked through the iron-railed, open end of the customs house, the sailors were greeted by cab drivers wearing smiles as radiant as the climate.

"Jambo! . . . Jambo!" They shook East African style, a tight clasp, then a firm grip of the thumb, and another clasp.

"Jambo! . . . Jambo!" was repeated over and over again as the crewmen piled into the cars.

Big Shot and Rinco had not long returned to normal relations with each other. They had fallen out, and gone days without hardly speaking following a heated argument, in which Rinco (later admitted, wrongly) had blamed Big Shot for Chitown missing the ship. Johnson and Brother Poe wanted Big Shot to go with them, but he decided to have a few drinks with Rinco first and meet them at the Beach House later.

"You gonna cop a cab, dad?" he asked.

"Naw." Rinco lit a cigar. "Let's walk. I want to see if I can notice any difference since Uhuru."

"Where to?"

"The Pot O' Gold. It's a good place to change money."

"Okay! . . . let's get going!"

They crossed City Drive and turned left in front of the magnificent sharp-domed Roman Catholic Cathedral. It was hot and humid with few people on the winding streets. When they reached Independence Avenue, the bicycle, scooter and small vehicle traffic thickened. Big Shot was impressed by the cleanliness, of the cafes, bazaars and teahouses, but most of all by the many different kinds of people. Most of the African women, except for the Muslims, in all black Bui-Bui's, wore long bright-colored Khargas made of printed cotton. The Muslim men were distinguished by tight, multi-colored skullcaps, the type Johnson and Brother Poe always wore.

"This is Broadway," Rinco flipped an ash, frowning at the Europeans lounging on the porches of the Splendid,

Spencer and New Africa hotels, eating lunch, drinking beer and sipping cocktails. Cold-eyed Arabs that sailed the Dhaus between Southern Arabia, Zanzibar, and the east coast of Africa, strolled in sloppy turbans, carrying jewel handled daggers in their wide sashes, while shifty-eyes Indians peeped from shop and store windows.

"These broads over here sho' got mo' ass than them in Bombay!" Big Shot tipped his hat to an Indian woman who ignored him. Rinco laughed as they turned off Independence and started down a narrow dusty side street.

"That grimy-ass Indian!" Rinco said, and threw his cigar butt at some dried red betel nut spittle in the dirt.

"I thought you said you was gonna stop talkin' 'bout Indians after they helped Chitown pull yo' ass out the vaps."

"I don't hate all Indians," Rinco softened his voice. "Although their stinking caste system is deplorable, I realize the majority of them are victims. It's that foreign Indian I can't stand. The British brought them here to build railroads, and they found a paradise. They got most of the small business, live in comfortable homes and air-conditioned apartments, with good schools and hospitals. Take that same son-of-a-bitch eating cow shit off the streets of Bombay and put him over here, within a year he'd be stretching his scrawny neck, and snarling down his pointed nose at the black man."

"What about gray broads?" Big Shot asked. "Many of 'em here?"

"Not too many. But with whitey controlling the big business, banks, resources and whatever industry, they lay up in fabulous pads in Oyster Bay. Houseboys do their shopping, so they hardly come out until the sun goes down. If you want gray broads you should have kept your black ass in Europe."

"Damn," Big Shot shook his head, "the white chicks ain't available, the Indians super bigoted, an' what I've seen of these Africans so far ain't hittin' on shit."

"A lot of these Africans may not look like much to you, but you can bet they got foxes, and all of them will wear

159

your ass out in bed. And these white boys will run over your ass to get to them."

Rinco led him across Lumumba Sreet to a large round intersection with roads spreading like spokes. In the center of the wheel, stood a tall stone monument adorned by the bronze statue of an African soldier holding a bayoneted rifle.

"This way." Rinco motioned down an extra-wide street filled with small shops, bazaars, and ten-story apartment buildings.

"That's it!" He pointed to a Pepsi Cola sign in the middle of the block with Pot O' Gold printed at the bottom in big black letters. They opened a squeaking gate at the front of a long gangway, climbed the dark steep stairway to the first landing, and made a right turn into the huge spacious ballroom.

Most of the early patrons were *Mitchell* crewmen who had taken cabs. There were about twenty of them, flopped back in beach chairs along the walls, with over half sporting their Bombay tailored shirts and Bermuda shorts. Since it was just mid-day, only a handful of women were scattered about, including the three waitresses. All of the women were short, and all wore gay-colored sleeveless dresses with Ballerina style shoes. The wide curving bar to their left was sprinkled with Malayan soldiers: already flown in from the Congo to board the *Mitchell*.

"What's the rate?" Rinco asked the short dark, mingled gray haired Indian owner.

"Seven to one," he answered from behind the bar.

"Okay, give me twenty dollars exchange and a Scotch and water!"

Big Shot threw a fifty on the counter, and ordered the same. "Damn!" he said, "these little wide-legged broads shaped all right, don't look bad either, but they hair ain't *that long*," he snapped his finger as his eyes shifted from girl to girl.

"Hey Shot! . . . come here!" Nelson shouted from a nearby table. He was decked out in his brown silk suit, green

160

shirt with a tan tie to match his socks, and sat between two giggling young girls.

"Say, man," he rubbed his process when Big Shot walked over, "the cat's been telling these chicks my hair ain't real!"

"Sure it is!"

"How you know?" asked the girl with tiny blue lines etched in her dark brown face.

"'Cause we soul brothers." Big Shot eyed the other girl whose face was smooth. Her hair was short but combed straight back, not like most of the others who wore small braids or little parted rows.

"What happened to you?" She pointed at his head when he removed his straw hat to wipe his brow.

"We had different daddies!" He rubbed his hair and everyone at the table laughed.

"Dig!" Nelson lit a big cigar, "sit down and take one of these broads off my hands." He nodded to the one with face marks.

"Naw, dude," Big Shot shook his head. "I'm gonna scout around."

The girls started speaking Swahili as they admired Nelson's and Big Shot's clothes and jewelry. Big Shot noticed they kept saying, "Wana Kuba," and asked Nelson what it meant.

"Big-time nigger?" Nelson laughed, and they slapped skin.

"Well, dude, have you noticed any changes since independence?" he asked when he rejoined Rinco who was now sitting at a small table by the windows on the other side of the room.

"Not so far," Rinco said. "Uhuru's not at all that I anticipated. I expected to see political rallies on every corner; a sudden fire of enthusiasm, like in Kenya. And they haven't even gotten their independence yet. All I see here are signs like that." He pointed over the jukebox to the opposite wall, where a giant picture of Prime Minister Julius Nyerere pointed back. Below the portrait was a message written in English and Swahili. It read, in big

161

block letters, "THE MANAGEMENT AND CUSTOM-ERS OF THE POT O' GOLD WISH ALL TAN-GANYIKA THE BEST OF LUCK ON UHURU. MAY GOD BE WITH US."

"Dig this shit!" Big Shot motioned to the apartment building across the street where Indians peeped from al-most every window of the middle floors. "Don't nothing but Indians live in town? Where the fuck the Africans live? Out in the bush in them goddamn huts?"

"Most of them," Rinco hated to admit.

"Jambo is a dumb motherfucker," Big Shot said. "An' speaking of Jambo, where yo' broad? I know long as you been coming here you got a broad. What she look like?"

"I had one, but I put her down."

"How come?"

"For two reasons: first, she tried to impress me with her sister, who's married to a white ex-South African. Then, the last time we were here, I found a picture of an Italian sailor in her closet."

"Ain't you some shit!" Big Shot laughed. "These ho's fuck anybody they want to. You carrin' that black bag too far."

"To each his own bag," Rinco signaled for a waitress.

A tall thin African in a clean white shirt, starched khakis, wearing an old straw hat with the brim turned all the way down, came through the door and scanned the crowd.

"Nambawni!" (number one) "Nambawni!" he shouted to Rinco and started over.

"Uh-Uh," Rinco chuckled, "here comes Slick. Now I'll find out everything."

"Nambawni!" he gave Rinco the thumb-grip handshake and took a seat, as a waitress with dark lines tattooed on her face came to the table. Big Shot and Rinco ordered another drink. Slick told her to bring him a bottle of Tuska beer.

Rinco introduced Big Shot and another handshake en-sued.

162

"You wanna get high man?" Slick asked him.

"What?"

"Yeah man ... I got good pot, man, the best. Right, Nambawni!" he nodded to Rinco who just laughed.

"Naw, dad!" Big Shot pulled out a pipe full of hash. "I carry my own."

"Well, how are things going, Slick?" Rinco asked.

He was an ex-seaman who hung around black crewmen when the *Mitchell* was in port. They called him "Slick" because his English had that slow hippish rhythm copied from the Negroes he had met in the Gulf ports while sailing for the Black Star line out of Ghana.

"Great man, great! ... Everything changed in Tanganyika, man!" When he smiled, his even white teeth glowed above small woolly patches of hair under his bottom lip and the tip of his chin. "Everybody same, man, no matter what color. Anybody go anywhere ... anytime. It's good, man ... very good!"

"History shows," Rinco said as the waitress returned with their orders, "very little is won without a fight."

Slick pushed his hat back and said, "Kenya, man ... they fight and fight. But no fighting in Tanganyika, man, we get Uhuru before Kenya ... they very surprised, man. They don't know what happen'." He took two quick swallows of strong beer with the elephant head label and continued. "City Governor, man, he go to big cafe; white owner don't know that's City Governor, man. That's Mayor of Dar es Salaam. White owner don't want him there. He say to his workers, 'I don't want this man's business. Tell him he will have to go.' Governor leave and say nothing. Next day owner get notice. He have to get out Tanganyika, man! He got to go back to Greece."

"That's good to hear," Rinco said, "How are things with you personally?"

"Great, man, great! I now have a scooter!"

"Ain't that a bitch," Big Shot grunted. "I got a Cadillac! Let's check out some more joints. I'm tired of this ... "

A loud burst of applause, accompanied by whistles and cat-calls, came from the door when the owner's wife

163

walked in. Big Shot jumped to his feet with his eyes bucked. "Who that fox?"

"That's Krishan," Rinco said, "she and her husband own the place."

"Wow!"

"Same thing with him, man," Slick pointed to the Indian behind the bar. "Long time ago, man, he same way Greek: he don't like Africans. He change when he know Uhuru coming ... but too late, man. He get his exportation papers. Soon he go back to India ... wife okay, she stay."

"What!" Big Shot grinned with a gleam in his eyes. "You mean ta tell me he gonna split an' leave that fine bitch here?"

Slick nodded yes.

"She's just your type, Shot," Rinco said. "They ain't about nothing but money, and she'll do anything for it."

As Slick and Rinco resumed talking politics, Big Shot watched Krishan who went behind the bar and put on an apron to help her husband as the crowd began to thicken.

She was in her early thirties, with a pretty face, nice figure and big legs. Except for age, she had all the attributes he desired in a woman. Instead of a sari, she wore a green sleeveless silk dress and high-heel shoes to match. With her fair complexion, the only things Indian about her appearance were the long shining black hair, the many rings on several fingers, and the countless bracelets.

"Ya'll can keep talkin' all the bullshit you want," he finished his drink and got up, "'cause I'm going over an' check this broad out."

"Hello Krishan," he sat at her end of the bar and gave her his special smile, "what's the best Scotch in the house?"

"The best?" she looked over her shoulder and studied the shelf.

"That Black Label will do!" he pointed. She took down a bottle of Johnny Walker and picked up a glass.

"I want a fifth, baby!"

"A fifth! How many glasses?"

"One!"

"Oh, come now! I know you're not going to drink that bottle alone. What is your name?"

"Big Shot, baby, Big Shot Sonny Collins. I'm new on the *Ghost,* an' I don't do nothin' small."

"As you wish." She smiled curiously while taking notice of his expensive clothes and jewelry. Then she exchanged the open bottle for a full one.

"Do you want a mix?"

"No, doll, jus' water. How much do I owe you?"

"You have American money?"

"Both!"

"Eight dollars ... American!" she scooped up a bowl of ice, and got him a pitcher of water.

He pulled out his roll and peeled off a ten. "Keep the change."

"Oh, thank you!" She gave him a warmer smile before going to the cash register.

On her way back a Malayan soldier called her and engaged in a prolonged conversation after being served.

"Damn!" Big Shot frowned, "why don't that rice-eatin' motherfucker lightin' up!"

When she returned, he told her to fix herself a drink.

"You wanna know why I bought this?" he held up the fifth.

She smiled "Yes!" as she mixed a cocktail.

"I said to myself. She way too pretty to be workin' like a dog in all this heat," he undressed her with his eyes. "I can see why most of the cats come here. You the finest thing I seen since I hit Tanganyika!"

"Oh, thank you!" She was more amused than flattered.

"From the second I saw you come behind the bar," he went on, "I was determined to sit awhile. So why cause you extra work by ordering one drink at a time."

"Now I see how you got your name. I wish all of my customers were so considerate." She raised her glass in a toast. "Here's to good living."

"Good living!" he toasted, and she rushed to a calling customer.

165

"Is this the usual size of your Friday crowd?" he asked when he had a chance to talk to her again.

"Heavens no!" She pulled a green handkerchief from her belt to wipe her brow as her sharp dark eyes scanned the whole ballroom. "We'll have a bit of a crowd shortly, and with the *Mitchell* in port, it can get awesome."

"Dig, baby! Since you have your best crowds when the *Ghost* is here, maybe I can give you some professional help . . . free of charge!"

"You're kidding," she took a drink from her cocktail.

"Naw!" he shook his head, "I'm a first class bartender. That's what I do in New York when I ain't sailing. I like the night life atmosphere: the loud music, bright lights and pretty women. Besides, I've got enough money!"

"Maybe so," she laughed. "I really will need some help soon. We'll talk about it some other time," she went to another waving customer.

Suddenly, an endless line of *Mitchell* crewmen with their giggling girlfriends piled through the door. Within seconds the juke box was blasting, a half dozen couples were dancing, while the rest filled the front tables, noisily getting their orders ready for the bar.

Big Shot poured another drink and screwed the top back on the bottle. He looked at his watch and remembered he was supposed to meet Johnson and Brother Poe. They said it was important. It didn't make sense for him to sit there drooling over Krishan with her husband on the scene. And all those *Mitchell* dummies were gonna keep her so busy, he wouldn't have a chance to rap. So he had better get out of this joint and look for something else to shoot at.

"Dig, baby," he handed her the bottle when she came to finish her drink before the onslaught, "I got a run to make, stash this for me. I know you ain't got time to talk now," he smiled, "but remember, when you ain't so busy, we gotta rap about me helping out."

"Sure thing, I come in at ten o'clock for inventory on Mondays."

"Mellow! . . . We'll rap then!"

166

They drank a parting toast, and he turned from the bar to go and see if Rinco was ready to split.

Chapter Eighteen

JOHNSON AND Brother Poe lounged on the beach snorting coke, smoking hashish and drinking Cherry Kijafa while the sweet smell of spice rode the soft western winds from Zanzibar. They had dragged four beach chairs to a remote spot in order to get high unnoticed and jam their portable phonograph out of earshot of the jukebox in the small bar which formed the entrance to the beach.

"This sho' beats that funky ship with all those smelly-ass Indians." Johnson passed the chello as they gazed out at the two tall bronze, bushyheaded Afro-Arabian girls they had brought with them, playing in the water.

"What I don't dig," Brother Poe took a long draw, "is why we had ta wait till tomorrow before movin' to the dock? We should'a come in an' unloaded them creeps from the get-go."

"Damn right!" Johnson poured a glass of wine and stretched out in his lounge chair. "Those damn Malayans are flying in from the Congo already."

"Fuck the Malayans, an' the Indians too!" Brother Poe pointed to the record that was playing. "Dig Cannonball get away!"

"Dig Nat!" Johnson said when the trumpet solo started, then looked at his watch. "I wonder what happened to Big Shot? He was supposed to be here over an hour ago."

"You know that cat." Brother Poe took another drag and handed him the pipe. "He must'a run into a broad."

"Yeah." Johnson pondered as he put his handkerchief over the mouth of the chello. "You still think it's a good idea to bring him in with us?"

"Hell, yeah!" Brother Poe said, "much bread as that cat handle!"

"I'm hip." Johnson spoke between long slow pulls. "But a dude that like trim as much as he do, might put wetting his wick before taking care of business."

"I don't think so," Brother Poe accepted the smoke. "Not him . . . I think he like bread more; he sho' know how ta make it. An' we could use another cat since Creed went home."

"You might have something there," Johnson agreed. At least we know he ain't narc, or we would have been busted in Bombay. And he ain't C.I.A. or Rinco would've hipped us."

"Yeah!" Brother Poe took three quick draws and passed the chello. "He sailed with Big Shot before. And he can sho' feel heat a mile away, like them dudes that used to hawk him preaching that 'stay in Africa shit.'"

"While we were smuggling right under their nose," Johnson laughed and they slapped skin. "It would be nice to have a three-man operation again," he sighed, "like old times."

"Let's hit on him," Brother Poe suggested, "an' see how he act."

"Okay!" Johnson agreed, then pointed to the girls. "Those bitches sure look good in them red swimsuits!"

"You can say that again, baby!"

When the chello went out they started snorting coke.

The long, privately owned beach was hidden from the road by tall thick vines, causing Big Shot to wonder, "if this dumb-ass driver knew where he was going?" The cab pulled up at an opening thirty yards from where the vines ended and the white sand became spotted with stones and shrubbery.

The loud European music made the girl he was with hesitate. Like most of the African women who dated sailors, she was now going places she had never been, before or after Uhuru.

"Come on, baby." He took her by the hand through the gate and paid admission to the French owner behind a small beer bar that sat on a long, shedded, concrete platform, with washrooms and jukebox.

As the girl followed Big Shot down the beach in search of Johnson and Brother Poe, she nervously noticed the frowns from whites and stares from Indians seated around umbrella-covered tables.

The girls had left the water and sat snuggled with Johnson and Brother Poe, drinking wine and listening to strange music called jazz when Big Shot and his girl walked up.

"Damn, baby!" Brother Poe gave him some skin, "where did you get that fox?"

"I met her in a joint down the street from the Pot O' Gold. Her name is Bell!"

"Sho' didn't take you long ta cop, did it?"

"Hell, naw! You know me."

Johnson poured Bell a drink while Big Shot went to find a chair.

"Where ya'll latch on ta these boss broads?" Big Shot asked when he returned.

"They come from some place close around Dar es Salaam, can't hardly speak or understand English," Johnson said.

"Hell, that's all the better!"

"But they go with a couple funky-ass Indians with greasy beards an' rags tied 'round their heads," Brother Poe complained. "Say, baby!" he yelled to his girl, "why didn't ya'll hip us you fucked 'round with them Santa Claus lookin' niggers?"

170

After a long pause, the confused girl answered as best she could. "Friends." She waved her hands. "Have big cinema."

"I'm hip," Brother Poe grunted, "so that's why ya'll always at the movies."

"So they own a cinema," Johnson snapped. "Big deal, what does that make them, the Warner brothers?"

"Motherfuckers look mo' like the Smith Brothers," Brother Poe shouted, and the laughter carried down the beach, turning heads in their direction.

Bell asked Big Shot if she could join the other girls when they got up to go back into the water.

"Damn right!" he said as his eyes rolled across the two red-clad beauties, "why you think I bought you that suit."

The other men watched Bell peel until her bold black body exploited the tight yellow swimsuit.

"Your broad ain't bad at all," Johnson observed when she dashed to catch up with the other girls.

"I'm hip, but her hair ain't long as mine ... when we cover up, I'll look like the bitch. Now on the other hand, run a hot comb through them chick's hair an' ya'll have some out-a-sight broads."

"You jus' hung-up on hair, baby." Brother Poe gave him the coke. "That little ole black girl fine as she wanna be." He put on a Charlie Parker album.

"You can have her dad, 'cause I'm gonna get Krishan."

"From the Pot O' Gold?"

"That's right, dad, I've hit already. She gonna let me work for her. An' soon as her man get kicked out the country I'm gonna take up the slack." He pointed toward Bell, splashing in the water. "An' put that suede head ho' down."

They all laughed again as he took two snorts of coke in each nostril with the tip of his knife and passed it to Johnson.

"You should've heard the bullshit rap I gave Bell when Rinco took us to the Sea Food House for lunch. That broad think I'm the richest dude in town."

171

"Yeah," Johnson said, "some of these chicks are kind of gullible, until they find you out."

"What Krishan gonna pay you in?" Brother Poe asked, lighting a small ball of hashish on the tip of his knife. "Pussy or money?"

"Both!" Big Shot laughed as he poured himself a glass of wine.

"Wasn't you an' Rinco kinda salty at each other for awhile, about what happened to Chitown?"

"Yeah, but that's over, we mellow now. But he so hung up on that 'let's stay in Africa' bullshit, an' readin' all them Swahili books, I was beginning to think he was losing his marbles."

"Rinco take things too seriously." Johnson started breaking cigarettes and pouring the tobacco into his other hand. "Chitown is American. I'll bet they put him on a jet the next day for New York. But that 'stay in Africa' shit could pay off. Me and my man Poe been looking things over here and in Kenya for a long time. And if a real good investment come along, we're ready. In fact we had our eyes on the Pot O' Gold until we found out they gonna let Krishan stay. Man that hotel's got about twenty rooms. We could gamble in a few and rent the rest for transits."

"While we supply the ho's," Brother Poe added.

"You mean to tell me you dudes done saved that kinda bread off booze, pot, an' crap games?"

"That's right, baby," Brother Poe said. "We ain't drawn any money off the books in two years, an' most of the bread we hustle is salted away. We wear mess clothes. We don't buy nothin' but highs, good jewelry, an' a little trim when we can't beg up on it."

"And we smuggle!" Johnson said, stuffing the black tobacco into the large end of the chello.

Their sudden silence brought the sounds of the giggling girls and soft waves rolling in to blend with the smooth cool horn of Charlie Parker, as the orange sunset turned the harbor a powder blue.

"We need another partner." Brother Poe lit the chello for Johnson. "You interested?"

172

"I don't know," Big Shot said, shaking his head. "A smuggling rap would be the end of our ass."

Johnson took two draws and passed the pipe to Brother Poe. "You don't get busted if you know what you doing," he said while inhaling. "We don't get greedy, just a little at a time. Everything's been going smooth for over two years." He finally let the smoke out of his lungs.

"And the bread is good," Brother Poe added between puffs. "Our other partner wasn't over here but a year, an' he split with fifteen grand, not countin' what he had on the books."

"And what he blew!" Johnson said. "That cat could fuck up some money, baby."

"That the dude who used to go with Freda?" Big Shot knew the answer, but asked anyway.

"Yeah!" he was just like you, a mellow dude all the way. That's why we want you to take his place. You game?"

"For that kinda dough, hell yeah," Big Shot answered. "What's the set-up?"

"We'll go into details later." Johnson stretched back in his chair and gazed up at the cloudless sky. "Right now let's enjoy this tropical paradise while those niggers back in the city freezing their balls off."

"This would make one helluva after-hour joint right here." Brother Poe passed Big Shot the pipe. "Enlarge the bar ta sell other stuff besides beer. And put some boss sounds on that square-ass jukebox."

"It wouldn't take much to get that owner kicked out the country, Johnson said, because he's a prejudice sonofa-bitch and the Africans know it. But he don't fuck with us. He tried to get funny last trip and the Ghost almost turned this joint out."

Big Shot took his puffs, passed the chello and said, "Dig dudes, I sho' would like ta know a little more 'bout this smuggling bit ... just' ta get a' idea what I'm in for."

"Coke, heroin, jewelry and gold," Brother Poe stuck out his palm and Big Shot slapped it.

173

"It's simple," Johnson said, "but you got to be cool. We buy gold in Africa, sell it in India. Buy dope in India, sell it in Africa; save the heroin for the States. Like I said, we'll break it down to you. There's plenty time," his eyes fell from the sky and settled on the three girls splashing in the ocean.

"Hell!" Big Shot said, "if the Africans kicking out the bigots, we can still get the Pot O' Gold. When I start humping Krishan, all I gotta do is go downtown an' tell the big chief she called me a nigger. Tell 'em she said, "Oh do it to me, nigger!" he snapped his fingers.

The loud sound of their laughter turned heads again as they finished off the hash.

"You better watch Krishan," Johnson warned. That old Indian broad pretty slick. She done already shot a couple supposed-to-be-hip dudes through the grease. Had those dumb-ass niggers ready to go to blows!"

"Hey, baby! . . . this the *kid* you talkin' to. Ain't no chick walkin' gonna shoot *me* through the grease!"

"Damn!" Brother Poe rubbed his hand between his legs, "ya'll talkin' 'bout women done got me hot. I be glad when it get dark so we can call them bitches out the water!"

Chapter Nineteen

SINCE THE first two days, nothing had been mentioned over the air or in the newspapers about the dead Skully found in the alleyway. Although Reba assured him that violence was common among gangland toughs who roamed the African, Colored and poor white sections of the city, Chitown found little consolation as the miserable days slowly drifted into miserable weeks.

The stitches had finally been pulled out by Reba, but his right side still felt numb and, when he moved a certain way, something within pulled like the claws of a cat. Most of the pain, however, came from the chipped bone in his shoulder, where the swelling refused to subside.

Reba lived in one of the special basement apartments provided by the luxury complex, so the maids could live close to the families for whom they worked. But like every African in the country, her home could be invaded without provocation, by the law at any time. So as soon as he began to gain strength, he drilled himself to quickly and silently scoot under the small bed where all of his possessions were hidden.

Only Reba's warm tender care had made his hell bearable. Yet he couldn't forget the shock on her face when he mentioned that he had forgotten to ask Rinco to write his wife in the message he sent by Anya. Until then, he had sensed her yearning for him to seduce her. Now she slept with her back turned and her face to the wall.

He wondered why she hadn't inquired about his marital status that night in the Zambesi. It could have been because she had drank so much, he theorized, but whatever the reason that attracted her to him, he owed her his life. So it was best not to ask questions. He would ease his arm around her to get more comfortable in the tiny bed, close his eyes and think about the last night he was home with his wife.

After hours of begging and pleading for him not to go, his wife, Jean, had dried her eyes and said she would stick by his decision, that no matter what happened, she would stay in his corner. He recalled how she had turned her back to hide further tears as she wished him luck and promised to pray for them each day. Then he would think about the time they met, the movies, night clubs, parties and the wedding. Even in this sad situation it was joyful for him to recall the sound of her laughter riding the air on quiet summer evenings as they strolled hand in hand through the park. It seemed so long ago, like years instead of months.

His eyes would try to water, but shame and guilt denied him the luxury of feeling sorry for himself. Instead, he would ask those same tormenting questions over and over: Why the hell did he give in to a selfish, egotistical whim and leave her for the Merchant Marine? Why didn't he go back to the ship after eating at the Zambesi? Or choose to go with Reba that night? He could have come here in a car with two other men, and be home by now. But he knew all the time his sudden, overwhelming desire for that bitch Janet was the reason he lay wounded and frightened in this small dark room with a woman whose affection he couldn't return. He would curse and damn himself into the wee hours before falling asleep.

The long lonely days were spent between merciful nods and mind-wracking opinions of what he should do. The first, and only idea Reba agreed with was to go to the American Consul. But then he thought about the incident at the airport, when black crewmen, before they knew who he was, had cursed the Consul out and talked about his mother when he tried to quiet them down.

Fear was valid enough reason in both his and Reba's minds to reject turning himself over to the authorities, after he told her about Nelson beating up that policeman on the ship. As bad as things were, he believed he could have roughed it out, until that frightful night last week he trembled to recall.

They had finished supper, heard the seven o'clock news, and were sitting quietly listening to jazz records when a sudden pounding on the door made their blood run cold.

"Open up! Open up! Police!" came a deep Dutch-accented voice. Reba answered in Afrikaans, stalling until he was out of sight before her shaking hands found the lock. From under the bed he watched the two pair of thick black boots follow her tiny feet and cringed at the loud, snapping voices he could not understand. They teased, pawed, and tried to degrade her for what seemed to him an hour, but was only a few minutes. One of them, maybe both was surely going to rape her, but they got a call over their radio and left in haste.

Reba also realized the danger and finally agreed that he should consult Etobi and Ihetu, then decide his next move.

He stiffened when he heard her key enter the lock, then heaved a grateful sigh. Reba was home at last, to break the stagnant silence with rattling pans and running water. He met her halfway and took the groceries.

"How do you feel?" she asked.

"Fine," he lied. "Did you see Ihetu?"

"Yes." She removed her coat and hung it in the closet. "He and Etobi will come tomorrow night for dinner."

"Good!" He didn't want to wait an extra day until Sunday, the only other time she was supposed to receive visitors.

177

"What would you like for supper, fish or chicken?"

"It doesn't matter, whatever you want." He sat down, lit a cigarette, and looked at his watch. Tomorrow night he had to decide to turn himself in, try to escape the country or look for another place to hide. The watch ticked as if it was his heartbeat: The second hand racing across the face of his life, edging the other two, destiny, and reality closer together.

"But you are American." Etobi picked up a glass of wine from the table where they sat while Reba washed the dishes. I still say your consular could keep you safe."

"Maybe he could, but would he?" Chitown filled three more glasses. "I live in a racist society also, maybe not as bad as here,but whoever they send to South Africa ain't too cool towards blacks in the first place. I can't see him going through any changes in a country that trades billions of dollars with the United States for a black seaman with a five-thousand-dollar tag on his ass."

"What else is there to do?" Ihetu hunched his shoulders and threw up his hands. Chitown watched as Reba finished the dishes, took her drink and sat on the bed. Then he turned back to the men. "I've had a lot of time to think, and I can see two other alternatives. How much would it cost to get to Tanganyika the way Anya went?"

"It is impossible!" Etobi shook his head. "You are in no shape to travel by truck, foot and boat through three hostile countries, hiding in the brush by day from patrols and border guards."

"I didn't know it was that rough," Chitown quickly agreed. He wanted no part of hacking through the jungle. He refilled the glasses as the Africans awaited his second alternative.

"Can you get me a passbook?" They could hardly believe their ears.

"That's right!" He took a long swallow of wine. "With a passbook and another place to hide, I've got more than enough money to last till Anya reaches Dar es Salaam and tell Rinco what happened. He'll know what to do. I need more going for me than a pissed-off consular. Besides, that storm we suffered won't allow the ship to cross the ocean again without returning to Capetown for a final checkup."

"My friend," Ihetu fingered his drink, "you are not fully aware of the way we must live."

"I told him this was the safest place," Reba said. "I know the policemen that come here. Out there he will be in much more danger. If he leaves, he should go straight to the consulate and take his chances."

The other two Africans agreed. Chitown got up and paced the floor.

"But didn't you also tell me that if they had decided to look under the bed, knowing them wouldn't do any good?"

She took a drink and dropped her head.

"Okay! Suppose I turn myself in and it made the news, it wouldn't be hard for them Skullys to figure I'm the guy they fought in the alley. The guy that killed their buddy! Suppose they went to the cops? This government don't dig blacks, American or otherwise. I don't want to give them a chance to make an example of me."

"If only that man wasn't killed," Ihetu frowned.

"It was me or him," Chitown said, "I'm not sorry. And I'm not about to rot in no South African jail for it!"

The word "jail" silenced the room. Nearly every urban black male, and countless females fortunate enough to reach maturity, had at one time or another spent part of their lives in prison, mainly because of the dreaded pass laws. They didn't believe he could long survive the subhuman terror, torment and torture, so decided to help him.

"Do you have a photograph?" Etobi asked.

"No, Chitown!" Reba sprang up and rushed across the room. "Do not leave! We should hear from Anya soon!"

"Dig, baby!" he grabbed her hands and looked into her eyes, "it's too dangerous for you to have me here. All of you have done too much already. I don't want to jeopardize you any more. I got myself in this mess, and I'll get out the best way I can. If I am caught, I don't want any of you involved. I wish I could stay, baby," he took her in his arms, "but this is like a cell. I wanna see daylight, smell fresh air, activate my mind to other things. If I lay here

179

day after day thinking about the same old things over and over, I'll soon crack up. I can make it this way 'cause the ship's got to return."

She shook her head, went back to the bed and picked up her drink. Chitown pulled out his wallet and gave Etobi his Seaman's Document.

"Too small," he said, "and our people seldom smile on passbooks."

"My passport!" Chitown snapped his finger. Reba poured herself another drink as he crawled under the bed for his jacket.

"How about this?" He pulled the thin blue book from the pocket. It was taken just before I left the States and I'm sure not smiling."

"Are you certain this is what you want to do?" Etobi turned to the photograph, then gave it to Ihetu.

"I'm positive," Chitown said. "I've thought it through."

"Trade an American passport for an accursed dompass." Ihetu shook his head sadly. "What will you do if you are arrested for any reason, and there are many?"

"I'll keep my Seaman's document in my shoe. It will prove I'm American. Now, I've got whatever money you need, so how soon can you get started?"

"Life will be very difficult." Etobi tried a last time to make him reconsider. "You must live, act and think as an African."

"And I would advise you not to talk to strangers," Ihetu said, "your manner of speech may give you away. "I will have it put on the dompass that you have lost your voice."

"How much will it cost?" Chitown's heart pounded as Ihetu carefully tore out the picture.

"I do not know for sure, maybe thirty, forty American dollars."

"Here's sixty, keep the change!"

"No! No! I could not . . . "

"Go ahead, man, it's the least I can do. I wish I had enough to get us all the hell out of this country. How long will it take?"

"I will start right away, tonight!" He folded the money over the picture and picked up his hat.

"And I will speak to the old man that lives with me," Etobi said, "perhaps you can share our quarters at Nanga. They are only searched when there's trouble; a suspect, or some white reports an employee absent without permission."

That would be great, Chitown reasoned, *much better than being alone all day.*

"I should have the passbook by Tuesday." Ihetu edged towards the door. Chitown shook their hands warmly. "I don't know how to thank you fellows, but if and when I get out of this mess, I'm gonna tighten you up. All of you!" He looked at Reba.

"I feel that young man is making a terrible mistake," Ihetu whispered as they hurried up from the basement. "Perhaps it was foolish for us to help him."

"But we must!" Etobi climbed into the passenger side of the car. "If he went to prison he would never return; a well-planned accident, or just disappear one night as so many we knew. They will not permit a foreign black witness of such horror to walk out."

"You are right." Ihetu bit his lip and stuck the key in the ignition.

Chapter Twenty

"THIS WILL be your badge of slavery." Etobi handed Chitown a black, wallet looking passbook as they sat in the back of Ihetu's car. He opened it to the first page and saw his picture pasted on an identification card.

"Your name will be Obo," Ihetu said over his shoulder while Chitown studied the strange looking book, printed in English and Afrikaans.

"Everything is filled out on the proper pages, and we picked an easy name for you to remember. To compensate for your lack of knowledge regarding local tribal customs, the book states that you are from Nyasaland. We are taking you to Windermere, so the woman whose address is on your book will recognize you in case you are ever forced to prove residency. I told her you lost your voice as a child. So remember, do not say a word!"

"Many Africans come from Nyasaland and Rhodesia to work the mines in Johannesburg," Etobi said as the car turned into what had to be the world's foulest slum. "They travel through lion country, and swim crocodile infested rivers, only to have their bodies broken in a few years, and end up in places like this."

182

In his worldly travels, Chitown had too often witnessed the adverse conditions in which human beings were forced to exist. But only the decaying flesh-pits of Bombay compared to Windermere. Whole families, many with sickly undernourished children, living in everything from mud huts and gunny sacks stretched over wooden poles to shelters made of cardboard and empty tar barrels. Large bloated flies swarmed over the countless piles of stinking refuse that cluttered the narrow streets.

To take his eyes from the destitution, he opened the book again. On the left of his picture, followed by a row of numbers, were two words: MALINK MALE. Below was his name; the last one he couldn't pronounce. The third and fourth lines were dates from 1959 to 1962. At the bottom was a scribbled signature under the word: DIRECTOR.

Ihetu stopped the car and got out in front of a small leaning, warped wooden shack.

"I'm going for the woman; when she comes don't say a word," he cautioned. Chitown nodded and lit a cigarette.

"Will I be able to talk to the old man?" he asked Etobi.

"Oh yes! I've known him all my life. He can be trusted, and will be a good companion for you during the day."

"That's great!" Chitown took a long draw, then looked sadly at Reba, who had sat silently in the front seat since they left Sea Point.

Ihetu returned with a big, black, musty woman who motioned for Chitown to roll down his window. She stuck her head in, looked him over, conversed briefly with the other men, then returned to her shack.

"Everything's fine!" Ihetu checked his watch before speeding out of Windermere, "but we must reach Nanga before dark!"

Chitown's stomach tightened as they entered the large shanty-town where twenty thousand black people lived row upon row in three and four room frame houses, stretching for nearly a mile on a sandy fenced-in wasteland. Ihetu parked by a small three room dwelling less than a block from the main gate.

The old man who greeted them inside was tall, thin, dark and jolly. His name was Silombela. The way he clicked his tongue when speaking English made him sound funny to Chitown. It was soon obvious that the old man hid arthritic pains with the help of bootleg Skokaan whiskey, which he poured for everyone. They sat on empty crates around a small table under a single lightbulb hanging on a long cord from the ceiling.

"I'll buy another bottle," Chitown said when the whiskey was gone. "Who wants to go for it?"

"Let's all go Shabeen," the old man suggested, "drink . . . sing . . . have good time!"

"No!" Reba said. "You stay, Chitown. I want to talk to you. It's very important!"

"Okay!" He gave Etobi five dollars and the three Africans left.

In the lingering silence Chitown tried to avoid her eyes but could feel them on him as he sized up his new home. The living room was bare except for a cupboard and face sink. In the far corner, near a beat up old wood-burning stove, was the narrow fold-away cot Etobi had purchased for him. There were two other doors. One led to the bathroom and the other to a tiny bedroom where Etobi and Silombela slept on double bunks.

It made him nervous to be alone with Reba. He knew she didn't want him to leave Sea Point, and he really didn't want to go. But the bitter memory of that night when those cops came convinced him he was making the right move.

"Chitown," her soft voice stiffened him. He turned slowly and looked into her dark eyes.

"Don't leave the house," she warned. "The streets are filled with dagga smoking, Skokaza drinking Tsotsis who rob, beat and kill the same as Capetown Skullys."

"I'm glad you told me, but I can tell by the silence there's something else bothering you."

"Yes!" she folded her arms. He lit two cigarettes and gave her one.

184

"This is the worst choice you could have made," she said between puffs, "because we all overlooked the date."

"I don't understand' what do you mean?"

"Today is the thirteenth," she finally finished her drink, "two years ago, on March twenty-first, sixty-seven men, women and children were shot dead in Sharpsville. Last year that day was declared a day of mourning throughout the land. The Pan-Africanists called for a general strike. It was a disaster."

"What happened?"

"The army and police bully-boys came in beating and arresting those who did not go to work. It was horrible. I only hope for all our sakes it doesn't happen again."

"I don't have a job," he said, "so that shouldn't affect me. But just in case, he pulled out his wallet and gave her all of his money except two hundred dollars, "I want you to keep this for me. And feel free to use any part you need, anytime."

"I will not need anything." She folded the money carefully.

"Will you come to visit me?" he asked.

"On the weekends," she nodded, "and bring the things you need but can't buy here."

He leaned over and kissed her on the cheek.

"I know in your mind," she looked him in the eye, "you must wonder why I do these things."

"Yes," he said as they put out their cigarettes in an old tin ashtray, "but I couldn't think of a proper time to ask."

She rose slowly, went to the window and stared out at the approaching darkness. He came up behind, grabbed her shoulders and gently turned her around.

"Go ahead, Reba. Tell me everything. I'll understand, because I'm so grateful for all you've done."

"About a year ago," she said, speaking with apparent difficulty, "one of my friends married an American seaman. She now lives in New York."

"And you wanted to do the same with me!" He looked down into her bewildered face.

"You knew?" she gasped.

"I had an idea, from the way you acted after you found out I was married."

"I'm so ashamed." She turned back to the window in an effort to hide her moistening eyes. "Had I not been so intoxicated, I would have asked you that night."

"It's all right . . . it's all right, honey." He put his hands back on her trembling shoulders. "I understand. And I don't blame you for trying to escape from this hellhole anyway you can. But why me?" He turned her around and held her close. "Most of the other crewmen are single."

"That is why I thought you were, also. When Rinco introduced us on the dock I had strong feelings and should have inquired then, but you left in such a hurry. That night in the Zambesi, I was only thinking of singing in New York. It was really stupid of me."

"Please don't say that, Reba. If it wasn't for you I'd be dead, or rotting in some stinking-ass prison. When I get out of this shit, I'm not gonna stop spending until I get all of you out of here. Maybe not to the States, but at least out of this slime-pit they call South Africa. And if anything happens to me, take what I've given you and get yourself out."

"I still want you to reconsider coming back to Sea Point," she looked him in the eye again. But in her mind she felt it would be better for him in Nanga.

He held her tight and kissed her in the mouth. When their lips parted he saw the three Africans returning from the Shebeen.

As Reba and Ihetu hurried their drinks because of darkness, she reminded them all of the date, and warned there may be another strike. She thought again of Chitown returning with her, but knew he would not give up constant companionship in Nanga for the fear and loneliness of Sea Point.

She gave him Ihetu's telephone number in case there was trouble, or he became separated. She told him to keep his Seaman's Document on him at all times because he would have to prove he was American before he could get out of the country.

The first few days went well for him in Nanga, but as time dragged, worry mounted. Etobi and Silombela did whatever they could to combat his despondency. During the day while Etobi worked, and he grew tired of the boring radio, Silombela would entertain him with exciting stories about Zulu chiefs and warriors of the past, and sat fascinated whenever Chitown talked about America.

They helped each other with the housework, and usually there was something needed to complete dinner. Before heading to the store, the old man would flash his wide friendly smile and suggest a little libation to round out the meal. Chitown just laughed and gave him the money. The Africans didn't let him be as generous as he wanted, because it was uncertain how long he would have to stay. However they were thankful for more, if not better, food, good soap and cigarettes, plus a little extra skokaan for the old man.

Chitown and Etobi often talked well into the night about their countries and childhoods. Etobi never failed to mention old man Silombela, who was now too broken to work, but had raised him from a child when both of his parents died. With each passing day Chitown felt closer to the Africans, whose social problems were not unlike his own.

On Saturday, March 17, Reba didn't come to visit, so he asked Etobi to call Ihetu and find out what happened. Etobi returned and told him that Ihetu's auto was being repaired, but it should be ready in a day or two. He also had good news.

"Reba's girlfriend, Joyce, a dockworker, told her that an American ship was in port. She wasn't sure what kind it was but was positive of the flag. As soon as Ihetu's auto is running again, he will come and take you there."

Chitown yelled and leaped for joy. "It won't be long now!" He hugged Etobi and Silombela. "It won't be long before I'll be heading home!"

The very next night his bright bubble began to burst under the heat of barn-fired speeches and rallies being held throughout the town. He cursed himself again while the three of them, from the darkness of their only window, watched a large gathering in the churchyard near the main gate.

If you had went back to Sea Point, you dumb bastard, you might be on an American ship instead of the middle of all this shit!

Several pounding knocks shook the door. There was a brief awkward moment of silence before Etobi turned on the light and unlocked it.

Two black men entered: a tall giant-like one with a wide nose that spread the length of his lips, and a short porkly bearded one, with small shifty eyes that settled on Chitown.

Silombela offered them seats and everyone sat down. The big man asked a lot of questions in Zulu, with a tone as commanding as his size. Etobi did the answering after explaining that Obo could not talk at all and only understood English. All the while the short one watched Chitown.

"Where are you from?" he finally asked him anyway.

Chitown hunched his shoulders and pointed to his throat.

"Nyasaland!" Etobi said.

"Nyasaland?"

Chitown shook his head yes.

"Let me see your dompass!"

Who the fuck are you to ask for my passbook? Chitown thought as they stared at each other. Then he looked at Etobi who nodded for him to comply. He took the book out slowly and held it in the air. The African snatched it, frowned through the pages, and handed it back.

"Where do you work?" he asked as if he expected an answer.

"He's looking for a job," Etobi said, "but we all will be at your rally."

188

"We will be expecting you!" The big man rose and shook the Africans' hands. Before he could shake Chitown's the short one stopped him and whispered something in his ear. He studied Chitown curiously, then pointed at him.

"Make very sure *you* are there, young man!"

They gave a tight fist salute and left.

"Now what was that all about?" Chitown asked.

They are members of the Spoilers," Etobi lit a cigarette, "the largest gang of Tsotsis in Nanga. Their rally will be held tomorrow night, so they are building support for violence, if the people are beaten again on the twenty-first."

The Spoilers can be very intimidating." Silombela got a bottle from under his bunk and passed it around.

"Damn!" Chitown took a long burning swallow, "first the coloreds, and now the Africans are on my ass?"

Chapter Twenty One

IT WAS just a coincidence that the band stopped playing when she walked through the wide glass door leading from the elevator into the patio bar of the Roof Top Garden.

But to Rinco, everything seemed motionless except that tall lovely brown woman with the graceful stride of a queen, dressed from head to foot in gold. She stopped to question a waiter who pointed toward some tables where a bunch of Americans were seated. Heads snapped as she passed, and even women took second looks.

From his seat near the bandstand he was entranced by everything about her. The narrow silk scarf tied Apache-style around her thick bushy hair. The large golden earrings that dangled on each side of a face molded by the gods, as her knee-length evening dress flowed like a magnetic cloud around her long, curvaceous figure.

All of the crewmen stood up when she stopped at the first table. They talked for a second, and the men started looking in all directions.

First one, then another, pointed to him. He glanced around; there was nobody else in the vicinity. She thanked them and headed his way. He couldn't believe it was happening.

I hope she's not coming to ask me about Big Shot, he thought, *or dude, as you say, you sure got competition!*"

"Good evening." Her soft voice sprang him to his feet. "Are you Rinco Styles?"

"Yes! Please be seated!" He quickly pulled out a chair. She sat down and placed her purse on the table.

"I have a message for you."

"I'm open for any message you care to convey," he smiled, "but first, may I have the privilege of buying you a drink?"

She gave him a strange look, then smiled back. "Thank you."

"What would you like?"

"A soda will be fine."

He ordered the soda and another Scotch for himself.

"What's the message?" he asked when the waiter had gone.

"It's from your shipmate ... Chitown."

"What!" he caught himself and lowered his voice. "Chitown is still in Capetown?"

"He was there when I left the night after your ship sailed."

"Where? The cops haven't got him, have they?"

"No, he was at Sea Point with Reba. She said you knew each other."

"Yes, but why did Chitown miss the ship?"

"He was stabbed in a fight with some Skullys."

"Oh my God! Did he get a doctor? How badly was he hurt?"

"I am a nurse. I treated the wounds in his shoulder and side. He had lost considerable blood, but no doubt he will recover."

"You *are* as beautiful as you look," he just had to say.

The waiter returned with their drinks and a five-piece Italian band started another number. The sadness masked by her pretty face was revealed through her dark almond eyes as he stole glances while they watched the couples dancing.

"Your friend ... " she took a sip and cleared her throat, "he killed one of them."

During the long pause that it took for the information to sink in, he finished his old drink and started on the new one, as she stirred her soda with a straw.

"Then he's in a lot of trouble, too."

"I'm afraid so. He wants you to contact the American consul for some help."

"Tomorrow's Saturday," he frowned, "the consulate may be closed. But I'll find his house."

"Please ... say nothing about a man being killed!"

"Don't worry, I'm not telling anyone but our roommate about that. And I'll seek advice before even revealing he's in Capetown."

"Meanwhile, he's in very good hands." She took another sip. "Reba will care for him. Etobi and Ihetu will help and advise as best they can."

"Other friends of yours?" He could sense the hurt in her voice.

"Yes, I wish they all could have come."

"I know." He patted her gently on the hand. "South Africa is a hell of a place to be trapped ... or born in. Unless you're white, then you're running scared." He took the hand in both of his. "I'm deeply grateful. You probably saved Chitown's life, and it was swell of you to look me up. When did you arrive in Dar es Salaam?"

"Yesterday." She withdrew her hand to restir her soda.

A seaman came over from that first table and asked her for a dance. She politely refused with the explanation that she was very tired. He apologized and left.

"If you just arrived yesterday, it must have been a long, hard journey," Rinco sympathized, glancing around in hope that Big Shot wouldn't make it. "How in the world did you find me?"

"I went to your ship, a man in uniform told me you might be here. He was very pleasant."

192

"I'll bet!"

"Thank you for the drink, Mr. Styles. Now I must be going. I am on duty at eight o'clock and still need rest."

"I understand." He touched her hand again. "But please stay and see the show, it should be starting any minute. I'll take you home afterward . . . Okay?"

"Very well," she agreed.

"And please call me Rinco. And tell me your name."

Her smile sent shivers through him. "My name is Anya," she said.

"By the way, Anya, where are you staying?"

"The Princess Margaret Hospital, but it's only temporary. I was told to expect a transfer soon, to some remote village where I will be needed more."

He ordered another Scotch, and wondered how she could escape from South Africa and have a job waiting on her, but dared not ask.

"Would you care for anything else?"

"A coffee perhaps," she smiled.

The band finished and started leaving the small red carpeted stage.

"The main attraction should be coming up next." He looked at his watch and squirmed nervously. The last person he wanted to see right now was supposed to meet him here twenty minutes ago. *I hope he doesn't show,* he thought to himself, gluing his eyes on the entrance. It had been a long time since he openly competed for a woman. But if Big Shot found out he had just met Anya, the competition would suddenly become relentless.

"Are you looking for a woman?" Anya asked with a hint of slyness in her voice.

"No!" he laughed, shifting his eyes to her's, "just the opposite. But if I were, and she walked through that door, I would throw rocks at her."

She laughed as he took her hand and made a promise to himself: *I'm going to do everything in my power to get you Anya. And when I do, I'm never going to let you go."

At that very moment, Big Shot was dashing down the gangplank into a waiting taxi.

"Step on it dude," he barked at the driver. "I'm a half hour late. Bet I missed the show. Nothin' been going right lately," he mumbled, reaching for a joint.

It had started that morning Krishan's old man came to the Pot O' Gold early, and caught him behind the bar rapping in her ear. He blamed himself, because she warned him that the little ass-hole might come in. But he had almost got in them drawers, and just couldn't leave her alone.

He lit the joint, smiled out of the window and thought back to the day she told him she took inventory every Monday morning at six-thirty. When she arrived the next Monday he was waiting. He bought a cold bottle of her best champagne, and promised to help her if she would join him in a drink.

When the inventory was finished, she decided to check the vacant rooms, and he eagerly followed. The third room was dark and she walked over to the window. She raised the shade, and when she turned around they were face to face. He kissed her passionately, grabbing at her soft flesh and combing his fingers through her long silky hair. She didn't resist until he started squeezing and fondling her plump round breast. When she turned her head, he wrapped his arms tightly round her waist, ran his tongue down the side of her neck and started kissing her bare shoulder.

"No! No! ... not now!" she panted, "my husband may be here soon!"

She had responded, and that was all he needed to know. But he was so eager to get next to her that he couldn't leave her alone, or keep his hands off her. That was the reason her old man had caught him fucking with her behind the bar a few days later. His smile turned into a frown as he took a long pull on the reefer. "Now I gotta beat the bush with these goddamn Jambos."

He ordered the driver to turn on the dome light so he could check himself out, while anticipating a grand entry.

He didn't like to dress fast, but those damn boilers were down again. That meant long-working hours, and every second he could be on the beach was precious.

"Overtime alright for those po' motherfuckers who need it," he grumbled, feeling to make sure the collar of his brown silk shirt fitted neatly over the collar of his ivory colored tropical suit. "But it's just puttin' shit in my game." After checking his watch, ring and ivory patent leather shoes, he told the driver to dash the light.

When they arrived at the Roof Top Garden, he gave the driver a five and told him to keep the change. As he started for the lobby he heard a voice shouting, "Hey man! Hey man!" He turned and saw Slick pulling up beside him on his scooter.

"What you want, dude? I'm in a hurry!"

"Krishan, man!" he winked, "she asked me to look for you. Her husband, he now gone, man!"

"What!" Big Shot's eyes lit up and he flashed his favorite smile. "You mean he's headed back to India?"

"No, jive man, he been deported. I told you so man!"

"I use to think you were full of shit, Slick," Big Shot said, "but you a alright cat. Meet me at the Pot O' Gold and the drinks on me."

"Mellow man!" The African putted off on his scooter.

"The little sawed off prick can't stop me now," Big Shot laughed, glancing up to the roof. "Fuck you, Rinco." He grinned and hailed a cab.

"I am glad I decided to stay." Anya drew up her long, shapely legs to sit erect in the small taxi.

"Princess Margaret Hospital!" Rinco told the driver and climbed into the back seat beside her. "So am I, much more than you could ever imagine."

They smiled at each other when the car made a sudden turn and their bodies touched.

"Where are you from?" he asked, "Jo-berg?"

"No, Orlando, outside Johannesburg. We can't live in the cities unless we are servants."

"That's right." He paused for a second, then changed the subject.

195

"What about the guy with all those different hats?" He imitated the African comedian, who wore a dozen hats, and a different face for each one.

"Oh, yes! I have never seen so many funny hats before," she laughed. The music was a lot different to me, but it was all wonderful."

The dimly lit city began to vanish rapidly behind them on the end of a long, narrow dirt road.

"You know, I've just figured out why I didn't immediately recognize you as South African."

"Oh?" she looked at him.

"I was too spellbound by the luscious maze of bronze and gold to recall any place I've ever been, or anyone I've ever known."

"Reba told me you Americans were quick to flatter women," she laughed.

"This isn't flattery, baby, this is honesty. You're the finest woman I've ever seen."

The road widened, and they were flanked by tall wooden fences. She rolled down her window and gazed out at the round tops of the huts within the fences that reminded her of her early childhood. Shouting voices from hut to hut and across the road battled the sound of night insects as Rinco rolled down his window, lit a cigar and wondered if he was coming on a little too strong.

The high-rise hospital loomed out of the green and black like a giant sandy ant-hill behind a huge circular wall.

"Wait here, driver, I'm going back!" He got out, hurried around to her side and opened the door. Beyond the swinging iron gates were three closed receiving desk facing a long double row of empty wooden benches. He stopped her in the light from the open air corridor that led to the emergency rooms and looked into her large brown eyes.

"This night has been filled with beauty and sorrow. I met you . . . then learned the bad news about Chitown. I want the ship to hurry back to Capetown only because he may still be there. But the thought of leaving Dar es Salaam now ... now that I've met you ... " He shook his head and threw his hands in the air.

"Your friend is much more important." She stepped out of the light onto one of the long concrete paths paved across the spacious lawn.

"I know!" he said, "but it doesn't help the hurt. May I see you again ... soon?"

"How soon?"

"Like tomorrow."

They both laughed.

"Since tomorrow's Monday, I guess you have to work," he said

"Only an indoctrination, and maybe one class, but I am going to rest tomorrow. I must also get a letter off to Reba. If Chitown is still at her house, he will be anxious to know if I have contacted you."

"Right! ... And tell him to get to the American Embassy as fast as he can. And stay there no matter what, until our ship gets back."

"I will!" she promised.

"You are truly wonderful," he said. "Now then ... when are you off? Nursing is a rough grind. You should have at least one day to relax, and enjoy yourself."

"True ... " she agreed, "because in the evenings I attend classes ... but perhaps Tuesday."

"Great!" He took her hand. "Tell you what, I'm going to rent a car so I can track down that consul. Then Tuesday we'll ride all over town, and out into the countryside without worrying about cabs. We can have dinner, perhaps even a show, and still get you back early enough for a good night's sleep."

"Very well. How can I resist?"

"Great!" He let go her hand. "What time can I pick you up?"

"About noon, will that be all right?"

"That will be just fine. Now don't eat lunch, and thank you very much."

"Thank you, Mr ... I'm sorry, Rinco, for a pleasant evening."

"The pleasure was mine."

She looked at her watch. "It's late, I must go!"

"Okay, see you Tuesday." He stepped back into the light and watched her stroll to the nurses' quarters on the far side of the grounds. Before entering, she turned and waved. He threw her a kiss.

Chapter Twenty Two

THAT CLOUDY wet Tuesday night, Chitown, Etobi and Silombela reluctantly joined a crowd of about four hundred people, including women and children, standing in the spacious yard of a tall wooden church.

The speaker stood on a makeshift platform waving towards last year's charred ruins of a school and administration building and shouted, "We alone suffer from this!" He reminded the crowd that no one had enough saved from their meager wages to tide them over in case of a prolonged strike and would again have to ration corn meal given by white liberals to survive.

But as the crowd thickened, other speakers shouted him down. They spoke of men being pulled from their beds in the middle of the night and beaten in front of their terrified families. Women spoke of sons and husbands that were dragged away screaming, never to be seen again. What was once the rear of the assembly was now the middle, and Chitown and his companions were swallowed by the frenzied crowd yelling slogans as they relived last year's horror from the lips of the speakers. The church was set on fire and the crowd roared its approval.

Chitown, Etobi and the old man were thrust toward the front as the huge throng spread out to surround the growing blaze, moving their bodies from side to side while chanting "Izwe Tethe (our land)!" to the slow, sorcerous beats of three large goatskin drums.

Some people up front picked up the platform and threw it in the fire, bringing another roar.

A tall, stout woman wearing a tam rushed forward and threw her passbook in the fire. That brought more cheers of "Izwe Tethe!" and a loud roll of the drums. A man did the same, then another, and another woman. With each extreme act of defiance came loud applause, a roll from the drums and shouts of "Izwe Tethe!"

As more and more burned their books, Chitown and his friends moved aside so others behind them could do the same. The crowd pushed forward. Chitown realized too late what was happening. The last thing he wanted to do was give up his passbook. He tried to squeeze backward, frantically searching his pockets for a substitute, but there wasn't any. The crowd pushed him forward until he faced the fire. His turn had come. He tried to move to the right and the short man who had paid them the visit stepped in his way. He turned, and there was the big one glaring down at him with his hands on his hips. Chitown had no choice. He pulled out the book and threw it angrily into the blaze.

The flames suddenly engulfed the church building and licked at the cross on top of the steeple. The crowd grew still and silent until the roof collapsed, sending up a great ball of smoke and fire.

The wild screams and shouts that followed were short-lived as whispers of "Isele . . . Isele" (frogs) echoed through the crowd.

Chitown searched for Etobi and Silombela through the dreadful sounds of cracking flame, nervous mumbling and approaching vehicles. Two frogs (armored cars) came through the gate and eased up to the edge of the crowd, each accompanied by a truckload of gasmasked police.

The policemen unloaded with their clubs and sidearms drawn as the frogs shot tear gas into the startled crowd.

"Ratissage (wholesale beatings)! Ratissage!" they shouted, charging into the coughing, crying Africans, swinging their night sticks.

"Teach the agitators another lesson!" yelled a voice through the loud-speaker of the lead truck. His sinister orders rang over the thud of wood and metal against flesh and bone as the screaming blacks fled in all directions.

Chitown saw Etobi and a few other Africans run between two buildings. He dashed after them. There they hid, choking and rubbing their burning eyes until the attack was called off. The white policemen hurried back to their trucks, kicking at fallen blacks along the way.

"We are giving you kaffirs a stern warning!" the magnified voice sounded. "If you try again to strike, as you have in the past, Nanga will be one puddle of blood. You bastards will pray to work!"

The deadly frogs started up with a noisy grind and left in clouds of dust.

Etobi and Chitown went back to the scene in search of Silombela. Although the ground was littered with battered, bruised, and bloody bodies, the Africans' spirit was not broken. Many had already returned to assist the wounded while humming songs of liberation, with rags tied around their faces to fight the choking and wipe the tears from their burning eyes.

Chitown spotted the old man lying quivering on his side and called to Etobi. It was evident he was seriously injured when they turned him over. There was a nasty swollen gash across his forehead, and bright red blood oozed from his nose and mouth. Etobi dropped to his knees and bent an ear to the slow moving lips, then stood up with tears in his eyes. "He wants to die at home."

Chitown nodded and grabbed the long, thin legs while Etobi carried him under the limp, swinging arms.

"He didn't make it," Chitown said as they placed his body on the bed.

201

Etobi closed the sad eyes and wiped the bloody face tenderly with a damp cloth. Chitown unfolded a blanket to cover him up. Then he said a prayer as Etobi stood silently recalling the endless suffering apartheid had visited upon his people.

Long ago it had separated Silombela's family by simply running a comb through their hair and classifying his wife and three children colored. The same slave-filled Johannesburg gold mines that stiffened Silombela's joints with arthritis had given Etobi's father tuberculosis who, unwittingly, had passed it to his wife, resulting in both of their early deaths. Silombela, with no one of his own left, raised Etobi and his younger sister, who didn't reach the age of twelve because of gastroenteritis.

Etobi suddenly let out a scream and banged his fist on the table. "This is it! This is it!" The tears ran down his cheeks. "They have killed my father, my mother and sister. They drove the woman I love with all my heart to a distant land and I may never see her again . . . now they murder Silom . . . " His voice broke and he began to shake and sob.

Chitown put a sympathetic arm around his shoulder, persuaded him to sit down, and got a half-full bottle of skokaan from under the old man's mattress.

As they sat silently smoking and drinking, Chitown felt somewhat ashamed for only thinking of himself after the way this man had helped him, but he had struggled too long and hard to stay alive. The Africans were headed for another, more violent, confrontation and he figured they didn't stand a chance. The time had come for Ihetu to get him to the American embassy.

"Can you make a telephone call?" He asked when the whiskey was gone.

Etobi looked up, "Tonight?"

"Yeah, as fast as we can! I want Ihetu to drive me back to Capetown tomorrow. I'm going to give myself up and take my chances. I want the three of you to have my money and try to get the hell out of South African."

Etobi got up slowly, and stared down at the dingy blanket covering the old man. "Since the night she left, I have dreamed of joining Anya, but not now." He shook his head. "Not anymore." The fury showed in his face. His hand trembled as he went to the dresser and got an eight-inch dagger. "They have done too much for me to run now. I would feel like a dog, with its tail between its legs. No . . . not now or ever." His voice became clear and calm, like the ring of doom. "All of my life they have made me run, bow, hide and crawl as if I didn't belong on earth. Not any more!" He rubbed the blade of the knife, tucked it in his belt, and put on his coat. "I am sick to my soul of being submissive. However, this is not your fight. I will go and make the call. We will bury Silombela when I return."

"Waitaminute! I'm going with you!" Chitown got his weapon. He didn't want to be alone with a corpse.

"What happened last year?" he asked as they hurried down the dark, narrow streets. When did the whites attack?"

"Midmorning, they waited to be sure we were not going to work, then came with whips, clubs and guns. There will be a great difference tomorrow."

"What do you mean?"

"Last year we chose to strike against the passbook law, to leave our books at home and allow ourselves to be jailed without resistance, but they wanted only to maim, torture and kill. This year I will fight with the Spoilers. We shall take some of the bully boys with us." He patted the knife.

"Did you burn your passbook?" Chitown asked.

"Yes! Did you?"

"Yeah, but I've got my Seaman's papers in my shoe."

For curfew to be approaching, there were many people still on the noisy streets, and several scattered fires blazed angry red against the black, moonless sky. Very few slept. Nearly every window had some kind of light, and the streets were loud with hidden voices.

Chitown felt they were being followed, but couldn't distinguish the shadows in the darkness. He stopped, lit a cigarette, and checked behind them, but still couldn't be sure.

"Will Ihetu be able to make it if they blockade?"

"Maybe! Reba knows the police that man a permanent barricade ... speaking of the devil!" They jumped aside as a speeding patrol car passed with its brights on and a spotlight glowing from side to side. Chitown thought about the cops that had invaded Reba's apartment.

"This is one of the telephones they always fail to disconnect." Etobi turned down the path of a house similar to their own. The door was opened by a little woman with three frightened children. He told her what he wanted, and gave her some money. Without a word, she led them to the bedroom, turned on the light, left and closed the door.

"I will speak Zulu." Etobi went to the far corner and pulled a phone out from under a big, stuffed, skirted chair. "Chances are the operator will not understand."

As he talked, the idea flashed through Chitown's mind to turn himself in at the police station, but the awesome way they beat those blacks, they had to be bigoted to the bone. He would rather fight than surrender to those redneck son-of-a-bitches. His only hope was for the Africans to go to work or somehow break the blockade.

"His auto is ready. As soon as curfew is lifted at six A.M.," Etobi said, hanging up and replacing the phone under the chair, "Ihetu promised to pick up Reba and be on his way."

Chitown felt a dim ray of hope, quickly thwarted by loud banging on the front door.

They emerged from the bedroom and stood face to face with the short bearded Spoiler, plus five of his cohorts. The Spoiler immediately started interrogating Etobi.

This is the meanest looking bunch of niggers I ever saw. Chitown squirmed nervously, hoping they wouldn't be searched. When the conversation seemed to take on a more friendly tone, he relaxed a little, until Etobi told him they had to go with them.

204

"I have vowed to fight and must be questioned by their leaders. They will let us bury Silombela later."

"What about you?" the bearded one asked. "Or can't you hear either?"

Chitown paused for a second, then hunched his shoulders as if dumbfounded.

"Come! Let's go!" the man ordered. The Spoilers surrounded them as they all headed out the door. As they left the house, the night was filled with distant sounds of armored cars tightening the ring around Nanga.

Chapter Twenty Three

NEAR NOON that Tuesday, the dusty road to the hospital was lined for a quarter-mile with tired sweating Africans. Most were children, being led or carried on the backs of women.

Although he was in a hurry, Rinco drove slowly to keep down the dust. He frowned at the absence of Indians and Europeans in the line. They didn't have to stand in line. They got their private and semi-private rooms without waiting. And these people were just getting clinical care.

Aw hell! he thought, lighting a cigar, *things don't change overnight. If it wasn't for Uhuru, many of these people wouldn't be getting medical aid at all.* He parked his rented Volkswagen near the main gate and got out.

While he waited for Anya in the shade of a small tree on the side of the road, he thought about all of the conflicting emotions this day had brought, and it wasn't over yet.

At eight-thirty that morning he took six days leave and checked into the Spencer Hotel. After a hurried breakfast, he rented the car, parked it in the hotel lot, and went shopping on Independence Avenue. As the bright sun began to warm the cool damp air, he figured it would be a beautiful day for a picnic. He purchased a battery operated phonograph and four jazz LP's. When he got back he told a waiter to have the cook prepare a special lunch basket, then went up to his room.

How different the day had seemed to him as he sat in the overstuffed chair sipping Scotch and soda, while birds sang in harmony with the smooth trumpet of Dizzy Gillespie. He had been looking forward to this day since the last time he saw Anya, and as the moment neared, even the fresh warm air from his open windows seemed to whisper her name as it gently fluttered the soft white curtains. After the record played, he cut off the phonograph and made the mistake of turning on the radio. Everything started downhill.

First, a communique from South Africa predicted minor insurrections by small bands of agitators in the urban areas throughout the union on March 21st.

"Minor my ass!" he had grunted.

Then it was announced that the USNS *General Mitchell* would be leaving Dar es Salaam for India on Sunday, March 25th. The same day his leave was up.

He waved, then stomped the cigar into the dust when he saw Anya emerge from the shadow of the receiving booth where the long line inched forward.

"Ah ... the radiant elegance of femininity in its truest form," he sighed as she approached. She was wearing a low-cut blue cotton dress and rose colored glasses, with the sunlight glowing on her smooth dark skin and dancing sparkles off her golden earrings.

"Good afternoon, Rinco," she glanced at the car, "I see you *did* get an auto."

"Your chariot no less." He opened the door for her. "How do you like it?"

She didn't hear him. She was staring down that long black line, knowing the receiving stations would soon close, turning most of them away.

"You know," he said as they headed toward town, "I've rehearsed all kinds of compliments, but now that you're here ... "

"It doesn't matter!" she cut him off.

"No, it doesn't!" he agreed, "because there are no words to describe how lovely you are."

"She gave him her coy smile, then asked, "Did you see the Counsel?"

"No! but I went to the embassy!"

"What happened?"

"They said he was out for the day. And they didn't have any report of an American seaman in Capetown. What's the matter?" He noticed a worried expression on her face.

"I hope for his sake he's gone before tomorrow," she answered. "If my people decide to strike, as I am sure they will, the whites are going to retaliate brutally. No one will be safe."

"Yeah!" He thought about the communique. "If he's there he could be in big trouble."

She gave him a reassuring pat on the arm, and said, "If he's discovered, perhaps his American citizenship will keep him out of trouble."

"I hope so, baby. Our ship was in Capetown this time last year, but we couldn't go ashore. It must have been pretty bad." He glanced at her.

"Yes, it was, so was Sharpeville the year before."

"I don't suppose you want to talk about it?"

"No!" She shook her head and looked out of the window.

"Would you like to eat now or later?"

"Later."

"How about a movie, or a nice drive?"

She turned to him and smiled, "Let's ride a bit."

"Good!"

He drove through town, then headed out to Oyster Bay. He gave her a tour of the splendid homes and breath-taking gardens behind low vine-covered walls, before turning north along the calm, glittering shore line.

They rode for a half-hour along a rough stone and bush cluttered stretch of beach caressed by pale blue water.

"You know," he said, "I've just thought of the perfect spot for our picnic."

"Picnic?"

"Yes! I hope you didn't eat lunch."

"Just coffee and a salad."

"Good!" He drove back to town, turned down a dirt road, and soon came to a dead end at the foot of a large steep hill. He got out first and opened the trunk in the front of the car.

"Can I help?" she asked.

"Okay, you carry the blanket. I'll take the rest."

He got the basket, phonograph and records, then led her up a narrow weedy path to the top of the hill, where a giant orchid tree shaded a secluded clearing that overlooked the harbor.

"There's the *Gray Ghost!*" He pointed down to the *Mitchell* where a long line of olive-clad Indian soldiers were climbing aboard.

As soon as the blanket was spread, Anya sat down, leaned her back against the trunk of the orchid tree and heaved a relaxing sigh.

"You're still tired, aren't you?" He sat beside her and put on a record.

"Yes," she said, "I really am."

"It must have been a hell of a trip."

"The hell was where I left."

"I know," he said. "What you really need is a few days off."

"That would be nice, but I'm afraid it's impossible at this time." She rubbed the back of her neck and smiled at him. "In fact, I am leaving Dar es Salaam tonight, and will not be back until Friday night."

"Why!" He was shocked.

"In a small village near Mozambique," she spoke slowly and deliberately as Jimmy Rushing sang, *River Stay Away From My Door,* "there is a wireless. I must know what will happen in my country tomorrow, so I will leave tonight." She closed her eyes and rocked with the music.

"I'm on leave," he said, "why don't you let me drive you?"

209

She looked him in the eye, smiled and touched his hand. "That would be very nice, but my comrades may not understand. They are very cautious."

"You mean they might think I'm some kind of agent?"

"I hope you are not offended!"

"Of course not! But I did want to spend more time with you because my ship leaves Sunday."

"Oh! . . . I didn't know."

"That's all right, but why will you be gone so long?"

"I have other things to do."

"Will you go out with me when you return?" he asked, determined not to show how upset he really was.

"That is a promise!" she smiled and nodded her head. "We can be together Saturday."

He opened the basket and pulled out a bottle.

"Champagne!" she gasped.

"That's right Anya, this is a special occasion." He filled two glasses and gave her one. After the second glass she began to talk more. By the time they started dining on steamed lobster tails, roast beef, rolls and salad, she had told him all about the South African musical King Kong, the cast, and the leading lady Miriam Makeba. Not to his surprise, she had been exposed to black American music, but had never heard Jimmy Rushing before.

"That is what Reba wants," she said, "to get out of South Africa and start a singing career like Miriam."

"Now that you are out of South Africa, what are your plans?" he asked. She didn't answer, and they finished their meal in silence. After they ate, he poured more champagne and changed the record. She started to wipe and put up the dishes, but he told her to relax and did it himself. Then he got his polaroid camera from the basket and asked if he could take some pictures of her.

"Certainly!"

"Thank you!" He took her arm and they walked near the edge of the cliff, where she struck her first pose. The bright sun blushed on her face and flared out over her proud shoulders across the dancing, sky blue water like a long golden cape. He was so entranced by her beauty that

210

a whole minute passed before he even raised the camera. His heart clicked with the shutter, and he knew he was in love.

She marveled at how quickly the picture developed and how well the colors came out. He plucked an orchid from the tree, put it between her ear, and took another picture.

"You shame that poor flower." He removed it and took a shot of her leaning against the tree.

"You want to take a couple of me?" he asked. She smiled, but shook her head "no."

"Aw come on Anya, you can't break anything." He explained how to use the camera, finding a good reason to put his arms around her. When she peered through the sight, he smelled and brushed his face against her hair.

The first picture came out perfect.

"You keep this one." He gave it to her. "I've got just enough film for one more." Then he gave her a silly pose, with his thumbs in his ears,and his eyes bucked. For the first time since they met, he heard her laugh out loud.

"I wish I could always make you feel this way," he said as they sat on the blanket examining the photos.

"Why?" her smile faded. "You have just met me."

"I know, and for that I am sorry because you are the finest woman I've ever known."

"Oh come now!" She laughed again and looked out to sea.

"I'm serious, Anya. I want to know all about you." He put the pictures in his case with the camera. "So I can bring more laughter to your voice and paint more smiles across your lovely lips."

"There is too little happiness in my life," she sighed. "It would be much more exciting to talk about you. I'm sure it must be wonderful to travel throughout the world."

"I used to think my life was exciting," he said, "but compared to now, it was really dull."

"I thought you said you were serious." She gave him a playful tap on the arm.

When Peggy Lee started a slow ballad he asked her to dance.

"Here? ... Now?"

"Why not?" He stood up and offered his hand. As they danced, he held her close, pressing his cheek to her temple.

"Anya," he whispered, "there's so much I want to tell you, and our time is so short I don't know how to start. The best way I guess is to tell it like it is ... I love you, Anya. I love you with a passion I've never felt before."

She started to speak but he cut her off.

"Please baby, let me get this out in the open while I can. From the moment I saw you at the Roof Top Garden, I haven't been the same. You've dominated my every thought and emotion, because you're much more than just beautiful." He held her tighter and moved his lips ever so slowly towards hers. "You're heavenly Anya ... nothing can compare, anyone I've ever met, or anything I've ever seen ... the neon lights of the Ginza Strip, the Taj Mahal ... not even the golden red glitter of sunrise, dancing across the rippling waves can hold a candle to your beauty ... or even the sea itself, on clear calm nights when the moon and the stars seem close enough to touch ... I love you Anya!" He placed his lips on hers. Their tongues invaded each other's mouths for a brief moment, before she broke his grip, turned and walked to the edge of the hill. He followed, grabbing her tenderly by the shoulders.

"Your cleverness has no doubt worked well for you in the past," she said, facing him again. "Perhaps when you return to Capetown, or wherever, the words you have spoken will vanish like those rippling waves."

"Did Reba tell you I had a lady in Capetown?"

She nodded her head "yes."

"What else did she say about me?"

"Only that you were a gentleman, and very nice. I am sorry I said that," she rubbed his cheek, "because I also have a friend in Capetown."

"Just one?" It was hard for him to say.

"Only one." She took the sun glasses from her pocket and put them on.

"I'm sorry," he apologized as they walked back to the tree and resumed their seats. "I was just implying that you could easily have many friends, anywhere."

He poured them another glass of wine, then said, "You told me what Reba wants out life. Now tell me what you want, now that you are out of South Africa."

"Maybe it would bring understanding if I did tell you a few things about myself." She took her first sip without frowning. He turned off the record player.

"For years I held the burning desire to become a doctor. It flamed during my childhood as I witnessed many playmates suffer and die before the age of fifteen with gastroenteritis, pneumonia and tuberculosis. However, to be black under apartheid, the chances of becoming a doctor was all but impossible. And being a woman, impossible indeed. So I settled for their inferior nursing schools reserved for non-whites. I remember, oh so well, the long tiresome monotonous details assigned by the arrogant whites. Upon graduation I went straight to Baragwanath, the largest hospital in the country for non-whites. It was always overcrowded, understaffed and ill equipped. My salary was meager compared to whites in the same position. But I continued my education, advancing only to discover I could not give orders to lower staff whites, who did not want to be there in the first place. But I gained a deep satisfaction in helping ... if only in a small way ... to ease the misery and suffering of many black children."

"It must have really been rough," he said.

"Yes, it was." She took another drink without frowning, and looked far away. "I told you earlier I had no family, but once I did. Now I'm only thankful to have made them proud of me before apartheid destroyed them. It began three years ago with the arrest of my father for no valid reason. We never saw, or heard from him, again. Despite added hardships, my mother and brother continued sacrificing and encouraging me to finish my post graduate studies. However, we all grew more bitter by the day about my father, and the nonsense the police gave us whenever

213

we inquired." She turned her head to hide the approaching tears. "My brother joined the Pan-African Congress."

"I've heard about their struggle to end the passbook laws," he said.

"Yes!" her voice trembled, "and gain full political rights using Gandhi's philosophy of non-violent civil disobedience . . . a sad mistake. Sharpeville was supposed to be the beginning." Her whole body shook as she broke into tears.

"It's all right, honey." He rose to his knees and took her in his arms. "I understand . . . go on and cry." He removed her glasses and pressed her head to his chest.

"I was on duty when they brought them to the hospital," she sobbed, "their bodies torn and shattered by filthy racist's bullets." He held her tighter, rubbing his face in her soft bushy hair, as her tears soaked into his shirt.

"Why were they murdered?" she asked. "It was only a peaceful demonstration for human dignity. Why were they slaughtered like animals?" She withdrew and stared him in the eye.

"Because they were slaughtered by animals," he answered, then took her back in his arms.

"I try," she sniffed, "but cannot drive that hellish day from my mind . . . searching through the countless wounded, until he called my name . . . when I saw him I fainted. When I awoke, he was gone." She cried for nearly five minutes.

"My mother hasn't spoken a word since," she said, wiping her eyes. "It was just too much. She is in the care of relatives, but doesn't know anyone." She regained her posture, pulled away and again wiped her eyes with a small handkerchief. He returned her glasses and she put them on.

"The plan was to march peacefully on police stations without passes and demand to be arrested. To overflow the jails, and make the white bastards sweep their own homes and streets, make their own beds and cook their own food. Make the farmers and miners perform their own dirty, back-breaking tasks. But instead they were shot down. From that day, I vowed to fight apartheid in any way I could. I joined a more militant group, made it to the government's wanted list and had to flee. Oh, I'm sorry," she pointed, "I ruined your shirt."

"Forget about that." He reached out and touched her hand. "These tears are now part of me." He rubbed the wet spot on his shirt. "I feel the pain and sorrow of your life, and beg for the chance to show you another side. I'd be more than willing to spend my life showing you better things, and painting smiles across that lovely face. You are out of South Africa now, and too much of a woman, inside and out, to let sad memories haunt you forever."

She saw the sincerity in his face, and admitted to herself that she could care for him. But she hadn't escaped to find peace, safety, romance or the finer things. She had left South Africa to join the courageous freedom fighters, facing incredible odds in the jungles of apartheid's outer shields, Angola, Rhodesia and Mozambique. For his own sake, it was best that he knew nothing about them.

"I am sorry I ruined your picnic," she sighed.

"No! . . . I'm the one who should apologize. In the first place you couldn't *ruin* anything. And so far, all I've done is cause you to relive your past horror . . . and express my selfish desire."

"Do not feel sorry. It was good to finally pour out some of the pain. Thank you for being so kind."

"I give thanks," he held her face in his hands and gently kissed her forehead, "for each precious moment you've shared with me. But since there's nothing we can do about what's happening in Capetown, let's try to throw it out of our minds, while I tell you a few things about me . . . agreed?"

"Agreed!" She nodded her head as they picked up their half-filled glasses and drank a toast.

"I bet you would never guess where I was born."

"Tell me." She tried to smile.

"I was born in Africa . . . " He laughed at the look on her face. "That's right. My father was a Liberian who married an American woman. They divorced when I was twelve and she took me back to New York. The only times I saw my father after that were the summers I spent in Africa with him. Those were conflicting years of being torn between Liberia, which my mother hated, and the America my father didn't like to the day he was killed in an accident."

"That is sad," she sympathized. "Do you have any brothers or sisters?"

"No, only my mother, who would like you because she's just as militant. My father died when I was eighteen. A year later I was drafted into the Army. She raised holy-hell because I didn't go underground, or even back to Africa. But I went and served my time, caught hell in Korea, got out and went to sea."

"What made you decide on the sea?"

"I'm not sure, but I guess it was those six summer voyages between New York and Liberia that gave me a latent love for the sea." He started to put on another record but she looked at her watch and stopped him.

"I am truly sorry, but I can't stay longer. I want to write Reba another letter and get some rest before my tiresome journey."

"I understand ... speaking of letters, I hope it will be all right for us to write each other. I want to keep in touch with you after the ship leaves."

"Very well," she said, "but I do not know exactly how long I shall remain in Dar es Salaam."

"Where will you go?"

"Perhaps to that remote village I told you about."

"No matter," he said, "I have a pad in the car so we can exchange addresses. Just answer my letters ... please! And I'll find you if I have to hack my way through every jungle in Africa. If that doesn't work I'll hire a safari."

After a good laugh, and a long kiss, they finished the champagne, packed up the gear and headed down the hill.

216

Chapter Twenty Four

THE FIVE Spoilers took Chitown and Etobi through the gate of a high, shaggy, bamboo fence, that circled three bungalow type houses and a large, unkempt yard. The bearded one shouted a code word and rapped a signal on the middle door. The voices inside hushed, the lights dimmed, and the door opened slowly. A bright flashlight beam motioned them past a bunch of Africans sitting on the floor sharpening knives and making short spears, to a thin, wooden table where a man in a black wide-brimmed hat sat behind the only lit gasoline lamp. He stared up at the two non-members who glanced back and forth into the many cold, dark eyes surrounding them.

"You I know!" he pointed to Etobi. "You I do not!" All eyes shifted to Chitown. "Where are you from? What tribe are you?"

"He is not supposed to be able to talk," the bearded man remarked sarcastically, "His friend says he is from Nyasaland."

"Is this true?" the man at the table asked Etobi.

"I'm an American!" Chitown said before Etobi could answer. There was a brief disbelieving silence, while the word American filtered through the crowd, which suddenly erupted into laughter. The big hat man got up and waved his hands for silence. It came slowly.

"He is American!" Etobi insisted, "He's from ... "

"He can talk!" the man snapped. "Let him!"

Don't show fear! Chitown repeated to himself before he spoke. "I had a fight with a colored gang and was bleeding to death in a alley when Etobi and his friends found me. They took me to Sea Point and saved my life. But my ship had gone by the time I regained consciousness."

"You expect us to believe," the bearded man challenged, "that you could not have gone to your ship, or back to America? You expect us to believe you preferred to stay in South Africa?" He grinned around at his chuckling comrades.

"I killed one of them," Chitown said, "and I don't like your jails!" The chuckles turned to mumbles, as some recalled reading or hearing about the dead Skully.

"I can prove I'm American. I only wanted to stay with my friends until my ship returns."

"Prove you're American!" the Spoiler in the hat snapped. Chitown took off his left shoe, got the Seamans' Document and gave it to him.

"It could be a forgery!" the bearded man snarled, the same as his dompass! I believe he is a plant!"

"Look, man," Chitown began to get angry, "how the hell could we be plants? We didn't ask to come here, you brought us!"

"Where is your passport?"

"It was disfigured to make that fake dompass you and your buddy made me burn."

"Liars!"

"He is not a liar!" Etobi glanced around for familiar faces. "Everything this man said is the truth. I had just finished a call to get him back to Capetown when we were forced to come here. Tonight ... " he paused to clear his throat as his eyes filled ... "many of you know the old man I lived with ... Silombela. Well, the ghost (whites) killed him in that baton charge! We were going back to bury him." The gang offered silent respect, but the bearded one wasn't finished with Chitown.

"This is the one I do not trust!" He pointed. "How many Skullys were there?"

"Four!"

"Four!" he laughed, "and all good with knives. This super American killed one, fought off the others, and is here to tell about it. Perhaps he can teach us to fight bullets with our hands."

While the Africans laughed, Chitown nonchalantly unzipped his jacket and folded his arms, slipping his trembling right hand under his shirt to the handle of the weapon.

"Very well then, Mr. American, tell us how ... single handed ... you beat off four, knife-carrying coloreds."

They moved in closer when Chitown told Etobi to remove the lamp.

"With this!" In the second it took to say the words, he snatched out the weapon, swung it over his head and down on the table, shattering it to pieces.

Two men grabbed Chitown from behind. The bearded one called him a name and popped out a long switch blade.

"That will be all!" shouted an authoritative voice.

The lights came on and everyone froze, except the ones who cleared a path through the crowd for a short thin man, too young to be completely bald, yet was.

"Let him go!" The man with the shaved head held out his hand for the weapon. Chitown was released and gave it to him.

"Do you have a weapon?" The man asked Etobi while he looked it over.

"Yes! I have a knife. The death of Silombela made me vow to fight the ghost."

"Why were they not searched?" he asked the bearded man, as he took the Seaman's document.

"They were well covered ... and we suspected no weapons!" The bearded man looked around sheepishly.

"If they were plants," the leader studied the document,

carefully comparing it to Chitown, "they would have had better weapons, and you probably would be dead."

The bearded one started another reply, but the leader stopped him with a wave, and turned to Etobi. "I knew the old man and have seen you with him often. I also believe what you say is true, both of you."

At last! Chitown felt relieved. *Somebody with some brains.*

"However!" the bald head man continued, "since you know our location and intentions, we cannot let you out of our sight." He named three men to help Etobi bury Silmonbela with orders to return immediately after. He told the others to disperse with the exception of three lieutenants to accompany him and Chitown.

Maybe he's too fuckin' smart! Chitown thought as he followed the little man out of the front room into a small bedroom. The light was turned on and the door was closed.

"Let me see your wounds!" the leader demanded.

Chitown took off his jacket, threw it on the bed and opened his shirt. When he showed them the wound in his back, they frowned.

"You are indeed a lucky man." The leader's voice suddenly took on a tone of sympathy. "Sit down." He motioned to the bed. Chitown sat down and he sat down beside him. The other men stood silently with their arms folded.

"That call to Capetown, who was it to?" He gave Chitown back his weapon, but kept the Seaman's Document.

"A lady name Reba." Chitown offered cigarettes, the leader accepted, but the others declined. "She's a friend of Etobi's and sings at the Zambesi."

"How . . . and what time was she suppose to get you out of Nanga?" he asked after they lit up.

"Her cousin Ihetu will drive her here when curfew is lifted in the morning."

"She will not get in, and you will not get out." He stood up and went to the table for an ashtray. "Nanga is completely surrounded. If the Pan Africans again let themselves be arrested without resistance, and the people

220

meekly return to work, the ghosts may lift the blockade. But that will not happen, and there will be no peaceful solution."

"Why not?" You gonna stop it?"

"*We* are going to stop it." He returned to his seat, putting the ashtray on the floor between them. "Being beaten, driven, arrested and humiliated is not a peaceful solution for the Spoilers. We will no longer stand by and do nothing. If we continue to remain docile, they will enslave us forever without giving an inch."

The other men voiced their agreement.

"When they decide to teach us another so-called lesson, many of the bastards will learn regret. Ny name is Nxaumalo," he put out the cigarette and offered his hand.

"Wilbur Kane."

The others were introduced but just nodded from their distance.

"Wilbur, my friend, fate has sent you here at a very bad time."

"Don't I know it!" Chitown put out his cigarette. "That's why I have to take my chances with the American Consul."

"Why didn't you do that at first?"

"Under South African law, I'm a deserter, an undesirable alien. The consul is white, he might have turned me in. This country doesn't have a monopoly on bigotry."

The African got up and took the ashtray back to the table.

"I am sorry Mr. Kane, but it is too late now. You should have gone long before curfew, and the blockade. Now you would fall into the hands of the ghosts. They hate and fear black people much more than Americans. There would be no mercy. To survive the torture, you would have to betray us and the people who saved your life. Then it is unlikely you could survive the jails until they ... in their own time ... checked your story thoroughly. But fortunately, we have eliminated that possibility," he patted the shirt that held the Seaman's Document. "You have only one chance to get past this blockade, and that is to fight with us. We need everyone we can get for the initial assault."

"Do I have a choice?" Chitown asked after a lingering silence.

"Yes! You can take the same shovel that buried the old man and dig yourself a hole. We are not murderers," he quickly clarified, "if you dig deep, and pray hard, you may escape the hell that will ring through Nanga when we start fighting back. Rather bitter choices I'm afraid, but they are all we can offer ... try and relax while you think it over. I will expect an answer when the shovel returns."

"I've thought it over already!"

"You have a fast mind."

"I've got a desperate mind. I wanna meet that car tomorrow, and I don't hide in holes ... but more important, I wanna know how the hell you expect to break a armed blockade with spears and knives?"

"First, the element of surprise my friend," Nxaumalo passed out cigarettes and everyone lit up. "Then the people, unarmed, but out-numbering the ghost by thousands, will rally behind us. When this happens, we shall crush the force at the gate, seize weapons from the dead, and for the first time since Cetshwago, fire will be fought with fire!"

The other Africans let out a cheer.

"I wonder if you realize how many people you're gonna get killed?" Chitown asked.

"I have more pertinent questions, my friend. How long shall we starve amid plenty, and be called Babtu, native, or black stinking kaffir in our own fatherland. How long shall we rot physically, spiritually and morally in the squalor of Windermere, the Sahara Desert and Nyanga West? How long shall we be a rightless, voteless, voiceless eleven million in our own fatherland? Yes many ... maybe all will be killed; if that is the case, so be it. You see my friend, apartheid offers *us* only two unpleasant choices ... fast or slow death."

Chitown wondered how he could call him friend, after being put in some shit like this, but sensed a sudden admiration for the thin, bald African.

222

"You must have some sort of plan."

"Yes! Plain and simple." Nxaumalo put out his cigarette. "Kill until we are killed. It is past time for the oppressive, white-man-boss to learn we will not forever be enslaved by his calvinistic doctrine of white supremacy; that many of us are gong to be free, or die trying."

"I can dig it." Chitown said, "because of just what little I've seen, I know it's hard to find another way."

"Perhaps, my friend, fate has sent you as an eyewitness to the never ending misery we endure under this sick society. If you can help spread the word to the outside world, I am sure decent people will become concerned."

"I think you are right," Chitown said, "and especially black people. If I'm a *living* eyewitness, I'll tell just as many as I can."

"The element of surprise will get you free," Nxaumalo smiled, "nothing is farther from their minds than the thought of *us* attacking *them*. The only major obstacles are three armored cars. But hopefully we will find weapons among their dead to fight them with. The other five are scattered outside the distant fences, with jeeps carrying bully-boys from Johannesburg waiting to start their hideous sweep through Nanga, clubbing and whipping."

Got Damn! Chitown thought, *three armored cars could raise havoc.* "I know how to fight the frogs," he said.

The Africans looked at each other, then back at him with dumbfounded expressions.

"Molotov Cocktails! I'll show you how to make them," he said.

"What do we need?" Nxaumalo prompted.

"Empty bottles, petro and rags. Something you said earlier gave me the idea. Fight fire with fire!"

Chapter Twenty Five

"COME WITH us!" Nxaumalo led them into the front room and started barking orders in Zulu. It was only a matter of minutes before two lamps, a pint bottle, and a dirty pillow case sat on a card table in the middle of the floor. They cleared a path through the whispers and mumbles. Nxaumalo told everyone else to stand back.

Chitown took the cloth and carefully removed the globe and wick holder from the lamp with the most oil. Silence prevailed as the Africans watched intensely. He poured it slowly into the bottle, not spilling a drop, until it was nearly full, then sat it down and ripped the pillow case into strips.

I sho' hope the hell I'm doing this right. "Come on outside," he said after it was finished, "I'll show you how it works." Another path was cleared and all twenty Africans followed him out into the yard.

"Now stand back everybody!" he tilted the bottle, soaking the cloth sticking out of the neck, and reached for his cigarette lighter. After igniting the cloth, he threw the bottle thirty feet down wind. A large puff of bright orange flame sprang from where it landed and lit up the faces of the cheering Africans. Nxaumalo quickly restored silence,

224

ordered the fire smothered, and rushed Chitown back into the house. Except for the few having a rough time extinguishing the fire, they all followed, whispering their amazement.

"You have given us exactly what we need most!" Nxaumalo shook his hand warmly and motioned him to a large soft chair in the corner of the room. "I am surprised to learn you have use for such things in America."

"Not yet." Chitown took the seat and tried not to show pain from the back wound he aggravated when he threw the bottle. "At the present, Martin Luther King is having some success with non-violence, but who knows. Molotov cocktails' been around since the Russian revolution. I'm surprised you guys didn't know about 'em."

"The government has always taken great effort to keep us from learning such things." He gave Chitown a cigarette and lit it for him. "They decide what we read and hear. The only movies we are allowed to see are made for twelve year olds."

When everyone was back inside, the leader told them to gather around.

"I want you to leave in small groups . . . quietly, at three minute intervals. I want all of the petro and empty bottles you can find, as promptly as possible."

The first three left immediately while others selected partners. Nxaumalo signaled for Chitown and the three lieutenants to come into the kitchen. The door was closed, and they all sat at the table.

"You seem to be in pain my friend. Are your wounds bothering you?"

"Not much!" Chitown played it down.

"I speak for all of us by expressing gratitude for the simple, but magnificent weapon you have given us."

The others offered their hands, along with smiles of admiration. Nxaumalo gave him back his Seaman's Document.

"In payment, we will get you and your friend to that car." He unbuttoned his shirt and pulled out a large piece of white paper.

225

"Your firebomb has caused me to change the original plan." He unfolded and spread the paper on the table. "This is a drawing of town with markings where the frogs, troops, and police are deployed. Now that we can attack the frogs directly, the people will be even more inclined to follow us." Using his pencil as a pointer and marker, he revealed a bold, ambitious new offense that not only called for destruction of the main force, but ambushing the bully-boys on their murderous mission through Nanga. He asked Chitown's opinion.

"I don't know, do you think the people will go that far?"

"Not all, but many. They will have no choice. From the time that first bomb is thrown, it will be a matter of life and death. How many bombs would you say a man could carry inconspicuously?"

Chitown scratched his head. "Not many, two . . . maybe three at the most, depending on the size of the bottles, and the kind of clothes he wear. They should work in pairs, one guy light the other guy's bomb, and vice versa. The lighter will have two hands to work with, and the thrower can keep his eye on the target. Etobi should be with me, so we can reach the car at the same time."

The Africans agreed.

"And tell your men to have good cigarette lighters full of flint and fluid. They don't wanna be fumbling around with matches."

"Very good indeed!" Nxaumalo outlined the second part of his plan. The women would be the supply line. They would wait at the rear of the crowd, hiding bombs in hand baskets and under long dresses, until the main force is over-run, then come forward. The men, armed with seized weapons, and more firebombs, would divide everyone they could into guerrilla bands and intercept the bully-boys."

I'm sure glad I don't fit into that part of the plan, Chitown thought as he rubbed his now aching shoulder wound.

"Come with me, my friend," Nxaumalo got up and motioned. "We watched you closely and know how to make

226

the firebombs," he said as Chitown followed him back to that first bedroom, "so why don't you try and relax for awhile. I can see you are in pain. The women are preparing a meal. Soon there will be someone to tend your wounds, and give you food and drink."

"Thank you!" Chitown opened the door, then paused.

"Tell me one more thing. If the people decide to go to work, and everything's peaceful, are you still going to attack the whites, just because you've got that firebomb?"

"Definitely not!" Nxaumalo shook his head. "We will be peaceful as long as they are. But do not expect, or even hope for miracles, my friend; it is their nature to react violently. They have the fierce weapons and expect no resistance. Tomorrow, however, violence will beget violence!"

"When Etobi returns, tell him I want to see him."

"Very well, now get some rest," Nxaumalo smiled and returned to the kitchen.

Chitown removed his jacket, folded it for a pillow, then took off his shoes. He eased down onto the bed wishing in a way he had chosen to dig that hole. *Nxaumalo's shit might look good on paper,* he thought, *but those Spoilers are headed for a lot more than they can handle.* It wasn't only pride that made him decide to go with them. It was Reba, Ihetu, Etobi and Anya. Whatever chance he had of ever getting home, he owed to them. He thought of the risk they had taken to save his life and keep him hid. Then there was old man Silombela whose companionship was so comforting those last frightful days when being alone would have cracked him up. If he had to die, he thanked them for the chance to die for something, not being murdered in a stinking alley for following a stinking bitch. He took the weapon Nxaumalo had returned, put it under his jacket, got up and turned off the light. He tried to catch a nap, but all of his hidden fears emerged in the darkness with the pain of his weary body: The fear of never seeing Jean's face again: Never hearing her laugh or feeling her body next to his.

227

My God! ... he prayed, I don't want to die ... I'm only twenty six years old.

Three loud knocks stiffened him until a female voice called out.

"Reba?" his heart pounded as he jumped up and opened the door.

"No!" smiled a dark, full-featured woman, shapely wrapped in a floor length dress and a tight head scarf. She held a tray of hot chicken curry and a bottle of Tshwala beer.

"Come in!" He hid his disappointment, turned on the light, picked up the little table and carried it to the bed.

"I will go for something to treat your wounds." She sat the tray down and started for the door.

"That's alright," he said. "I'm okay. The food will be just fine."

She stopped, gave a puzzled look, then came back and sat beside him as he stirred the curry with a fork to cool it. His stomach ached and growled because he had not eaten all day.

"Are you sure you do not want me to treat your wounds?"

He shook his head no, and dug into the food.

"I saw your bomb burning in the yard. It is very good for us that you came along."

"Maybe for you, but not for me." He washed down a mouth full of food with two swallows of beer and belched.

"Excuse me!"

"Nxaumalo told me to make you as comfortable as possible." She touched his arm and smiled again. "Is there anything else you want?"

He took a long second look, wondering how she meant that, but his mind was too preoccupied to give it much thought.

"I only want to eat, then try and get some sleep." He hoped she wouldn't be offended.

"Very well." She looked him up and down and waited patiently until he finished, then took the tray, leaving him the rest of the beer. "My name is Cammara. If there is anything else you want, I will be happy to serve you."

He thanked her, smiled and opened the door. The light remained on as he sat sipping beer and listening to the sounds of the Africans returning with empty bottles, petro, and women.

Soon there was another knock. Etobi entered, the sorrow in his face replaced by excitement about the bomb. Chitown explained the Spoiler's plan, plus one of his own. They would stay back far enough to avoid the first assault and would concentrate their bombs on the foot soldiers, take their weapons and break into the clear.

"I sure hope Reba makes it," he sighed, "or we're gonna have to take a jeep."

"She will be there ... you will see ... By tomorrow's end," Etobi slapped him on the knee, "you will be headed back to your country!"

"Hey! ... What about you?" Chitown touched him on the shoulder. "I gave Reba enough to get all three of you out of South Africa. If it's just to the nearest border."

"Ihetu and Reba perhaps ... I am not going."

"What? ... man you gotta be joking!"

"No, Wilbur, tonight I have learned why the Spoilers stopped mugging, beating and robbing their own people. When Nxaumalo became leader, he made them realize how much they aided the government's overall plan of genocide. Instead, he began building a force to buffer our people against the oppressors ... to fight ... and even die when the time was right. The time is tomorrow, and with the new weapon, we shall teach the ghost a lesson they will not soon forget!"

"Look, Etobi, don't get carried away. Those firebombs can only do so much, until the surprise is over. Then that honkey's gonna throw everything he's got at you ... tanks, planes ... everything! Our only chance is to get away while we got 'em by the ass ... don't you want to see Anya again?"

"There is nothing in the world that could make me more happy." He started pacing the floor, holding the handle of the knife in his belt. But I have made a solemn oath to avenge Silombela, her parents and mine."

"Look, man, I figure we gonna have to kill a lot of grays to get to that car. You'll have your revenge. It would be stupid to go back. Maybe by tomorrow's end you will be on your way to Anya. And as a man worthy of her, one who has repaid your tormentors."

Etobi shook his head in agreement, then said, "If all goes well, some day I will repay you."

"Forget it. Have you eaten?"

"No, have you?"

"Yeah, now I'm gonna try an' sleep."

"Good, and do not worry, things will work out. I will eat now, then help with the bombs." Etobi turned off the light and left.

Chitown finished his beer and eased down on the bed. For a long time he lay in limbo, smelling gasoline and listening to the growing voices, until the roll of drums brought an eerie silence that shook him from his trance. A loud, deep voice began reciting an old Zulu poem. "Thou who art great as the mountains ... cleaver of the heads of enemies ... "

"Bayete! ... Bayete!" the crowd responded.

"Thou whose wounds emit gunsmoke!" the voice continued, "thou of the elephant ... thou who art black ... Bayete! Bayete!"

"All hail ... all hail ... " the crowd roared and started a slow, mournful hum to a single drumbeat, accelerating the shuffling feet into dancing feet as the lamenting voices began to sing and shout. More drummers joined the fastening pace that became so torrid Chitown could no longer resist.

He got up, went to the door and cracked it open. The floor was filled with perspiring dancers, while others lined the walls, chanting, clapping and drinking. The four drummers took turns pausing to refresh, as laughing women refilled their cups with beer. They beat faster and faster; the sweat poured from their bodies. The chanting grew louder as the people against the walls started edging onto the floor with their own individual or tribal dances. Chi-town closed the door and returned to bed.

He couldn't understand why they were dancing and drinking instead of preserving their strength for tomor-row's supreme task. The drums pulsated to a furious, frightening pace, and soon he got their dreadful message.

Why sleep or worry! ... Tomorrow you may sleep for-ever ... And your worries will be over!

He got up, went to the door, and called for the woman.

Chapter Twenty Six

RINCO PARKED the car at the end of the long pissy-smelling gangway that led to the entrance of the Pot O' Gold. Behind half drawn curtains of the adjacent buildings whole Indian families sat watching the loud-talking, booze-drinking Africans and Americans who filled the narrow rear balcony. He could hear the jukebox blasting as he climbed the stairs and walked into the ballroom.

The floor was packed with blacks, Malayans, Arabs and whites from the *Mitchell* and a Norwegian vessel in port but no one was dancing. He eased his way to the edge of the crowd to see what was happening.

They were gathered around a stocky young girl with tiny lines carved in her dark face who was dancing the twist with a quart of wine on her almost hairless head. She jerked her arms and shoulders and twisted in every direction to the hasty beat of the music, but the bottle never wavered from its upright position, as the flashbulbs began to pop.

The louder the crowd applauded, the wilder she danced. With her arms spread out beside her, she wiggled her hips and shoulders while squatting until her buttock almost touched the floor, then sprang up again. Her audience showed their approval with stomps, claps, shouts and whistles.

With sweat pouring down her face and spotting her pale-blue dress, the girl covered all of the space allotted her by the cheering crowd. When the record ended she was almost exhausted. Rinco hurried to the bar and found an empty stool.

"'Bout time you dropped by," Big Shot grinned from behind the counter. "How you want it? Soda, or on the rocks?"

"Soda!"

Big Shot mixed a drink that was mostly Scotch. "On the house, dude!"

Rinco took a sip and frowned. "Look, can you spare a few minutes? It's important," he glanced around, "and concerns Chitown!"

"Damn right!" Big Shot called a waitress to take over and adjusted his apron. He poured himself a drink and joined Rinco at a small, isolated table far from the jukebox.

"Now dude, what's this all about?"

"I met a woman Sunday night who escaped from South Africa."

"So ... what's that got to do with Chitown?"

"She saved his life. Some Skullys cut him up, the night you left him at the Zambesi."

"Now wait a min ... "

"Forget about that!" Rinco interrupted, "what's done is done. We've got to find a way to help him."

Big Shot took a stiff drink, then cleared his throat.

"Let me get this straight. Just how did this chick save Chitown's life?"

Rinco sipped on his drink to keep from getting impatient.

"She's a nurse. She patched him up at her girlfriend's house in Sea Point."

"Then she came all the way to Dar es Salaam to tell you, huh?"

"Hell no, man, she was wanted by the police for political reasons! Now let's stop playing silly games. Chitown's probably still at Sea Point, afraid to turn himself in because he killed one of those son-of-a-bitches!"

"No shit!" Big Shot's eyes bucked. "You mean he dusted a du-flamy?"

"Damn right! Four of them tried to waste *him*."

"Four! How the hell he manage to get away?"

"That's not important, we've got to figure out some way to help him."

"You right, dude, but what the hell can we do for him here?" Big Shot finished his drink. "Be right back." He went to the bar and got a half-full bottle.

"Who all know 'bout this?" He poured them another drink.

"Just you and I, and I think we should keep it cool until the purser gets back from that safari. He may know the right way to handle this."

"Don't even tell *him* 'bout the dead motherfucker!"

"Hell no, the less anybody know about that, the better! I went to the Embassy this morning, for the second time in two days, but the damn Counsel was playing golf at the Country Club, so I asked a stooge if they had received any word about a Mitchell seaman missing in Capetown. No soap!"

"Damn!" Big Shot lit a cigarette and glanced around at the crowd. "The ole man wired Capetown and New York the first night out, so something tells me all you gonna get from the Counsel is a lot of red tape and bull-shit."

"Chitown told Anya he wanted me to go see the Counsel, but I got my doubts too." Rinco took a drink and pulled out a cigar. "I sure don't trust that one in Capetown."

"I'm hip!" Big Shot lit it for him, "not after what happened at the airport. You know what I think?"

"What?"

"If the cops ain't got him, he's laying right in Sea Point waitin' till we get back."

234

"How do you figure?"

"It's his best bet, dude. The broad must dig him, she ain't gonna turn him in. The way the vaps an' engine room got fucked up in that storm, he know we comin' back to Capetown before crossin' the deep six. Who was the broad anyway? The singer?"

"Yeah!"

"I thought so."

They looked at each other, clicked their glasses and turned them up.

"You say this chick Anya wrote a letter?"

"That's right."

"Mellow! She should get an answer before the ship leave. If the Americans get him, cool. But if them South Africans got him, we tell everybody, the crew, the Counsel, the newspapers, an' then raise enough hell to light a fire under *somebody's* ass. If he still there when the ship pull in, we get as many dudes as we can an' go after him."

Rinco thought for a moment.

"That's the best we can do I guess, because otherwise we would have to tell where he is; and if he's caught at Reba's, she's in trouble too."

"Leave it to me to come up with the right answers dude," Big Shot winked.

"It's always amazing when you can think of something else beside money and women."

"I was jus' thinkin' 'bout Janet. Sho' figured Chitown was gonna split with her."

"You're something else," Rinco shook his head, "but you've helped take a load off my mind."

"Hey, baby!" Brother Poe shouted as he, Johnson and the half-Arab girls walked up and joined them. He slapped Big Shot's open palm and asked, "How you making out with Krishan?" before getting two chairs for the girls.

"He must be doing all right," Johnson said. "I see she got a apron tied around his ass."

"That's right dude," Big Shot bragged, "but you can bet I ain't bustin' my balls for nothing. I'm gonna wrap up that hoe, her tough ride an' boss pad. An' man, you should dig her pad. She live in one of them modern high-rises with wall to wall carpeting and air conditioners in every room. She got a plush couch the length of a whole wall, a big hi-fi record player an' a boss Zebra skin marble top wet bar. An' baby, you should dig the bedroom!" He kissed his fingertips. "An' she sho' know how to take you to joyland when you get there!"

"She's got enough experience." Rinco welcomed a chance to cut him off.

"Maybe so, baby, but now she dealing with the Shot, I got plans for her ass."

"An' we gonna buy the bitch out after the war!" Brother Poe added.

Rinco burst out laughing.

"That's right!" Johnson pulled out a hash pipe. "First we're going to rent the whole top floor; two rooms for gambling and the other five for tricking. And the way these gray dudes dig these black broads, our bread should turn over fast."

Rinco laughed again, longer and louder.

"What the fuck so funny?" Brother Poe asked. "You the one preaching all this stay-in-Africa shit."

"I know." Rinco finished his drink. And I can just see Krishan letting you jive cats beat her out of this gold mine. But what really gets me, is how the hell you figure the government's going to let you dudes operate a whore house and gambling den?"

"Bread, baby! That's how!" Brother Poe snorted. "That good ole American green is a bitch. We can buy off a few cops till we make enough to turn legit."

"Dig, man," Johnson said, "we're not going to hustle off Africans, just seamen. Besides, Dar es Salaam isn't any different from anyplace else. The people in power want that dough. And big Jambo's gonna bullshit little Jambo."

"Nevertheless," Rinco said, "Africa needs people who can build, teach and farm; people with some kind of trade or knowledge that can help a nation develop. They've got enough imps and pimps of their own."

"How the hell you know so much 'bout what Africa need?" Brother Poe snapped, "Jambo need all kind a hustlers 'ta keep that funky-ass Indian from soppin' up all the gravy. An' who the fuck you 'spose ta be anyway? Marcus Garvey or some motherfucker?" He slapped Johnson and Big Shot's palms and the three of them laughed. The two girls looked at each other, then felt they should laugh also. Rinco lit a cigar to hide his anger and blew smoke toward the ceiling until they finished laughing.

"I don't give a damn who you are," he pointed the cigar at them, "where you are or what you think, but as long as you're black you better hope Africa gets over. Because what happens here is going to affect you and your children's lives in one way or another. Man, it's a brand new day. If you weren't blind you could see, hear and feel it all around. These people are finally shedding Mr. Charlie's yoke and you dudes still trying to be little black hunkies."

"Well you can say what you want," Brother Poe countered, "but I'm glad the hunkies took my ancestors away from here or I might be out there dancing 'round pots with the rest of them dumb motherfuckers! An' I don't give a wet-dream what Africa do. I'm jus' gonna hang here an' make this bread. When I get back to the Apple, I'm gonna get me a new Hog, a three-grand wardrobe, a penthouse apartment in upper Manhattan, an' be a stone freak!" He held out both palms and got them slapped by Johnson and Big Shot. Johnson sensed Rinco's anger and quickly changed the subject.

"Say, man, where's that boss chick you left the Rooftop with Sunday night?"

"You mean the nu ... " Big Shot caught himself and winked at Rinco. "You didn't tell me all-that!"

The thought of Anya mellowed Rinco.

"No, I didn't," he said. "She's the most beautiful woman I've ever known, a real African Queen."

"She must be black," Big Shot said.

"Black enough!" Rinco agreed. He wanted to leave but Big Shot told them all to sit while he stopped a waitress

237

and ordered a fifth of Scotch, a quart of soda and four more glasses. Johnson and Brother Poe lit up their ready packed pipes. The Afro-Arab girls grew tired of talk they couldn't understand and accepted offers to dance.

"Why you in such a hurry?" Big Shot asked Rinco. Going to get that fox? Why don't you bring her by?"

"Yeah!" Johnson seconded, "and introduce us. What's the broad's name?"

"Her name's Anya." Rinco didn't like the word broad. "She's a nurse and a lady! She works and goes to school, so she'll be busy the next few days."

"Well, you better hurry up and cop baby," Johnson said. "The *Ghost*'s loaded with those Hindus, so we'll be leaving on time."

"He probably done copped already." Brother Poe handed Big Shot his pipe. "'Cause we dug him puttin' her 'round yesterday in his little beep-beep!"

Big Shot noticed Rinco doing a slow burn and tried to lighten the conversation.

"What!" he said, "you rented a ride . . . what kind?"

"A Volkswagen."

"Come on, dude." Big Shot bucked his eyes. "You Big Shot Sonny Collin's roommate. Don't tell me you chauffeur yo' main squeeze 'round in a little funky-ass bug. Didn't they have no Hogs or Mercedes?" He held out his palms for Johnson and Brother Poe to slap.

Rinco refused Johnson's pipe and took a stiff drink to keep from losing his temper.

"I not only rented a car," he said, "I took leave until the ship gets underway. I'm going to spend every minute I can with her, not to cop, but because she means that much to me. So I wish you cats would quit this fucking yapping!"

"Man I gotta dig this chick," Big Shot took another long pull on the pipe.

"She's sure boss," Johnson said.

"Go on, get the bitch an' bring her back," Brother Poe snapped, "we ain't gonna eat her up . . . not here in front of you anyway." He laughed. Rinco was getting ready to knock the hell out of him, but everyone was distracted by a loud commotion three tables down, where a flashbulb had gone off.

"I told you not to do that, you son-of-a-bitch!" Smitty jumped up from the table where he and another white crewman sat with two African girls.

"Wait until your old lady see this," the other sailor started to laugh, but Smitty punched him in the mouth with a round-house right that sent him and his camera sliding across the floor. Smitty pounced on him and starting throwing lefts and rights into his face as the crowd gawked.

Suddenly, the seven-foot Watusi bouncer appeared, towering over the customers in a long dark green robe. He lifted Smitty first, then the victim, and held them at arms' length by their collars.

"That dirty son-of-a-bitch!" Smitty yelled, "he took a picture of me kissing a girl and was going to send it to my wife!"

Those in ear shot roared with laughter.

"Gee, I was only kidding buddy!" the other sailor pleaded.

"You're a goddamn liar!" Smitty tried to reach him as the bouncer cussed them both in Swahili. He let them go and pointed to the door. When the other sailor stopped to retrieve his camera, Smitty kicked him in the rump, and he scrambled toward the door. Smitty started stomping the camera.

This infuriated the bouncer, who shoved him to the exit, shouting cuss words.

"You know that Swahili shit dude." Big Shot said, "What was my man saying to them cats?"

"The best I could figure," Rinco hunched his shoulders, "he threatened to put a foot in their ass!"

Brother Poe laughed so hard he almost choked. "Did you see the foot on that motherfucker, Jack!"

From the rear balcony came the sound of breaking glass followed by the loud crash of a window pane.

The customers on the porch had grown tired of the Indians peeping at them, and had tried to scare them from their windows by throwing empty beer bottles against the walls. But Party-Time, drunk enough to see double, threw a bulls-eye right into a kitchen window. The crowd stampeded straight into the bar room, knocking down dancers and setting off a vicious free-for-all.

Rinco used a small chair as a shield against swinging fists, flying bottles and glasses until he eased his way to the door.

While descending the long narrow stairway, where the scent of Lysol battled the odor of musk and urine, he knew the last place he'd ever take Anya would be the Pot O' Gold.

Chapter Twenty Seven

BY SEVEN o'clock on the chilling gray morning, over two thousand Africans had gathered near the main gate of the shantytown, with hundreds more merging. Among them came the Spoilers, concealing Molotov Cocktails, knives and short spears.

The female supply line, wearing long dresses and carrying big baskets, stopped in front of the burned out church to hide their oil-filled bottles, as the men paired off, spread out and moved forward.

At the head of the crowd, an African National Congress speaker was being shouted down by the more numerous Pan-Africanists. Soon their spokesman took the rostrum. He yelled the Pan-Africanist creed despite the sound of the white forces' clicking weapons and starting motors outside the compound. The crowd repeated after him.

"Government of the African ... by the African ... for the African ... owing it's allegiance to Africa ... and to accept the rule of the African Majority!"

As pre-planned, the Spoilers stopped about twenty yards from the front of the loud angry crowd, and waited to see how the whites would deploy.

Chitown and Etobi strained their eyes, looking beyond the fence and between a long line of empty buses ready to take workers into Capetown, but didn't see Ihetu's car.

Three armored vehicles rambled through the gate, spread out and rolled up to the edge of the crowd. Then came four trucks filled with heavily armed soldiers and attack dogs, followed by a jeep of officers who stopped at the platform. A big, round, red-faced Colonel jumped out and ordered the African to come down from the rostrum.

"What is the meaning of this?" the Colonel demanded, pulling his pistol.

"It is only a peaceful demonstration, sir!" the African answered.

"Demonstration for what?"

"For our God-given rights as human beings."

The Colonel grabbed him by the collar with his free hand and shouted, "Don't you fools know that Emergency Regulations have been imposed!"

A hush fell over the crowd as the Spoilers moved in closer. The rhythmical chant of "Our Land! ... Our Land ... " grew louder and louder as more Africans took it up.

Chitown glanced around to check the size of the crowd. It now numbered nearly three thousand, including women and children. But any comfort he derived was offset by the police erecting a barricade just outside the gate.

The other officers jumped from the jeep, ordered their soldiers out of the trucks and told them to fix bayonets. Chitown felt his slim hope for a peaceful settlement fastly vanishing.

"Are you their leader?" the Colonel scolded the African speaker.

"No sir, only a spokesman." He turned and waved to the crowd.

"Face me when I talk, you knotty-head bastard!" The soldier snatched him around. "As of this moment you are under arrest for inciting peaceful blacks to break the law. You will give the names of your fellow agitators. But first ... " he signaled to the jeep. Another officer turned on the

242

loud-speaker and handed him the microphone. The Colonel passed the mike to the African.

"You kiffirs have ten minutes to get started for work, or I promise blood will flow ... beginning with yours!"

"Listen to me, my people!" the Pan-Africanist's voice echoed through the noisy throng. "This officer says we are breaking the law!"

"Arrest us! ... Arrest us! ... " came loud shouts followed by loud laughter.

"They gave us ten minutes to get on a bus."

"Nine minutes, kiffir!" the white man snapped, "or suffer the consequences."

"We are breaking the law whenever we object to the indescribable injustice heaped upon us."

The crowd let out a roar.

"Or seek enough wages to hold our families together, and keep our children from dying ... " The angry red-faced Colonel snatched the microphone.

"Please! ... Please!" shouted the Nationalist's speaker, "I will get them to work!"

"Wait!" the soldier told him, then addressed the crowd.

"You people have ten more minutes to decide your fate. My orders are to make you start for work now, or beg to work later. And I shall carry out my orders regardless of the force I must use. And I shall defend my country to my death." He then gave the mike to the African.

"My friends!" the Si-tron magnified a trembling voice, "please go to your places of employment. Our blood is to precious to be wasted ... no matter how noble the cause!"

The crowd reacted unfavorably, and the Spoilers began reaching for their bottles.

"I know our road is hard and our burden heavy. But we must seek other ways to voice our grievances!"

Another Pan-Africanist grabbed the mike and shouted. "No matter how mildly our grievances are voiced, we will be breaking the law. Send your women and children home, and let us bare up to whatever follows. Hell below could be little worse than the hell we live in now!"

243

"You asked for hell!" the Colonel hit him over the head with the pistol knocking him to his knees, then ordered the troops to prepare for a baton charge. The dogs were released, and they tore into the Africans biting and ripping. But soon they ran into the knives and spears of the Spoilers, and their growling snarls became final yaps.

Nxaumalo's tin whistle signaled the rest of the gang into action, as he threw the first bomb. It landed in front of the Colonel, exploding him into a screaming ball of flame. The deadly torrents of the armored cars swept the crowd, sending unarmed blacks scattering and falling in all directions under a hail of bullets. Then they roared full speed into the retreating mass, tearing skin, shattering bones and snuffing screams beneath their wheels. Behind them came the yelling soldiers, shooting, stabbing and beating.

The Spoilers retaliated with arching streaks of fire, that stopped the frogs in their bloody tracks, turning them into blazing coffins.

Inspired by the burning frogs, the Africans took the offensive. They charged back over their dead and wounded into bayonets, rifle butts and point blank gunfire. Automatic firepower permitted the vastly outnumbered troops to begin an orderly withdrawal, but those unlucky enough to be caught were hacked, stabbed, or stomped into ghastly pulps. The buses took off in full speed, leaving thick clouds of dust.

Etobi and Chitown started the next barrage of fire bombs that turned the orderly retreat into fiery panic, then rushed to search for abandoned weapons as the Africans overran the barricade.

In response to urgent radio calls, soldiers and police in neighboring positions rushed to meet the spearhead of the frightening black horde, while the more distant armor and jeeps rambled through the streets of Nanga, closing in on the crowd from different directions and shooting at every African they saw.

A helicopter buzzed angrily overhead as it alerted the Air Force. American made Sabre jets with napalm under their wings began warming up. *To teach those black bastards how to play with fire!*

When the first reinforcements arrived, they were greeted by fire bombs and captured weapons. The Commander deployed his troops in a wide circle with orders to hold the blacks until the armor arrived at their unarmed flanks. *Then we shall box them in, and wipe out the stinking kaffirs!*

The Spoilers who were left received a fresh supply of bombs from the women, and Nxaumalo whistled for another attack. The whites were spread too thin and began another nervous retreat while firing frantically, fumbling to reload as the bloodthirsty blacks kept coming through a merciless barrage that heaped bodies upon bodies.

Chitown and Etobi crept close to the ground, rising at intervals to fire quick shots with captured pistols, then ducking back without checking results. Nxaumalo was in the act of throwing a flaming bottle when a hail of bullets tore him apart, spraying blood and fire. A woman's basket was hit, turning her body into a blistering torch that ignited other people. Etobi started to rise and fire again, but Chitown pulled him back down.

"You got any bombs left?"

Etobi shook his head.

"I've got one. Let's use it on that Command car."

They crawled a few feet closer whenever the enemy's firepower was concentrated elsewhere. When Chitown figured they were close enough, he took the bottle from under his coat. Etobi lit it and he threw. It landed on the hood of the car engulfing it in flame. The burning Frogs began exploding one by one, as the holding circle collapsed and combat became hand to hand. They fought ferociously, with gun-butts, knives, sticks, rocks and spears. They fought with feet that smashed faces and crushed groins, while hands gouged eyeballs and choked off life.

The Africans, by sheer numbers, quickly overwhelmed their adversaries, and chased after those trying to escape. But they started rejoicing prematurely, leaving the few surviving Spoilers saddled with the gigantic job of trying to organize them for upcoming battles.

Chitown's eyes were searching the road for Ihetu's car, and he didn't see the wounded policeman rise on one elbow and aim his pistol until the hot slug slapped him through the air. When he yelled, Etobi turned and administered a coup de grace to the cop with two close shots in the head.

"How bad does it feel?" Etobi kneeled beside Chitown, who squirmed and kicked in the dust. "Can you walk?"

"I don't know." Chitown gritted his teeth and squeezed his upper left arm, as the bright red blood poured through his trembling fingers.

"Stay here and play dead." Etobi reloaded his gun, and departed in search of Reba and Ihetu.

Chitown's numbness quickly wore off, and an unbearable pain shot through his whole body, making him gasp for breath. He no longer smelled the deathly air reeking with the sickening odor of gunsmoke, burning flesh and singed hair. No longer could he hear the sounds of war, or see the bloody ground around him, covered with mangled, mutilated and, ironically integrated, bodies.

Reba and Etobi ran ahead of Ihetu's car that slowly honked it's way through the noisy confused crowd. She dropped to her knees beside Chitown, and with tears in her eyes, tore a large piece from her clean white slip. When she removed his hand to stuff the rag into the gaping whole, he let out a scream and bit his lip until it also bled.

"I'm sorry," she placed his hand back afterward, "but we must try and control the bleeding!"

He nodded but could not speak.

"Oh Chitown!" she wept, "this is too much like the last time." She took a small bottle of brandy from her pocket and poured some in his mouth. He strangled and coughed it up.

When Ihetu finally reached them, Etobi signaled for help.

"Please be careful!" she said as Etobi and Ihetu lifted him gently and put him on the back seat. Ihetu rushed to the front and started the motor as Reba climbed in the back with Chitown, Etobi stayed out.

"Thanks to Wilbur, you two may have a chance at a new life. See that he gets aid as soon as possible."

"Don't be a fool!" Reba pleaded. "There is nothing but death here!"

"She's right Ihetu seconded. "Think of Anya!"

"Please!" Reba begged.

"No!" Etobi shook his head. "Anya knows there is no time in our lives for romance. She told me long ago that we should devote ourselves to the freedom of our people, and now I know she was right. Without freedom there is nothing but poverty, sickness, fear and death. I have pledged to see this battle through. Never again will I get a chance to kill so many whites. With Nxaumalo gone the Spoilers will need every man they can get. If I survive I will join you later. Please write Anya," he touched Reba's hand through the open window, "tell her about Silombela and what happened here today. She will understand why I chose not to leave. Tell her I love her, and may join her someday when the cause is won."

Again, the sound of heavy gunfire filled the air as the armor arrived at the unarmed rear of the Africans and began cutting them apart.

"Go! And good luck!" Etobi waved and ran back into the scattering crowd.

Ihetu eased back onto the open road and speeded up. "How bad is the young man?" he asked through the rear view mirror.

"Awful! . . . Please hurry!" Reba gave Chitown another drink, and took the scarf from her head to wipe his perspiring face. Then she twisted the scarf until it was as tight as a rope.

"What will we do if that bastard doesn't let him through the roadblock?" Ihetu asked.

"He's too big to fit in the trunk, but we must hide him as best we can." She tied the ends of the scarf together and asked Ihetu for something she could use to make a tourniquet.

"Good!" We should have thought of that sooner." he handed her a screwdriver from the glove compartment. "But I am still worried about that roadblock."

"If he's discovered I will think of something, or tell the truth and bare the blame. But I am going to get him to that American ship!"

Chitown screamed when she removed his sticky hand from the blood soaked rag just above the elbow, and made him grip the handle that held the tourniquet tight.

"You are losing too much blood," she quieted him. "I know the wound is bad, but how do you feel over-all?"

"It's bad Reba," he coughed. "I feel like hell. Sometime it feels numb, like there's no left side of me at all. Then it hurts all over my body!"

"Do you have your American Identification?"

"Yeah ... in my shoe!"

"Then do not worry. We will get you to that ship." She wiped his face again. "We are going to hide you now. Just remain still and silent. Everything will be fine."

Ihetu pulled the car off the road into the bush and got out. They eased Chitown to the floor and covered him with their coats. Then Reba sat in the front.

"Tragedy has followed that poor fellow from the time we met him," Ihetu said, as Reba's eyes began to fill with tears for Etobi.

"Yes," she sighed, "this is so much like that awful night in that alley. If he doesn't get medical aid soon, he will certainly die."

Ihetu stopped the car about fifteen yards in front of the blockade, and was approached by a big robust sergeant, while the other police stayed at the barrier.

"I told you not to go to Nanga!" he snapped, then motioned her to roll down the window. "Damn stinking kiffers want trouble do they!" He stuck his head in and looked around.

"Can we go?" she asked impatiently when he withdrew.

248

"I will say when you can go." He peeped in the rear window, saw the blood on the seat, and snatched open the door.

"Want to leave, eh!" He pulled the coat from Chitown, who lay on the floor shivering and mumbling incoherently, but still gripping the tourniquet.

"Who is this? . . . One of those intimidators?"

"No! . . . No!" she insisted.

"He is the man we went to Nanga for!" Ihetu spoke up. "He wanted to go to work, but was hit by a stray bullet."

"Shut up!" the sergeant barked. "You two are in a lot of trouble!"

"It is the truth!" Reba looked him sternly in the eye. "He must work because we are going to get married. He will be the father of my baby, the one I am carrying in my stomach right now. The baby who is going to look very . . . very white."

"Get out of the car," the sergeant grunted, then threw the coat back over Chitown. He motioned for Ihetu to also get out.

"I don't think that son-of-a-bitch is going to make it," he said as he pretended to search them. "But don't you ever dare mention anything to anyone about us." He glanced around at his men to make sure they were out of ear shot, then pointed his finger in Reba's face. "And never . . . ever relate your little bastard to me!"

After they both promised to keep his secret, he let them get in and signaled his men to raise the barrier.

"How did you think of that?" Ihetu laughed when they were out of sight.

"When I saw that fat swine walking toward us I thought of it. There is no way I would ever conceive his child." She climbed over the seat into the rear.

"Oh my God!" she gasped when she saw Chitown's face. He's delirious. He's going to die . . . I feel it!" She loosened the tourniquet for a few seconds.

"He will make it now," Ihetu tried to assure her, "the last obstacle is out of the way."

Chitown felt himself drowning in a misty, blue-gray haze of pain, grief and fear. The speeding car hit a bump, and his whole aching body trembled. Suddenly he is riding a Greyhound bus from New York to Chicago. They pass through Jackson Park on a clear bright sunny day, and the driver asks, "If anyone wants to get off at 63rd?"

"I'll take 63rd!" he shouts.

Reba wiped his face again, but this time she saw no pain. He is running up the long iron stairs to the Stony Island "L" platform with his bags in his hand. His breath comes in heaping gasps, as the train passes the four stations before 59th street, then gets even shorter as he runs the half block to his house, and up one flight of stairs.

"I told you I would make it, baby! ... Didn't I?" He smiles into Jean's glowing face.

Then everything darkened to the thunderous roar of jets overhead.

Chapter Twenty Eight

ANYA WAS feeling downhearted, but since she had promised Rinco to go out with him, she gave a last glance around the small tidy room and left. She hurried down the long narrow path and, just as the last time, he was waiting near the gate. And as always, so was that long dusty line of black patients waiting to be served.

"Hello, beautiful," he greeted her with a kiss and hug. But he quickly realized she was in a somber mood and didn't say another word until after they had pulled off slowly to keep down the dust.

"Did you find out anything about Capetown?"

"Very little," she said. "Only that the Pan-Africanists may strike. And there was a bloody baton charge in Nanga."

"Damn!" he grunted. "I'm very sorry to hear that."

"However," it seemed hard for her to continue, "after you called this morning, I received a more alarming letter from Reba. Chitown is in Nanga with my friend Etobi."

Rinco was so stunned he had to pull off on the side of the road.

"Silombela," she said, "the old man who raised Etobi, was killed in that baton charge. She learned about it by phone, then wrote me. She said that she and Ihetu would drive out and try to rescue Chitown and Etobi before any more conflict. Now I am worried about everyone involved."

They sat staring straight ahead, each wrestling with the problem, for nearly five minutes. He half-wished he hadn't brought up South Africa. But, really, there was no way around it. Apartheid hung over them like a dark, menacing cloud. In a way, Anya welcomed the silence to gather her thoughts and fight anxiety.

Perhaps if she helped him, he told himself, he could indeed temporarily shut out the agonizing plight of her people, and drive some of the misery from her heart. Therefore, when she spoke, he merely asked: "Have you eaten yet?"

She shook her head, no. "But I would like to do a little shopping before the stores close."

"Anything you say, lovely, is fine with me." He started the car and speeded down the road.

"Rinco," she reached over and touched his shoulder, "thank you for making these days less difficult for me."

"The pleasure's all mine!"

He parked the car near his hotel and they strolled hand-in-hand down Independence Avenue. He felt ten feet tall, as heads turned and eyes followed his gorgeous companion in her brown dress, just a shade lighter than her smooth spotless skin, clinging to her luscious figure. Even the policeman, directing traffic from a barber-striped stand in the middle of the street, watched her for nearly a block.

They went into a woman's clothing store, and while she was busy selecting lingerie, he asked an Indian saleslady to guess her size, and sneakily purchased a swimsuit.

"What is in the package?" Anya asked after they left the store. She couldn't help but laugh when he told her. Then he asked her if she liked to swim.

"Oh yes! I love the water."

"Good, after dinner we'll take a refreshing dip while the air is still warm."

252

"That sounds great." She smiled as they crossed the street and headed toward the hotel. "I haven't been swimming in a very long time."

They climbed the short stairs to the porch and took a small table overlooking the main street.

"The food here is really nice," he said as the waiter gave them a menu.

"I'll have the same as you," she said. He ordered prime rib, baked potato with sour cream, tossed salad, white wine and coffee.

"After we eat," he suggested, "you store your packages in my room. I have a private bath, so you can put on your swimsuit. It would be much more comfortable than changing at the beach house."

She agreed and as they dined, he tried to take her mind off South Africa by talking about his early childhood in Liberia.

First, he gave her a brief history on the three hundred ex-slave families who settled there after the American Civil War.

"They came with their chocolate-coated Christianity and assumed the role as masters. Now thirty thousand people subsidized by United States interest have risen to form an elite that regard the nation as their indisputable inheritance."

He then talked of times when his father would drive him from their luxurious home in Monrovia out to the remote villages where they were treated like royalty by people who had virtually nothing. But as he grew older and with his mother's help, he could clearly see the contempt in the eyes of the indigenous people who were bossed and taxed by the black bourgeois.

"The black bourgeois could not in any way be as cruel and ruthless as the foreigners who run my country." Her eyes were fixed straight ahead.

"No true human beings could be as cruel and ruthless as the animals who run your country," he agreed.

"Africa is many countries," she said, "with many different cultures and problems. The struggle will be long, hard and bitter, until we all are free."

He followed her gaze. Directly across the street, five loud-talking Mitchell crewmen with cameras had stopped four young Masai Warriors.

"I'll put an end to this." He got up when he realized his shipmates were bribing them, so they could take their pictures.

"Please Rinco ... no!" She grabbed his arm, "No please!"

He looked into her eyes and sat back down, but could not hide his embarrassment.

The Masai, though no longer fierce, was still a nomadic tribe. They lived on the milk and blood of their cattle, that determined wealth, and strongly resisted all outside influence. They were rarely seen in the cities, and always attracted attention with their long wooden staffs and loose-hanging robes.

The apparent leader in bright scarlet lit up the street, his garments clashing with those of the other three, who were dressed in black. Their braided hair was plastered in pale red clay, with one braid dangling a cloth ornament between their eyebrows. The tops of their ears were pierced with thin brass rings that hung down to the bottom of their long flopping earlobes.

When the cameras started clicking she began to frown.

"I can stop it," he said, but she shook her head, no.

"They're all new crewmen," he whispered as the waiter approached with more wine. After he left, Rinco continued. "Four of them I think I could talk to. But you see that little yellow peanut-headed one," he pointed, trying to make her laugh. "I may just have to fight him. It wouldn't be much of a fight, but then, how would it look?"

"Not very good," she sipped from her wine, "so let us ignore it." He patted her hand. "I know how you feel."

"It is not those people there," she tore her eyes from them. "It is the sight of cameras and tribal dress that make me vividly recall the day I learned to hate." He gave her hand a squeeze and she went on.

"My twelfth birthday was on a Sunday. My father could afford no present, so he took me to see the tribal dances performed by the miners on their day off. I was thrilled by the huge coliseum-like structure, even if we did have to sit on concrete in crowded bleachers on the sunny side. On the other side, the whites sat comfortably in the shade coddling their expensive cameras. I will never forget how the arena vibrated with African music while we waited for the dancers to appear: the throbbing drums, the mellow marimbas and the shrill flutes and tin whistles. There were scores of tribes represented among the dancers, who were all miners from throughout the union and many surrounding countries. They finally thundered onto the hard dirt floor. I was thrilled by the many traditional costumed dances and music."

"When my father directed me to the segregated washrooms, I passed close to the white section and saw them laughing and clicking away with their cameras. Then I saw the sign: THROWING MONEY, CIGARETTES, ET-CETERA, IS PROHIBITED."

She shivered as if suddenly swept by a cold wind.

"I hated all of those smug bastards. They were not in an open-air theatre watching an exhibition of folk culture, as we were. They were at a zoo ... and we were the exhibits. And the sign meant, DON'T FEED THE ANIMALS."

"Let's get away from here." He hurried his drink. She finished hers as he called for the waiter.

"How do you like your swimsuit?" he asked when she came out of the washroom fully dressed.

"Just a little tight, but very nice. It must have cost a small fortune."

"Naw!" he laughed. "Swimsuits don't cost that much. But it will be worth a fortune to see you in it."

"However," she said, "I must buy you a present in return. It is our custom."

"You are present enough!" he insisted, but to no avail. "Okay, I'll tell you what. You can buy a record, something we can both enjoy."

"What do Americans say?" she smiled, "It's a deal?"

"It's a deal," he winked, then got his swim trunks from his grip and went into the washroom to put them on.

Enroute to the record store they passed the five seamen who had taken pictures of the Masai.

"You damn Toms act like you've never seen Africans before!" Rinco shouted as he drove by.

"Motherfuck you, nigger!" the peanut-headed one shouted back.

Rinco wanted to get out and kick his ass, but in no way would he embarrass Anya. In the short time it took to reach the store he had pushed the incident from his mind. He was strictly in a romantic mood, and was very pleased when Anya picked a Nat Cole album.

Upon their arrival at the beach house, they found the entrance blocked by six gray-clad, short-pants policemen in long white socks. A fight had erupted inside. He heard Party-Time cursing, and decided to swim elsewhere.

He drove out to Msimbazi Bay, rented a small boat with an outboard motor, and paid the owner extra to help him load his gear. After starting the motor, he motioned Anya to sit on the back seat beside him. He slipped one arm around her and used the other one for steering.

"You know, Anya!" he said, as they sailed along a rough, stone and bush cluttered stretch of shoreline, "all those conflicting years of being torn between Liberia, which my mother doesn't like, and the American my father hated, I was searching for something."

"What were you searching for?"

"A place to really belong, I guess. I wasn't sure, not even after I returned to Africa as a man. There was too much chaos and confusion. But now my search has come to an end." He tightened his grip around her. "There is no place I'd rather by than here in Tanganyika, or maybe Kenya, where I can see the great potential of our people begin to grow and spread. I'd like to stay here after the war. There must be some way I can aid in the struggle. I wish you would stay in Dar es Salaam, because there is no one in the world I would rather be with than you."

256

She did not comment. Her thoughts were far away as she gazed up toward the glowing red sun beginning to fade in the west, sending wide orange beams dancing across the powder blue waters.

Rinco spotted a small isolated clearing on the beach, got in as close as he could, then cut off the motor. After stripping to his shirt and trunks, he jumped into the waist high water and she threw him the line. He tied his end to a stout bush, came back and carried her onto the dry sand. She waited and helped him by taking the blankets and camera, while he carried the phonograph, records and ice chest to a cozy spot under a long, leaning palm tree.

After placing the Jimmy Rushing album on the player, he took the top off the ice chest.

"What's in there?" she asked.

He pulled out a bottle of French champagne and two glasses wrapped in plastic. "And just in case we get hungry," he pulled out a bag containing four ripe mangos. "The best of two worlds!" he laughed.

"I think you are a little crazy," she joked as he popped the cork on the bottle.

"How would *you* act if this was one of the grand days of *your* life?" He poured them a glass and put the bottle back.

"Oh come now." She took a sip of wine and smiled at him. "Be serious."

"I am serious. Because after tomorrow, it will be a long, sad and lonely time before I see you again. My heart is going to ache every moment."

"No brooding," she said, "We must enjoy this day! Is it a deal?"

"It's a deal." He proposed a toast. "Here's to the Rooftop Garden, and the unforgettable moment you walked into my life."

She paused for a second, then drank with him. They laughed, talked and drank through the Rushing and a Dizzy Gillespie album, then prepared to go in the water.

When she peeled off her dress he was spellbound. His

257

eyes savored every inch of her resplendent brown body that wasn't hid under the pale green swimsuit.

She reached into her bag, got a little bottle of olive oil and began oiling her arms and legs. She almost had to put the bottle in his shaking hands when she asked him to do her back.

"Honest, baby," he sighed as he gently rubbed her smooth flesh, "you could be a movie star anywhere!" He felt her body shake and knew she was laughing, but it didn't stop him.

"That's what I said to myself the first time I saw you. The short time I've known you as been the most exciting of my life, but you still refuse to take me seriously."

"Your earnestness has long ceased to be doubted," she turned to face him, "but you are overly concerned."

He couldn't help but kiss her. For a few seconds she surrendered, then, as usual, she broke it off.

"I'll beat you in!" She leaped up from the blanket and ram for the waves. She was fast, and shoulder deep in the water before he caught her. She let out a laughing scream when he pushed her under. But when she didn't spring up he panicked, until he felt her hands on his ankles.

Before he knew it, he was upside down. When he righted himself and wiped the water from his face, he saw her swimming away. He stroked after her. She was a strong swimmer, and they were nearly a hundred yards out into the Bay when he went down, grabbed her legs and pulled her under. When he came up for air, she did the same to him.

They swam, chased, played and splashed each other for nearly an hour before he began to get winded and headed for shore. She caught up, splashed him again, then beat him back to the beach.

After they dried off, they ate mangos, drank more champagne and listened to Nat King Cole.

"I had no idea you could swim so good or run so fast," he said as he opened the second bottle.

"There was only two years between my brother and

me." That far-away look appeared again. "We were very close, and he taught me to be rough."

The loathsome thought of what happened in Sharpeville had risen again and he put his arm around her.

"No brooding . . . remember?"

"It's a deal." She tried to smile.

"To save Chitown, the way he was cut up, you must be one hell-of-a-good nurse. Tell me . . . how does it feel to be so attractive and have all those talents?"

She just shook her head and took a long slow drink.

The sun was now only a faint glow on the horizon, and a huge round fluorescent moon harbored over the still, silver water. It was getting dark fast, and he really wanted a picture of her in that bathing suit. But after what happened today, there was no way he would ask her to let him take one.

The wine, soft music and velvet voice of Nat Cole began to mellow her. She talked about Reba, Etobi, Ihetu and her brother, when they were kids in their village. She told him of the games they played and how much fun they had together, until their families were forced into a shantytown so the men could work the mines.

As she spoke he stared into her dark almond eyes and felt a relentless desire to possess and protect her forever.

At one time or another he had cared about other women. Some he even thought he loved, but he had never before experienced anything like this feeling for Anya. He realized his adult life had been filled with travel, and he was never in one place long enough for anything lasting to develop. With Anya it didn't matter. Time wasn't needed. He knew he loved her more than any woman he had ever met.

"It's getting cold," she suddenly began to shiver, then picked up her clothes and headed for the brush.

"I must get out of this wet suit."

While she was gone, he removed his trunks and put on everything but his shoes. When she came out he sensed her steps were kind of deliberate and hurried to assist her.

259

"Are you all right?"

"Sure . . . just a bit woozy. I can walk," she giggled when he swept her up in his arms and carried her back to the blankets.

"I don't want to take any chances." He sat her down and kneeled beside her. "Are you sure you're all right?"

"Of course, I'm just not very accustomed to drinking."

"Is there anything I can do?" he asked.

"I have some aspirin in my purse," she pointed.

He gave her the bag, apologized and filled an empty wine glass with ice water from the chest. She took two pills and he poured the rest of the water over a clean towel, squeezed it out and placed it on her forehead.

"Hold this," he said, then pulled out his knife and cut up another mango.

"Do you treat all of the women you date so nice?" she asked.

"Not nearly." He handed her a cool slice of melon. "But you're special to me. Nothing could please me more than to care for you."

She could feel how bad he wanted her. And until she met him, there had been a long time between moments of laughter. Even though happiness shared during this trying period in her life wasn't reason enough for her to sleep with him, she was worried that he was leaving tomorrow. It was very unlikely that she would ever see him again.

"Aw hell!" He jumped up as she bit into the fruit. "The tide's going out. We better head in before we're beached. Not that I would mind at all," he dropped back to his knees, "but it gets pretty chilly. How do you feel now?"

"I am all right, you will not have to carry me." She smiled and helped him get ready to leave.

The boat and car ride didn't make her feel any better, and by the time they reached the hotel she was a bit nauseous. He took her straight up to his room.

"Why don't you relax here for a moment while I get you something." He motioned her toward the big chair.

Before she could object, he had left.

When he returned with a pot of coffee, cream, sugar, tomato juice and Alka Seltzer, her package was open and she was in the shower. He sat the tray on the night table and put on a George Shearing album.

She came out of the bathroom wearing a plain blue cotton gown she had bought that afternoon, and a hotel towel wrapped around her head. To him, they were Paris creations worn by a high-fashion model.

"I sure hope you are feeling better," he had to clear his throat before he could speak.

"A lot better." She sat on the edge of the bed. "I didn't realize how tired I really am. The shower helped tremendously."

He picked up the table and tray together, took them over to the bed and sat them down beside her. She drank the tomato juice but shunned the Alka Seltzer as he poured her a cup of coffee.

"You take lots of cream and two sugars . . . right?"

She threw back her head and laughed.

"What's so funny?"

"Oh nothing."

"Come on, let me in on it."

"I just remembered something else Reba said about you."

He thought for a second, and asked, "Was it about the way I like my women and coffee?"

"Yes!" she said and they had a long laugh.

"This is the way I wish you could always feel." He kissed her softly on the lips, then gave her the coffee on a saucer. "Drink this while I take a quick shower."

He rushed as if she were an exotic dream or desert mirage that could suddenly vanish, and was only half dry when he put on his robe. But when he returned, she was stretched out on the bed, fast asleep.

"Damn!" he shook his head disgustedly, "she must really be beat." The album had played out. He flipped it over, poured himself a cup of black coffee and flopped down in the big chair.

261

Time seemed to hang in a state of nothingness as he sat sipping and wondering if he should lie down with her. All at once she began to moan, and he hurried to the bed.

She groaned louder and louder, jerking and twisting, perspiration pouring out of her forehead, as she shook her head from side to side. He woke her up and took her in his arms again.

"You were having a nightmare," he whispered.

"I know," she sobbed softly, "it recurs from time to time. Ever since that day in Sharpeville." She removed the towel from her head, wiped her face and lay back down.

"Did I scream?"

"No."

"Thank goodness!"

"Anya, baby," he rubbed his cheek against hers, "it pains the hell out of me to see you hurt."

"As I said before, Rinco, you are overly concerned." She tried to smile as his mouth moved closer to hers.

"I have to be. There is no other way. I'm mad about you!"

"How can you be sure of that?" she sighed, as their lips nearly touched.

"I can't answer how, but I'm sure of my love for you . . . more sure than anything I can see, touch or even dream of. I love you because you're the most beautiful woman I've ever known, inside and out. I can't answer why, but I know destiny brought us closer for a reason. And I never want to let you go."

"Let us speak only of tonight," she said as their open mouths met in a blistering kiss. Their tongues probed, explored and caressed with mounting passion until he pulled away to kiss her lovely face. He kissed her forehead, eyes, cheeks, the tip of her nose, then settled again on her waiting, parted lips. He felt this moment was the reason for his being born. His frantic fingers pulled at her gown.

"Rinco," she whispered as he sank his face softly into the base of her neck.

"Oh Rinco! It has been so long." She sighed as he slowly kissed downward to her resplendent brown breast.

"Just a moment," she said.

It was difficult for him to control himself as she removed her gown and turned off the table lamp. Now only the dim light from the street and the silver rays of the moon covered her divine body.

He ripped off his robe, threw it on the floor and started kissing her again. The torrid tempo of George Shearing's *Latin Escapade* filled the room with maracas, claves and Congo drums, matching the vigorous pace of their grinding, twisting, sweating bodies.

"I love you," his words came in gasps, "with every heartbeat I love you more. I love the ground you walk on, the sky above your head, the very air you breathe ... I vow to love you forever, and will follow you wherever you go ... because we were made for each other."

Chapter Twenty Nine

"DAMN, DUDE!" Big Shot grinned when Rinco came into the compartment, "I thought you was gonna pull another Chitown."

"When I found out we were going to leave late I had other things to do." Rinco sat his garment bag, record player and camera case on the desk, slid his overnight case under his bunk and stated changing clothes.

"I'm hip you had other things to do, and they all was with Anya. Hell dude, yo' leave was up at eight o'clock an' it's almost four. You sho' musta had a boss time, 'cause you jus' took you another day. And you wouldn't even let me dig the chick."

Rinco reached into the camera case and handed him the pictures he took of Anya on their first date.

"Wow!" Big Shot bucked his eyes and kissed his fingertips when he saw the first one. "She is most super boss!" He complimented every picture with words like, "out of sight ... maaan ... outrageous!" until he got to the one of Rinco. Then he shook his head, grunted, gave them back and went to his locker.

"How 'bout a parting toast to our lovely ladies, Anya and Krishan."

"Good deal!" Rinco slipped into a fresh set of dungarees.

"What will you have, scotch, bourbon or wine?" He opened the locker and showed Rinco ten fifths of liquor. "This of for Bombay dad."

"Yeah," Rinco said, "And for Johnson and Brother Poe. Wine will do."

"Nothing but the best, dude." He filled two water glasses with Harvey's Bristol Cream. "My personal stock, compliments of the Pot O' Gold."

"You got another place to hide that shit? You never know when we might have inspection."

"I'm gonna stash it in the vaps, now that I work with you."

"What!?"

"That's right! I'm yo' new watermaker. The Third Engineer don't want it anymore."

"Mellow!" Rinco said and they slapped skin. "He didn't know his ass from a hole in the ground anyway. Smitty and I have been carrying him ever since Chitown left."

Their names came over the P.A. system with orders to report to the Evaporator Flat.

Rinco took a drink and asked, "Who the hell is having us paged?"

"That silly-ass first Engineer, who else! They been paging you all day. I'm suppose to be looking for you."

"Well, you found me, so what do they want?"

"Can't you hear? They want us down in the hole!"

"You mean they're stupid enough to think I'm going to turn to, and it's almost four o'clock."

"Hell yeah! Old chief wants everything in the engineering spaces repaired at sea ta shorten our stay in Capetown."

"And I know you are all for shortening our stay in Capetown."

"That part went over like a fart in church. But since we gonna be at sea, we might as well make the overtime, dude. With all these funky-ass troops aboard, we gonna have ta run them hot screaming bitches all the way to

265

India. Smitty lit off, an' makin' feed water. Gonna start the fresh soon as we get out 'a port."

"Well they can stick the overtime up their ass today." Rinco raised his glass. "Here's to my lovely Anya!"

"An' here's ta that bad-ass Krishan!" Big Shot joined him and they both gulped down a half glass of wine.

"So you and Krish are really hitting it off?"

"That's right, dude." Big Shot kissed his fingertips and took another drink.

"If I told you something, would you keep it between you and me?" Rinco asked.

"Damn right!" Big Shot tried to look serious.

"Now I mean this is personal." Rinco paused for a second, then dug into his shirt pocket and pulled out a tiny box. When he showed Big Shot a beautiful jade ring, it was the first time he had ever seen him lost for words. But it didn't last long.

"You done flipped, man ... That cost a nice taste a bread! I can dig the leave, ride an' hotel, but not this. You really blew yo' cool. Why didn't you go all the way for the okey-doke? Buy a diamond an' ask her ta marry you?"

"I may just ask her when she comes to see the ship off."

Big Shot dropped his head in disbelief. "Well ... since Smitty lit off, I suppose you want me ta take the Four to Eight so you can get engaged."

"You got that right! But I don't know about getting engaged right now. She's got something else deep in her mind."

"Lucky for you. You want my honest opinion?"

"No, but I figure you're going to give it anyway."

"Forget that chick. Hit the beach hard in every port. Chase every broad you can until she's out of your mind."

"Not a chance! I'm in love man, win or lose. She's the first thing I think of upon awakening, and the last before sleeping."

Big Shot gave a sigh and shook his head. "You sho' got it bad, jack."

The wine was making them feel good, so they poured more and sat on top of the desk.

"Here's ta yo' good luck, dude . . . 'cause you sho' gonna need it!"

"If she'll have me, that's all the luck I need."

"You remember what marriage did ta me, don't you?" Big Shot stuck a cigarette in his holder. "Remember all the changes I went through with Pam? But that was way back when, dude, an' ain't no broad had my nose open since. Look, I ain't saying matrimony can't be mellow. I'm jus' trying ta help you the way you helped me. The only way you can make it half way work would be ta give up the sea."

"Fuck the sea!" Rinco snapped.

"What!" Big Shot jumped from the desk and pointed. "That gangplank out there is the doorway ta the world. You gonna give that up for a mortgage an' a bunch a crumb crushers ya gotta feed, clothe, educate an' worry 'bout the rest a yo' life. Look, dude, I'm trying ta hip you like a brother. Don't do it! I been through that shit, an' I know what I'm talkin' 'bout. Most cats get hooked jus' ta lock up that trim. An' after while they both start slippin' an' slidin', peepin' an' hidin'. So you better forget 'bout wedlock, dude. An' stay away from chicks like Anya, they dangerous. Do like Big Shot Sonny Collins. I play the fast flip fancy broads, who jus' in it for the good times an' what they can get."

The Boatswain's whistle blew for early chow, and Big Shot put out his cigarette. "You ate yet?"

"I'm not hungry." Rinco didn't want to be in the messhall when Anya came.

"All the symptoms huh?" Well, I ain't gonna stay here wastin' my breath on you. Since I got the next watch, I'm gonna chow-down, then call Krish."

"Wait a minute!" Rinco said as they drained their glasses, "I'll go topside with you."

Big Shot's advice had failed to change his plan for Anya, but as departure time neared, her absence caused Rinco grave concern. He nervously paced the crowded fantail checking his watch and looking down the road for approaching vehicles. With each passing second the desire

267

grew stronger in him to see her again. He had to hold, kiss and tell her again how much he loved her. His eyes left the road as he felt the ring in his pocket and dreamed of putting it on her finger. When he looked back she was stepping out of a taxi.

He dashed through the passageway, past the quarter-deck and down the gangplank.

"I can't tell you how glad I am that you finally made it!" He hugged and kissed her, but didn't like the look on her face.

"I have news from Capetown," she said. "Is there some place we can be alone?"

"Sure!" he took her by the hand and started up the long narrow path to where they had their first picnic.

"This is the best spot to spend our last moments. Plus I can see you better and longer from here when the ship leaves," he said when they reached the top. But her silence still worried him.

"Would you like to sit?" he offered.

"No, thank you." She walked to the edge of the clearing as she had done before and stared out across the water.

"What's the matter, honey?" He slipped an arm around her shoulder. "What happened in Capetown?"

"I cannot tell you these awful things," she reached into her purse, "so I will let you read the letter I've just received from Reba."

He took the envelope and slowly removed the pages, searching her face for some kind of hint before dropping his eyes to read. *MY DEAR ANYA, I HOPE THIS LETTER FINDS YOU SAFE AND WELL, BUT ABOVE ALL STRONG. THIS MORNING IHETU AND I WENT TO NANGA TO RESCUE CHITOWN AND ETOBI. WHEN WE ARRIVED THERE WAS NOTHING BUT BLOOD, FIRE AND DEATH. OH ANYA! IT WAS HORRIBLE! CHITOWN HAD BEEN SHOT!"*

"Chitown, shot!" he stiffened, then looked at her. "Those dirty son-of-a-bitches killed him?"

"No! He didn't die," she said, "but he lost one of his arms."

The loud ship's horn signaled preparations for getting underway. His jaws hardened as he read on. *ETOBI DID NOT COME WITH US. HE SAID YOU WOULD UNDERSTAND. IF HE IS STILL ALIVE WHEN THE FIGHTING ENDS, HE WILL SOMEHOW TRY TO JOIN YOU. OH ANYA, I FEAR SO MUCH FOR HIM, BUT WE MUST KEEP FAITH. FROM NEWS SMUGGLED OUT, NANGA HAS BEEN SET ABLAZE AND INVADED. BUT WE CAN BE PROUD WITH HEADS HELD HIGH. BECAUSE FROM WHAT I SAW, THEY FOUGHT BRAVE AND WELL AGAINST ALL ODDS. WHEN WE GOT BACK THE SICKNESS HAD SPREAD TO CAPETOWN. EVERY BLACK OR COLOURED MAN WE SAW WAS BEING CHASED, BEATEN OR ARRESTED. AT EVERY STOP LIGHT WE FROZE IN TERROR. IHETU IS WITH ME NOW AND WE ARE AWAITING WORD FROM ETOBI. CHITOWN LEFT MONEY. AND THANKS TO HIM ALL THREE OF US MAY HAVE ENOUGH FUNDS TO ESCAPE FROM THIS HELL. HOWEVER WE CANNOT LEAVE UNTIL WE FIND OUT WHAT HAPPENED TO ETOBI. BUT AS TIME PASSES, HOPE IS FADING AND I AM PREPARING FOR THE WORST. IF YOU SEE RINCO, OR ANY OF CHITOWN'S SHIPMATES, TELL THEM THAT WE GOT HIM TO AN AMERICAN SHIP IN TIME TO SAVE HIS LIFE. BUT HE LOST HIS LEFT ARM. I HAVE SEEN SO MANY PEOPLE KILLED AND MAIMED TODAY, THAT MY HEART IS SICK WITH SORROW. EVEN AS I WRITE THIS LETTER I AM SHAKING IN FEAR. BECAUSE AS YOU KNOW, WE ARE NOT SAFE ANYWHERE. THERE IS SO MUCH MORE I WOULD LIKE TO SAY, BUT I AM TOO LOW IN SPIRIT TO WRITE ON. SO I PRAY FOR THE DAY WE SHALL ALL BE TOGETHER AND FREE. UNTIL THEN, MY HOPE AND LOVE GO WITH YOU." YOUR FRIEND, REBA*

The ship's loud whistle sent her sobbing into his arms. He searched for words of comfort but they were not there.

Numbed by the grief that had befallen them, he just held her in silence until she stopped crying.

"Now I understand why you were so late." He gave her the sad letter. "This must have torn you apart!"

"Yes." She put it back in her purse and pulled out a handkerchief to dry her eyes. "Etobi means so much to me!"

"I can see." He followed her to the giant orchid tree they had once sat under. "So I'm even more grateful for your coming."

"I really didn't feel up to it, but I had to tell you about Chitown."

"I hope you are not ashamed." He turned her around. "Don't ever feel guilty or ashamed about what happened last night. This is no quick cheap affair. I want you for life!"

"It wasn't because of you, Rinco, or what happened last night. You have been nothing less than wonderful, and your kindness has helped me bear a lot of pain. I am awfully sorry you are leaving."

He took her face in his hands, kissed her forehead, then settled on her soft full lips. The ship's horn blew again, and he cursed it.

"Anya . . . " He grabbed her shoulders and looked into her eyes. "I wish I could delay what I'm about to say, but it has to be said now."

She started to speak but he cut her off. "Please baby, let me get this out while it's coming. I don't know how long this Congo war is going to last, but I'm staying in Africa when it's over. Aw hell! I've told you all of that before. Oh baby . . . what I'm trying to say is hard because this is not the time or place . . . but it's all I got. I want to marry you someday!"

Her mouth opened, but she was lost for words.

"I love you, Anya! I've loved you from the moment I saw you. I love you so much it can't be measured. And if given the chance, I know I can make you happy."

"I'm very flattered, but . . . "

"You don't have to decide now!" He cut her off again, "You'll have plenty of time to make up your mind after your friends get here. Just give me a little time when I get back. Then if Etobi is the one you prefer, I'll bug out. But as of now," he reached into his shirt pocket, pulled out the ring, and offered it to her. "This is just for friendship, to let you know my true feelings. There are no strings or pressure."

"No, Rinco! . . . I can't!" She shook her head, and after getting over the shock, smiled for the first time.

"Please accept it," he exhorted, as she looked out to sea in deep thought, "it would make me very proud!"

She had no plans to marry anyone. Her only rooted concerns were the struggle for freedom in Southern Africa, and the escape of her friends. She adored Rinco, but fate had given them no future together. She wanted to tell him, but knew it would spoil his departure, so she decided to accept the ring. He smiled when she turned and held out her hand.

"There is plenty of time," she repeated his words as he slipped the ring on her middle finger. "Perhaps it is best you learn my true direction when you are far on a distant shore, within each reach of other women."

"There can be no other women. And whatever your true direction is, someday we will be going the same way. All I want you to do is write . . . and let me know where you are. We laughed when I said I would hack my way through every jungle in Africa to be with you, but it was no joke."

"Oh Rinco," she said. "You can't follow me. Where I am going is very . . . very dangerous!"

"I don't care! . . . I'll search!" he vowed.

"If and when you eventually find me, it could be too late. I may be killed. And it would all be for nothing."

"Please don't say that, Anya! Don't even think it! But if, heaven forbid, you are dead, I will find your grave and stand over you. I'll remember your face, and how it shames the daylight. I'll think of your warm giving smile, and the way your noble body can mold simple things like that plain white uniform into a royal gown. But most of all, I'll remember the tears trying to fill your deep, dark eyes that tell me I have truly touched you, and relive this moment forever."

They stared at each other for a long moment. Then he asked. "Does it fit?"

"What! ... Oh the ring ... Yes! It's perfect, and very beautiful." She held it to the sun. "It has a warm glorious feeling, and if I might add, much too expensive."

"Forget about that. Just promise that whatever destiny holds for us, you will write me and always wear my ring."

"I will do both, Rinco!" She hugged him.

The *Gray Ghost* gave a final warning to all concerned. He wrapped his arms around her as tight as he could without inflicting pain. Then he grabbed her shoulders and started kissing her face.

"I will miss you, Rinco," she sighed, and fought to hold back tears. "Please take care of yourself."

"I will," he kissed her neck.

"You had better get to your ship before it leaves," she whispered. "I will stay and watch it until it is out of sight."

"Thank you, honey," he forced himself away, "and I'll watch this hill until my world disappears."

"Thank you for the ring!" She shouted when he headed for the edge of the clearing, "I will wear it always!"

He turned for a last lingering look, threw her a kiss, then dashed down the path.

When he reached the quarterdeck, Ludlam was barking orders to raise the gangplank. "Another minute, by-god, an' you'd hafta stay here where you belong."

"Fuck you, redneck!" He waved to Anya then hurried through the passageway.

By the time he got to the crowded fantail, the last lines were being pulled aboard. He glanced up at that lovely figure dressed in white and realized it was practically impossible for her to recognize him in this swarm of blue clad sailors. So he climbed ladder by ladder, deck by deck until he was at the top, standing beneath the stack. He waved frantically with both hands, until she saw him and waved back.

The main throttle of the *Mitchell* opened slowly, sending superheat steam across her giant turbine blades. The still water erupted, then churned snowy white around her wide oval body as she inched away from the dock.

He had no idea how long he had been standing there, gazing out at the cloudy coast line slowly fading on the horizon. Time had vanished like the end of the wide foamy track that trailed the ship. He bitterly recalled the day after his father's funeral thirteen years ago in Liberia, as the last time he had cried. It had also happened at sea, on a vessel bound for New York but still in the shadow of Africa. All the years since he had fought and hid all the agony that swelled inside him. Now he felt the need growing stronger by the second to relieve some of it. He wanted to cry for Chitown and his wife ... for the millions of blacks enslaved by the South African government ... and all the human beings he'd seen in many countries of the Third World searching the ship's garbage cans for food. He wanted to cry for the countless people he had seen suffering and dying on the roadsides of Korea and the streets of Bombay ... but most of all for himself. He hurt because he could no longer comfort Anya, who was alone, heartbroken and depressed somewhere in that distant haze.

The grief swelled in his stomach and went upward through his chest into his throat. He gritted his teeth, but could not stop his lips from quivering. The tears finally came in pouring streams, and the swift swirling winds washed them across his face.

THE END